THE COMPLETE CASES
OF JEFFERY WREN, VOLUME 1

G.T. FLEMING-ROBERTS

THE COMPLETE CASES OF

JEFFERY WREN ™

G.T. FLEMING-ROBERTS

INTRODUCTION BY

JAMES T. ROBERTS

ALTUS PRESS

BOSTON • 2015

EDITED AND DESIGNED BY

Matthew Moring

PUBLISHING HISTORY

"Growing Up With Pulp Master G.T. Fleming-Roberts" appears here for the first time. Copyright © 2015 James T. Roberts. All Rights Reserved.

"No Haunting Allowed" originally appeared in the April, 1944 issue of *Dime Detective* magazine. Copyright 1944 by Popular Publications, Inc. Copyright renewed 1970 and assigned to Steeger Properties, LLC. All Rights Reserved.

"The Spirit Was Willing" originally appeared in the August, 1944 issue of *Dime Detective* magazine. Copyright 1944 by Popular Publications, Inc. Copyright renewed 1971 and assigned to Steeger Properties, LLC. All Rights Reserved.

"A Sleight Case of Murder" originally appeared in the October, 1944 issue of *Dime Detective* magazine. Copyright 1944 by Popular Publications, Inc. Copyright renewed 1971 and assigned to Steeger Properties, LLC. All Rights Reserved.

"Dig a Grave for Me" originally appeared in the November, 1944 issue of *Dime Detective* magazine. Copyright 1944 by Popular Publications, Inc. Copyright renewed 1971 and assigned to Steeger Properties, LLC. All Rights Reserved.

"The Turn From the Trite" originally appeared in the May, 1943 issue of *Writer's Digest* magazine.

THANKS TO

Joel Frieman, Rick Ollerman, Stephen Payne & James T. Roberts

Printed in the United States of America.

TABLE OF CONTENTS

GROWING UP WITH PULP MASTER
G.T. FLEMING-ROBERTS

JAMES T. ROBERTS

"BE QUIET Jimmy! Your Father's writing!"These were the words that introduced me to the world of the pulps. Our family unit consisted of Aggie, Mimi, Aunty, Tsin Wah (a Tibetan Pekinese) and my father. Writing ten or eleven hours a day, my father, G.T. Fleming-Roberts, was for me the invisible man, the Captain Zero of the household. My early memories date from the age of about two and one half years. At that age, my father was thirty-three years old and (as I have now learned) producing a huge volume of Mystery, Terror, Hero, and Detective fiction for the pulps. To my toddler mind, he seemed to be writing all the time. Had I at the time known the terrors flowing from the Underwood "Noiseless" typewriter in his basement study in our North Meridian Street home in Indianapolis Indiana, I might have never ventured down the stairs to see my father. His study was off limits to me. A visit to my father's workplace was a rare thrill.

He had taken a single room in the basement and decorated it in an oriental motif. There was a red leather chair and a smoking cabinet emblazoned with a dragon and topped with a huge brass Buddha. Twelve feet of special racks held his collection of briar pipes. The smoking cabinet held dozens of half pound tins of Edgeworth pipe tobacco. I now know that "Tommy," as GTFR was known to me, supported this vice by writing testimonials for Edgeworth tobacco. (If you ever see the Edgeworth ad in which Bing Crosby waxes eloquent about his favorite pipe fuel, you are reading GTFR fiction.) A bookshelf held some of his favorite fiction. The books that I remember coming from those shelves were mostly Sax Rohmer's wonderful tales of Naylon Smith and Dr. Fu Manchu. The focal point of the room was "Toots," a voluptuous, bound, blonde babe straddling a ship's anchor. A grim-faced dark-haired man was firing a huge pistol over her shoulder at an unknown foe. I couldn't take my young eyes off this picture! Who were these people? What was the pretty girl so afraid of? Was that dark-haired man my father? "Toots" was the original oil cover painting from the cover of the February 1940 issue of *Double-Action Detective.* GTFR always said that she had been given to him in lieu of payment for a story. Should I believe that?

There was so much fiction in my family history as I learned it from my father, that I now question things that I took for gospel as a child. For example, when asked how he met my mother, GTFR would embark on a lengthy narrative that started, "William Wallace Cook's Chinese houseboy forgot to take out the trash…." I know that Lewis Storr of Marshall, Michigan was an avid reader and collector of pulps, and that William Wallace Cook was a prolific writer who was well enough known to Storr to be called "Wally" at dinner conversations. I know that Storr married a wonderful woman who was like a sister to my mother. Somehow those connections yielded the union that produced my existence, for which I am eternally grateful. But the "Chinese Houseboy"? Probably as real as Bing Crosby's endorsement of Edgeworth.

I've been told that the names that I learned to call my parents were strange. My mother was "Aggie," short for Agatha Halcyon Amell; my father was "Tommy," short for George Thomas Roberts. "Mom" and "Dad" were not in my juvenile lexicon. My childhood friends thought this was extremely weird. I was very comfortable being on a first-name basis with my parents. The "Fleming" in my father's literary name was not an affectation. My grandmother Margaret Roberts was a "Fleming." The hyphenated "Fleming-Roberts" was out of respect to the distaff side of the shield. The "Flemings" were said to have descended from a brave medieval knight of Flanders. More GTFR fiction? You be the judge! Ian Fleming may have descended from the same armored loins. His James Bond had some similarities with GTFR's Secret Agent X, such as unlimited funds from secret sources, multiple false identities, beautiful bad girls, fast cars, and a plethora of gadget weapons. Maybe they both got it from Sax Rohmer! There is one commonality between Ian and my father that is factual: they both drove Studebakers, GTFR a white Hawk; and Ian, a black Avanti.

As a young child, I would hear my parents talking about the characters in my father's stories. Jeffery Wren, George Chance, and Pat Oberron, seemed to me to be distant members of our family. To me, they were as real as Uncle Rob and Aunt Helen. Later on, when I was about five, I was introduced to a local artist, Georges La Chance, and thought for years that he was the Ghost!

My father was drafted towards the end of WWII. At thirty-five years of age, married with one child, he was "the bottom of the barrel." He was able to elect to serve in the Army Air Corps. He was stationed at Shepherd Field, Texas. I am sure he had hopes of learning to fly. I have a letter that he wrote to my mother in which he wistfully commented, "They have plenty of kids here who can fly planes, but I'm the only guy here who can fly a typewriter! So they've got me filling out all the darn forms!" As the "old man" of the barracks, he described his service time as being a "father figure" to a bunch of scared kids. He may have contributed more to the war effort than he realized.

His absence from the home was hard on my mother, she had to deal with Grandmother (Mimi), Aunt Margaret (Aunty) and a yappy Peke (Tsin Wah) and a spoiled child (me). I think she had a little breakdown. Our Congressman secured a hardship discharge for my father and commented, "I think his stories do more for troop morale than his service down in Texas." GTFR's story "The Pin That Killed Hitler" (*Thrilling Detective*, May 1943) may have inspired that comment.

After his discharge, GTFR had a hard time getting back in the swing of cranking out stories. He was restless, and I remember many trips to the country in our 1941 Chrysler. These trips resulted in my parents finding a beautiful log cabin in Brown County, near the artist colony of Nashville, Indiana. In June of 1946 we moved. In retrospect, I feel the move may have been bad for his writing career. In Indianapolis he associated with other writers and newspaper professionals. His closest friend C. William Harrison, "Chet" to me, was a successful writer for the western pulps. Another close friend, a professional stage magician, George Paxton, was a source of reference for the magician detective stories. For a short time, GTFR and Chet had an office in downtown Indianapolis that they shared for writing. I believe the office was in or near the old Claypool Hotel, which had been the prototype for the "Hillary Building" in the Pat Oberron stories. The move to the country separated GTFR from these sources of inspiration and encouragement. Chet Harrison decided to move to California at about the same time as we moved to rural Indiana. In hindsight, I believe a California move might have been a real game changer for my father. At that time, he had sold two stories that had been produced on the big screen. The first of them was *Lady Chaser*, originally printed as "Lady Killer" in the July 1945 issue of *Detective Tales*. The second was *Find the Blackmailer* which first saw print as the novella "Blackmail With Feathers" in *Detective Novels* (August 1945). He may have become a successful Hollywood screenwriter, but I may have become a drug-addled Hollywood brat. You can't change history! (Except in a good Pulp story!)

Something big was brewing in 1947 because we were invited to go to New York City to visit August Lenniger, my father's agent. We stayed for several days in their beautiful home in Scarsdale and did the tourist things while GTFR met with editors and publishers. The names that I remember were Leo Margulies and Daisy Bacon. I don't know what was accomplished on that visit, but I expect that was the period when Captain Zero was hatched. Forgive me if I didn't get more details, but heck, I was only six! I know Lenniger, known to me as "Gus," and his wife Beatrice came to stay with my parents for a few days during the summer of 1948. My impression was that Gus and my father were very close. They certainly should have been. They had had a mutually lucrative relationship for more than fifteen years at that time.

The early postwar years were full of excitement; the technology of the war years was spilling over into civilian life. I saw my first television image on the New York trip. At Radio City Music Hall, they had a camera focused on a little platform and a small black and white screen built into the wall. Aggie and I stood in line for a long time to get up on the platform. I looked up at the flickering screen and there we were—television stars! I remember telling of this experience to my first grade class in a one-room schoolhouse with a coal stove for heat. I felt like a spaceman! Little did I know that the flickering image was a harbinger of the demise of the Pulps and my father's writing career.

The Atomic Age brought a lot of good science fiction to the Pulps. GTFR had flirted with futurist fiction but had produced only one salable story "The Golden Barrier." SF writer Jack Williamson visited my parents and gave me a Chesley Bonestell print of a rocket landing on the moon; he also left a copy of Heinlein's *The Man Who Sold the Moon*. I think he was encouraging my father to get into SF. Although he did not write science fiction, GTFR put a lot of science in his fiction. Medicine, poisons, chemical reactions and little known scientific phenomena were the staples of his stories. What seemed like the supernatural always had a rational explanation in arcane science. No wonder! Grandfather, George Horice Roberts, was a distinguished professor of Veterinary Medicine at Purdue University, and my father had graduated there with a Bachelor of Science degree in 1932.

Captain Zero was really a remarkable mix of superhero, detective, and science fiction. GTFR took one of the science headlines of the times, radioactive medicine, and used it to turn a mild-mannered, half-blind shrimp into an invisible crimefighter. Contact lenses were part of the new science of the day, and Zero used them to see when he was in his invisible state. My father kept up with the science of the time by reading *Mechanix Illustrated* and *Popular Science* magazines. I know that the Geiger counters described in the Captain Zero stories are the same as the instruments offered in the "Atomic Energy" set offered on the back page of A.C. Gilbert's 1950 American Flyer Electric Train catalog. I had spent hours touting that set to my parents as a perfect Christmas present. I never got it. Maybe they thought I'd blow up the house! I now realize that the checks from Captain Zero probably bought me some fine American Flyer Trains from that catalog instead.

The names of the characters in the Zero stories were borrowed from people that my mother and father knew. Eudora Kelly was a very sophisticated lady who lived near Nashville. She lent her name to the beautiful Doro Kelly. The villain in *The Mark of Zero*, Henshaw, was taken from a local artist Hinshaw. The Lockridge Institute was a homage to father's fellow Hoosier author, Ross Lockridge, whose *Raintree County* had been a national best seller in 1947.

Eudora and Lockridge might have been flattered. Hinshaw might have sued!

I never read the Captain Zero stories as an adult until their recent republication. Although some critics have accused Zero of "no pizzazz," I think they miss the point of the stories. They certainly miss the humor and strong character development. Lee Allyn, Doro Kelly, Ed Cavanaugh and Captain Zero were a love triangle, no, a quadrangle. Throw in Lee's multiple handicaps and his unintended invisibility. Toss that with the political criminal conspiracies that surfaced in *The Mark of Zero*, and you get the makings of great Pulp fiction. Too bad the declining Pulp market didn't permit the series to grow the way GTFR's Green Ghost and Secret Agent X had. In retrospect, I don't think GTFR liked Captain Zero very much. I think there was editorial pressure to turn Zero and his friends into an invisible army of crimefighters, sort of a Fantastic Four or Avengers type of superhero story. Certainly, *The Golden Murder Syndicate,* the last of the Zero stories, seems like a hash with the story development badly cut, and the momentum of *The Mark of Zero* totally lost. Maybe it was short-ened editorially because of space constraints, or maybe GTFR was just tired of Zero. Too bad. I feel that Zero and his friends deserved to have a few more adventures.

GTFR didn't give up with the failure of Zero. He did a pilot television script for Ralph Bellamy's *Man Against Crime* TV series. It was rejected because of suicide references in the plot, which of-fended the sponsor's family. GTFR felt that the half hour TV format didn't permit sufficient plot development. Too bad he didn't stick with the TV idea because formats eventually extended to one hour or more, then mini-series and series. He would have been a natural for a show like *Mission: Impossible.*

Politics dominated the last years of my father's life. He was the Republican county chairman in a strongly Democratic county, and was selected to be one of Indiana's delegates to the 1952 Republican National Convention. As history knows, the Convention overwhelm-ingly nominated the next President, Dwight David Eisenhower. GTFR voted for Taft. He loved underdogs. He was a compulsive off-brand buyer. He would choose a rusted out Studebaker over a shiny new Chevy, order anchovies on his pizza and bet on the Cubs. He didn't just march to a different drummer, he often was the *sole* drummer. He drew on his political experience for a good sale. Head-lined "Politics and Murder,""The Brass Halo" sold to *Bluebook* in 1956 and was his last originally published work.

I think writing took its toll on my father. When he stopped, he just stopped! It was like he had just run out of gas! When he died at age fifty-eight, he had not written a word of fiction for twelve years. He served as the editor of the *Brown County American,* a short-lived newspaper in our home town, did press releases for the Indiana Department of Public Education and helped me with some college papers. Sadly, there would be no more Captain Zeros or Secret Agent Xs. I could tell that he was done with writing. Reading his work now, I marvel at how much he was able to accomplish at a relatively young age. Where did he get all those great story ideas? How was he able to produce so much work, three hundred or more published stories, novelettes and novels in a brief span of twenty four years? I have a lot of regrets about my relationship with GTFR, but the greatest is that I can't show him the list of his books that are now being sold on Amazon, and share with him the enthusiasm that his stories still generate among fans of the Pulp genre.

James T. Roberts
February 2014

NO HAUNTING ALLOWED

"MY HUSBAND'S DEVOTION BECOMES UNBEARABLE WHEN IT IS NOT EXPRESSED IN DOLLARS. WHEN HE DIES I WANT TO BE ABLE TO MOURN LUXURIOUSLY," FLORENCE TAVELL TOLD WREN. NO EASY PICKINGS FOR LITTLE FLORENCE WHEN FREYA, THE VALKYRIE TABLE-TAPPER, AND WILFRED DOAN WITH HIS "SURE THING" SCHEMES WERE ALSO SHEKEL-INTERESTED IN THE BABY-TALKING MR. TAVELL. AND WHEN POOR OLD BOBERT TURNED UP, STRANGLED BY THREE YARDS OF BEST-GRADE ECTOPLASM, SOMETHING WAS REALLY COOKING—WITH THE FLAME TURNED UP TOO HIGH!

CHAPTER ONE

TABLE-TAPPER

J EFFERY WREN frequently mentions the man who was choked with ectoplasm, especially at meetings of the Indianapolis Chapter of the Society of American Magicians where he has more listeners than are good for his ego. When he talks about the body his deep voice hangs crepe gently as though the corpse were that of someone dear.

It was not. He had never seen the man before, alive or dead.

"My first body," he usually explains to preclude the idea that he has suffered a personal loss. "My baptism in murder. Or call it a ducking. Quite!"

After which he'll begin at the beginning—that dark five o'clock of a November afternoon when Florence Tavell and her pedigreed mink coat entered a glittering hole-in-the-wall shop on West Ohio Street.

Before the door was entirely closed behind her, Florence Tavell drew a shallow breath as if the air within were poison, and her eyes went slumming from counter to counter.

Souvenirs of leather, plaster, china, and pot-metal, flash jewelry, comic novelties that ranged from the inane to the obscene, patent potato peelers, jokers' items that pricked, snapped, stamped, damped, soiled, startled, smarted and generally out-smarted the unwary—all were included in that disdainful glance that swept on to the thin, bloodless-looking clerk named Horace.

Horace's gaudy necktie lifted and waved, apparently of its own volition, but Florence Tavell ignored this minor miracle.

"Is Mr. Wren in?" she asked, producing an immediate fall in Horace's barometer.

Horace sighed. "Boss's upstairs with coupla suckers." He showed Florence Tavell the way with a gesture of his faintly blue hand.

SHE plunged through green curtains redolent with cigar smoke, hurried up a stairway to a door that bore the legend *Wren's Magic.* Beyond this was a small reception room. The walls were decorated with framed publicity photos which had appeared in newspapers when Jeffery Wren had played Keith's circuit—Wren at the climax of "The Linking Rings," Wren escaping from a strait jacket, Wren cheerfully decapitating a shapely young woman in black silk tights, and many others.

Wren was feeding cobs into the stove
when somebody shot through the shutter.
The figure on the bed bounced under the
impact of the heavy-caliber slugs.

Florence Tavell poised like a swimmer about to plunge into Lake Michigan in mid-January, then pushed open the glass doors to enter the shop itself. Behind one counter, Wren, with a suggestion of being bored or a little tipsy, had reached the climax in a demonstration of "The Twentieth Century Silks" for a pair of customers. He gave Florence Tavell a heavy-lidded glance. His smile broke against his bronzed skin, twitched, and was gone—a slight and perhaps inadequate tribute to a lady of Mrs. Tavell's face and figure.

Wren was dark-complexioned, of medium height, with a heavy, squarish body. There was about him something of the sleek ostentation so admirably portrayed by Edward Arnold of the movies. Large, deft fingers ripped open a paper tube from which he took a green silk, previously vanished, which now appeared securely tied between a red and yellow one.

His customers glanced back at Florence Tavell, then huddled over the counter as though plotting to blow up the State House.

"No pulls?" one whispered. "No double silk?"

Wren shook his head. "It's clean. You can work it close." He chuckled warmly. Leaving the silks for examination, he came around the counter to Florence Tavell.

"Mrs. Urban Malthus Tavell," she pronounced, her voice as cold as new-fallen snow. She gave him a little time to recover.

Wren's chunky black eyebrows elevated slightly. The name of Urban Malthus Tavell meant money—a lot of money.

"A policewoman…" Mrs. Tavell frowned, making heavy business of excavating from memory a name that was of no importance to her, "a policewoman by the name of Osbourn suggested that you might be able to help me. Of course I shall pay you well."

The offer of money had all the earmarks of an explanation as to why Mrs. Tavell happened to be discoursing with the likes of Jeffery Wren. He concluded that she was of the sudden-rich. He looked into her eyes. They were long, tapering, gray eyes with something of chilled steel about them, a suggestion of temper acquired by quenching in the cold waters of disillusion.

"My husband," she explained, "is being victimized by a table-tapper."

"Ah? One of those?" He led Mrs. Tavell into that thoughtful brown room that was his office and placed a chair for her.

"Cigarette?"

Florence Tavell had reached halfway toward his extended hand before she realized it was empty. And then, immediately, it was not empty, but held a lighted cigarette at fingertips. She drew back, startled.

"Come now," he said. "Magic shouldn't frighten you. Something of an illusionist yourself, aren't you? You haven't a lorgnette, yet you seem to be looking at me through one."

SHE flushed, drew a startled breath through parted lips. It was as though she had been slapped. Wren, having spanked her verbally, said, "Now, now," in his gentlest voice. Her sensuous mouth curved up at the corners, and she demonstrated contrition by accepting the cigarette.

"The table-tapper?" he prompted.

"Her name is Freya."

"Ah! A Norse goddess."

Florence Tavell's slender eyebrows peaked into arches of surprise. "You know her then?"

He shook his head. "The name was originally that of a Norse goddess. Rode a billy-goat or something equally uncomfortable. Freya would be tall, blond, statuesque. Strictly from Wagner. How's that?"

"Perfect."

"You might tell me how Freya operates," he suggested.

"She, my husband and I sit about a table in a fully lighted room, with our fingers resting lightly on the top. After Freya has established contact with her spirit control, the table taps. My husband then asks questions and the answers come, one tap for 'no' and two taps for 'yes.' The table is an ordinary card table, except that it has a glass top, so it's evident Freya doesn't kick the table leg."

His smile twitched. "She wouldn't do that. Too obvious."

"My husband has perfect faith in her. He even consults her in financial matters."

Wren's eyes became shrewd. "That's what gets you down."

"Naturally. For example, there is a man named Wilfred Doan who is trying to get my husband to sign some sort of an agreement whereby Mr. Tavell will give him financial backing to the extent of a hundred thousand dollars. Doan has designed some sort of a prefabricated, low-cost dwelling for war workers. Freya and her table recommend that Mr. Tavell back Wilfred Doan."

"I see." Wren waited for Mrs. Tavell to continue.

"We live out of the city limits," she said, "not far from Carmel. Our nearest neighbor is a simple country woman, a spinster, by the name of Mary Maley. A few years ago her brother, for whom she kept house, died of some malignant stomach ailment and left Miss Maley quite a lot of money."

"Excuse me," Wren interrupted. "I fail to see what this has to do with your problem."

"You'll see in a moment. Village gossip has it that Mary Maley was responsible for Eben Maley's death because her cookery did not adhere to the rigid diet rules set forth by Eben's doctor. As a matter of fact, Eben liked rich food so well that he wouldn't have dieted anyway. But the gossip has so affected Mary Maley that she built herself a small house and erected a steel fence around it. With a single Negro servant and two vicious Great Dane dogs, she lives virtually as a hermit."

"Why the fence and the dogs?" Wren asked. "Going to extremes to avoid callers, wouldn't you say?"

"That's because Mary Maley doesn't trust banks," Mrs. Tavell explained. "I understand she keeps all her money in the house.

"But the point is, Mary Maley trusts my husband. From Mr. Tavell she has heard of Freya and now she wishes to have Freya attempt contact with her dead brother, Eben. Mary Maley wants to know if her brother holds her responsible for his death. Freya has arranged a sitting for tonight at nine at the old Maley farmhouse which has been vacant since Eben Maley's death."

"Cheerful idea," Wren mused. "You're afraid that Freya may somehow manage to rook Mary Maley out of her inheritance?"

"It's a possibility, of course," Mrs. Tavell admitted, "though my chief concern is for my husband and myself. It occurred to me that tonight at this sitting you might manage to do something about Freya."

"When she's doing her table-tapping is the table placed on a carpet or on the bare floor?" he asked.

"On the bare hardwood floor."

"Then put Freya and her table on a thick rug. Don't think the spirit will cooperate then. Not on a rug."

Mrs. Tavell raised a shoulder, shrugging aside his suggestion.

"That wouldn't do, I'm sure. Freya would explain that the rug insulates the table, or something equally absurd. My husband is in his foolish fifties and receptive to such suggestions."

SHE opened her purse, removed a fountain pen and checkbook. Her gray eyes priced Wren coolly.

"A thousand dollars?"

He laughed shortly, annoyed. "For what?"

"I want you to discredit Freya in my husband's eyes—tonight. I won't have her swindling him. You see, Mr. Wren, I have every intention of outliving him." She leaned forward a little in the chair. "My husband is completely devoted to me, but such devotion becomes unbearable when it is no longer expressed in dollars. When Mr. Tavell dies I want to be able to mourn luxuriously."

"Black from the skin out," he said. "Probably becoming."

"And if it should become necessary to murder Freya to protect my future I shouldn't have to hire anyone to do it for me."

Wren said: "I see, I see." He drummed on the desk top while she wrote the check.

Shortly after Florence Tavell had left, the ringing of the phone brought Wren away from the latest edition of the City Directory. Zoe Osbourn was calling him from police headquarters to learn how he'd got on with Mrs. Tavell. When Wren told her of the check, the police-woman uttered a prolonged whistle.

He said: "I think Freya's real name is Gladys Frye of 1123¼ Alabama Street."

Zoe Osbourn grunted. "So you know her?"

"I'm afraid so. She's listed in the directory as a notary and public stenographer. Last time we met, she was doing seances—with trumpets, with ectoplasm materializing all over the place. If anybody could tell you what your late Aunt Hattie wanted done with her Postal Savings account, it was Gladys Frye. Let's meet at Tenth and Alabama around seven. I want to talk to you."

CHAPTER TWO

DEAD—AS IN MURDERED

WREN'S SLOW, bouncing stride took him down Alabama Street. At Tenth, the appointed corner, Zoe Osbourn was waiting for him in a fur-trimmed coat and matching shako that contrived to make her look like the least dashing of cossacks.

"How are you?" Wren touched his hat vaguely. "How're all the dirty crooks?"

"I'm fine." She had a husky bellow. "And there's no reason to suppose the dirty crooks aren't fine, too."

Zoe Osbourn was a copper's widow in her late forties. She was taller than short, more than pleasantly rounded, with hair that had frequently met henna. She owed her assignment of picking up fraud fortune tellers to prominent pale blue eyes that lent a wholly gullible expression to her heavy face.

"Look," Wren said. "It's big of me to help the police catch their spook-crooks. Don't you think?"

"It's wonderful." She was walking fast. "We should crack the Orphans' Fund to buy you a loving cup to keep your thousand kopeks in!"

They turned up the approach walk of a square-faced, red brick building with blackened limestone trim. Inside the foyer, Wren pointed to a tarnished brass mailbox plate set in sea-green marble wainscoting. Gladys Frye's neatly-typed card was in its holder, proclaiming her a stenographer and notary public. Up carpeted steps and down a hall, they came to a door where a similar card was thumb-tacked to the panel.

Zoe Osbourn asserted her authority to the extent of knocking at the door. It was an imperative knock, but there were no takers. The door was locked.

"She's probably out at the Tavell place tapping the gold out of Urban Malthus Tavell's back teeth," Zoe suggested.

Wren took a hand out of his trouser pocket and wedged himself between Zoe and the door.

She said: "Here, no breaking and entering."

"No," he replied, already working on the lock with the cautious haste of Houdini escaping from a Chinese water cell in nothing flat. "Of course not. Who's breaking anything? Closer investigation simply reveals the door not locked, contrary to first supposition."

He twisted the knob, threw the door wide open. He stepped into the apartment, brushed a gloved hand up and down the wall to locate the light switch. Zoe Osbourn was right beside him. When the light came on, there they were, caught flat-footed with their tonsils showing.

A man was waiting for them.

HE STOOD beside a connecting door and against the west wall of the living room. A derby hat and a long dress overcoat lent height to insignificance. An automatic held low in a pigskin-gloved hand kept him from being a pushover for a pack of hungry rabbits. Above the up-turned coat collar was a narrow wedge of face with close-set eyes and a pinched looking nose. The end of the nose twitched. The muzzle of the automatic didn't.

"Put it down," Zoe Osbourn said steadily. "I'm from the police."

The man's attitude indicated clearly that the police could go kiss Santa Claus. He waved them away from the door with his rod and started across the room toward them. His eyes were narrow and desperate. When he saw Zoe Osbourn fingering the clasp of her purse he right away got the idea she was going to pull a gun.

"Drop it, sister. No kiddin'."

Zoe dropped her purse. She had got the clasp of it open and the butt of a revolver showed against the floor.

"Really, Zoe," Wren chided. "Don't you know jiujitsu or something?"

"That's for defending my virtue!" she snapped at him.

"I'm gettin' out of here," the man said. "Right now."

"Obviously." Wren bowed slightly. "Goom-by. Bon voyage."

The man drew a shivering breath. "I just want to get one thing off my chest. I didn't have nothin' to do with it. But I ain't gettin' railroaded neither."

"Zoe," Wren said, "for your education, those are double negatives he's tossing around. He's lousy with 'em."

The gun swiveled, covering them as the man took sidling steps. He stooped quickly, snaked Zoe's gun from her fallen purse, straightened, took another step. He was as close to Wren as he'd ever be.

Wren led with his right. The blow was straight out of the boiler but it came a long way and had an air raid siren attached. The man pulled out of the path of it. As Wren's hundred and seventy pounds followed through, he got rammed below the belt with the muzzle of a gun. He backed, seeing red, but feeling pea-green. The man had skipped out the door and slammed it.

Zoe Osbourn went for the doorknob like a West Indian diver after a penny, but didn't turn it because of the whispered warning that came from the hall.

"Don't neither of you show a hair out that door for three minutes. You got that?"

Wren kneaded his tummy with one hand, drew Zoe Osbourn back from the door with the other. The policewoman turned on him.

"He can't do this to me! Where's the back door out of this dump? I'll show the—"

He held onto her. "Don't try it. You're the weaker sex."

The name she gave Wren provided a family tie between him and the little gunman. She knocked down his detaining hand with a gloved fist and went pegging toward what had to be the kitchen door of the flat.

Wren said: "Aren't you interested in that 'I didn't have nothin' to do with it' stuff?"

She didn't hear. "You call headquarters and have a prowl car sent around." Then she plunged into the kitchen and slammed out the back door.

WREN looked around the room. It didn't spell home in any language except Neanderthal. There were no rugs. A chair of oak upholstered in brown leatherette, a desk that held a typewriter comprised the entire furnishings. He didn't see a phone.

He went through the connecting door that led to the bedroom, felt for the light switch while picturing Gladys Frye's buxom figure draped across the bed, gashed and hacked into any number of pieces. The light on, he found the bed empty, clean, smoothly made, and the dresser in order. He turned to the first of two doors placed side by side and recalled that sometimes the corpse was in the bathtub, swimming in gore. But in the bathroom white tile glared at him, innocent of stain.

The second door operated a light that switched on automatically to reveal a closet beyond, a closet large enough to have served as a dressing room. Wren couldn't see the back of the closet because of a folding frame of gilt gas-pipe hung with pleated black velvet drapes. The frame was a mediums' "cabinet" folded for packing. It had fallen sideways across the closet, and because of its height had wedged diagonally between a wall and the opposite baseboard.

Tumbled on the closet floor in front of the cabinet were three telescoping "reaching rods" and several spirit trumpets of aluminum. A pile of slates used for receiving spirit messages had been disturbed by a careless foot. One of them was broken, disclosing the secret of its inner flap.

Wren shifted to the left a foot or so to try and see over the mediums' cabinet, but as he did so the toe of his shoe touched one of the gas-pipe members and the whole contraption collapsed with a crash like a bull in a plumbing shop. A section of pipe fell across his toe but he scarcely noticed because of what showed up in the space beyond. Not much space, certainly, but brim-full of death by violence.

Between the fallen frame and the rear of the closet was a straight chair placed a little to one side of, and a foot back from a small window. In the chair slumped an old man, his rusty black coat drooping to the floor, his battered black hat at his feet. His head reminded Wren of a dandelion gone to seed. It looked as though one good puff of wind would dislodge the fragile white hairs. The face of the dead man was evident in the extreme, but something to be avoided. He'd been strangled—garroted, to put it properly—and by a three-yard length of cheesecloth twisted to attain strength and thickness and pulled tightly about his scrawny throat.

It was stagy. It smelled of herring. The way that mediums' cabinet had been balanced between the walls… why, if it had actually fallen that way it would have collapsed to the floor. And how could the killer have got back through the door without disturbing it, just as Wren had disturbed it? The whole scene was set up to look as though there had been a brawl in the closet. There hadn't been. Nobody would have stood in front of that window and strangled a man. Well, not with the light on.

Wren reached up to the electric socket in the ceiling, unscrewed the bulb far enough to darken the room. The picture was worse in the dark. Much worse. The cheesecloth glowed with white luminosity. The synthetic moonlight of it bathed the ugly profile death had left, bringing the highlights into sharp relief.

He screwed the bulb back to make contact. That hunk of cheesecloth was ectoplasm, the stuff that spirits are supposedly made of. Fake ectoplasm, of course, because it was always faked. Gladys Frye had probably used the stuff to wave in a dark room during a seance to convince the customers they were seeing grandpappy's ghost.

Wren stepped forward cautiously, dropped on one knee beside the dead man. The crystal of a watch on the dangling left wrist had been smashed, stopping the hands at 9:28. Wren looked at his own watch, and it was not yet 7:30. He touched the dead man's hand, found it stiff and stone-cold.

"So it could have happened this morning," he muttered. "Or last night."

Anybody, he decided, as he straightened to his feet, could break a watch crystal, stopping the hands at any desired time. Either the broken watch marked the time of death exactly, or falsified it to provide the killer with an alibi. He had a hunch the watch breaking was deliberate in either case, because of the attempt at setting the stage to indicate that a struggle had taken place. And he thought he knew why the closet had been chosen as the scene for the death tableau. Living and bedrooms were all but barren, with only minimum essentials of furniture. Plenty of room to brawl in, but there was nothing in the rooms to upset or disorder to show clearly that a fight had taken place.

He went back into the bedroom and from there into the living room. On the desk he found, in addition to the previously noted typewriter, an empty pen stand, a notary seal, and one of those appointment calendars. Nothing else. The facing page of the calendar was that of November 23rd. And today was November 24th. A single appointment was noted on the page, lettered in pencil rather than written in longhand: MARY MALEY 9:30 P.M.

"Ah," he murmured. "The lady who inadvertently killed her brother with too much pastry—according to Mrs. Tavell."

Wren turned back a few leaves of the calendar, saw that other appointments had been printed rather than written. He looked up quickly from the desk and across the room. One chunky black eyebrow lifted as slowly as the door of the flat was opening.

A HEAD, bald except for a fringe of yellowish-white lamb's wool above pointed ears, showed itself. The face was smooth, ageless, and untroubled. The man looked at Wren from the corners of round, shining brown eyes. The eyes, the button nose, the pointed ears—all combined to lend the face a Puckish expression that was out of this world.

"I knocked," he said in a voice almost too soft to be masculine, "but you didn't hear, did you? Probably not. I hope I'm not intruding."

"Not at all," Wren said.

"That's good." The man came in and closed the door. He had a pear-shaped torso and pot-hooked legs. His dark overcoat was too long for his shortish body, and he carried a gray felt hat in his hands. He came pussyfooting over to the desk and Wren noticed that he wore old-man shoes of pliant black leather. He breathed audibly and as he stood beside Wren at the desk his head was shyly downcast.

"You're Freya's brother, no doubt?"

Wren shook his head. He watched the man's gray-gloved fingers scamper across the desk and close on the handle of the notary seal. For some reason Wren was slightly startled. The man lifted the seal and looked at it.

"Notary seal," he said absently, and put it down. "So you're not Freya's brother. An uncle possibly? No, you are too young to be an uncle."

"Name is Wren, Jeffery Wren."

The man put a forefinger in the exact center of his chin and again examined Wren out of the corners of his eyes. His face was more than bland, it was blah. He clucked with his tongue.

"Why, you wrote a book about spirit mediums! I read it, to prove I'm broad-minded. But you're prejudiced about mediums, aren't you? All magicians are."

"Except Will Goldston, an English magician, who said…" Wren broke off, realizing that he was allowing the little bow-legged man to syphon off information without giving anything in return.

"Who are you, if you don't mind?"

"Urban… Malthus… Tavell," said the man with distinct spacing between the parts of his name. He smiled a futile sort of smile. "I am looking for Freya, as you possibly surmise. She has been a house guest of ours since last night."

"Ah? When did she arrive at your house last night?"

"I couldn't say really. I was busy in town until rather late and when I came home my wife and Freya were chatting in the drawing room."

Which did not provide Freya with any sort of an alibi.

Wren said: "If she's your house guest—"

"Why look for her here?" Tavell interrupted. "A logical question. She seems to have disappeared during the past two hours. I drove into town thinking that she might have returned to her apartment for something. Is she here now?"

The man was a whole radio quiz show, the questions and most of the answers delivered in the same breath. He was exhausting.

"Not here," Wren replied. "No one here but the dead man."

"Then I've drawn a blank. And I do hope that Freya will show up in time for that sitting tonight. No one here but—I beg your pardon." Tavell looked askance at Wren. "What kind of a man did you say was here?"

"Dead—as in murdered." Wren took hold of Tavell's thick arm and tugged him toward the bedroom. "You should see."

CHAPTER THREE

ALAS, POOR BOBERT!

IN THE bedroom Urban Malthus Tavell looked around dazedly until Jeffery Wren turned him to face the open door of the lighted closet. Tavell said nothing for a moment. He teetered up and down on the toes of his soft shoes. He blew his nose inoffensively, shook his head.

"Poor Bobert! Poor old chap!"

Wren reeled slightly. He removed his hat, took a handkerchief from his pocket, and patted his expansive brow.

"Now," he said with an elaborate show of patience, "once more. What did you call him?"

Tavell blinked. "An old chap—oh, you mean *Bobert.*" He smiled shyly. "As a small child I was always troubled with the letter 'R' sounds. Hence 'babbit' for 'rabbit' and consequently 'Bobert' for 'Robert'."

"But you're a big boy now, aren't you?"

"Well, of course. But I distinctly remember the pleasure it gave him the first time I called him Bobert, and I was determined not to give up the practice to his dying day.... But of course this is his dying day."

"Yesterday, I think." Wren took a deep breath. "Now that we've established beyond a shadow of doubt that you were a cunning child, who in hell is the corpse?"

"Why, Robert Parkinson, of course. He was my father's lawyer. He gave up his practice to devote himself entirely to my father's interests and with the passing of my father, he became my financial adviser. Does that make everything clear?"

"Not quite. Roughly estimated, not by a jugful. What's Bobert doing here besides sitting in a chair with rigor mortis? You act as though he were part of the plumbing."

Tavell's lower lip trembled. His round brown eyes took on a tearful glisten. "But I'm deeply shocked! Mr. Wren, I was on the verge of investing a large sum of money in a new enterprise. I have consulted Freya and her table about the matter and through Freya's spirit control was advised to make this investment. But I wished to be absolutely sure that Freya was sincere and genuine, for I'll grant you there are many fraudulent spiritualists. So I asked Bobert to investigate her for me...."

Tavell let that hang. He seemed hit by a sudden inspiration. He fingered the center of his chin and looked sharply at Wren.

"Why, you're the very man—you, with your skepticism!"

"I am?"

"Of course! You can take over the job that Bobert was doing for me!"

"When he was so rudely interrupted," Wren amended.

"You will observe one of Freya's sittings, and if you can offer proof that the phenomenon is produced by trickery then I shall suspect that Freya and Wilfred Doan are in cahoots and I shan't back Doan's project."

"You'll begin to suspect that, will you?" Wren took Tavell's arm and led the man from the bedroom back to the desk in the living room. He pointed to the name of Mary Maley penciled on the appointment calendar.

"A neighbor of yours, isn't she?" he asked. "Lives practically inside a cage with two man-eating Great Danes. Keeps her inheritance in a sugar bowl."

"Eh?" Tavell gave Wren a piercing look. "One couldn't very well keep three hundred thousand dollars in a sugar bowl, could one?"

Wren chuckled. "Figuratively, of course. D'you know if Miss Maley kept that appointment last night or not?"

Tavell shook his head. "How should I know?"

THE BACK door of the flat opened and slammed gustily. Zoe Osbourn's heavy tread shook the floor even as her husky voice rattled the paper on the walls.

"Jeff, you doggone light-fingered son of the woman-sawed-in-half! Why the hell didn't you call a prowl car? With a little help I'd have nailed that dirty little—"

She came out of the kitchen and into the presence of Urban Malthus Tavell, puffing and blowing like a donkey engine. Her efforts to gulp back unseemly words and at the same time summon a smirk were nothing short of convulsive.

"Why, it's Mr. Ta—vell!" she whinnied.

"Don't mention him," Wren said, absently making false knots in his handkerchief and dissolving them with a wave of his hand. "Look, rather, upon the late Bobert. Then at me, heir-apparent to the shroud."

Zoe Osbourn followed Wren's pointing finger into the bedroom. She came out a second later in a scowling dither. Mashers, moll-buzzers, shoplifters and phony fortune tellers she could take in her heavy stride. But this was something else. With no phone in Gladys "Freya" Frye's apartment, Zoe had to go to the flat across the hall to phone headquarters. Before she got back two uniformed cops of the radio patrol had taken over.

After that came Homicide with its detectives and photographers, and a bit later the assistant coroner. Wren found himself shoved off in the corner like a piece of old bric-a-brac to be given to the washerwoman next Christmas. A few perfunctory questions were asked of Urban Malthus Tavell and then he was practically kissed good-by.

Finally a plainclothes cop with pinkish hair and puffy eyelids discovered Wren in his corner suffering from neglect. He took Wren's name and address, writing with a stub of pencil, his mouth screwed over onto one side of his face.

"You know," Wren said casually, "the victim wasn't killed in that closet. Not actually."

"No?"

"No. He was posed in the closet because that's the only place in the flat where evidence of a struggle could be faked. There had to be evidence of a struggle to account for the breaking of the man's watch crystal. But the gimmick in the murder trick, the little item that could lead us straight into a sucker climax, is why the watch was broken at all. You see?"

The plainclothes cop brought his mouth around front and center and scowled at the knot in Wren's necktie.

"The watch got broke when they was fightin'. Don't leave town without notifyin' headquarters, Mr. Wren."

Mr. Wren groaned. He stuffed his hands deep into the slash pockets of his greatcoat and left the flat at the slow bouncing gait of a bus negotiating a rough detour in comfort. Nobody stopped him. Nobody noticed him. He was the Invisible Man and it was killing him.

A few minutes later he sauntered into a cheesy taproom in the neighborhood of the murder flat and asked for a glass of tawny port at the bar. The barkeep asked right back what that was—something like beef, iron and wine? So Wren drank whiskey which he despised, then went back to the phone to summon a cab.

THREE-QUARTERS of an hour later Wren's taxi turned off a county road somewhere between the villages of Nora and Carmel and into a sweeping white horseshoe of a drive that lay before the Tavell mansion. It was a red brick, two-and-a-half-story Colonial house with gray slate roof, white shutters and towering white columns on the portico. The cab stopped directly behind one of those long, superpowered convertible coupes that pedestrians glare at and mutter: "I wonder where *that* guy gets his gas."

Wren paid his fare plus tip, got out, started up the short approach walk. Halfway to the door he stopped, attracted by a glittering something half concealed in the frosted grass along the edge of the walk. He stooped, picked up a man's mechanical pencil with a barrel of chased gold. He put it in his pocket, went on to the imposing door. There was a knocker and an electric chime. Wren played them both with all the vigor of a bill collector.

A butler opened the door. He was a stocky man with a spatulate nose and a toupee that resembled an underdone pancake.

"Ah. Good evening." Wren stepped into a marble-floored reception hall and began stripping off his gloves. The servant closed the door without a sound, turned, self-consciously patted the right-hand pocket of his coat. The pocket bulged somewhat and sagged. The man packed a gun and he wasn't used to it.

"Your card, sir?" he suggested.

"Card?" Wren's smile twitched. He dipped into a pocket, brought out a whole deck of playing cards which he spread face down between his two hands. "Take one. Take any one."

Almost unwittingly, the butler had a card in his hand, and Wren said: "Nine of spades." He squared the deck, pocketed it. The butler looked dazedly at the card, turned it over, looked at the face of it. He uttered a dry little chuckle.

"Oh, but it's not, sir. Very sorry, sir. It's the queen of diamonds."

"Impossible." Wren took a sidling step to look over the butler's shoulder and incidentally to get his left hand near the man's right pocket.

"But it is, sir. The queen of diamonds."

Wren took the diamond queen from the butler's hand, held it at arm's length, facing them. "That? That's the queen of diamonds?"

It was, of course, and then it wasn't. Wren showed the back of the queen, flipped it around again. The card was now undeniably the nine of spades. And in Wren's left hand was the butler's automatic.

"It's a trick, sir!" the butler cooed. "Quite a trick. You must be Mr. Wren, the magician."

"Exactly. It's a trick. I'm Wren." He took off his coat and under cover of the bulk of it got the gun into his trousers' pocket. He handed coat and hat to the butler who took them across his left arm.

"If you'll step this way, sir." The servant pushed open a solid looking door beyond which was a dim, compact little room with oak paneling and bookshelves.

Wren shook his head. "Where's Mrs. Tavell?"

"Just step into the libr'y, sir."

"Don't like libraries. My mother was frightened by a bookworm."

"Don't be unreasonable, sir, I warn you. Into the libr'y!" The butler crowded into Wren. His right hand dropped to his coat pocket, groped, found nothing. He swallowed, backed off, looked dully down into his pocket. Wren dropped both big hands on the servant's shoulders, waltzed him around so that his back was toward the door of the snug little room.

"Tell you what, Jeeves. *You* go into the 'libr'y'!" He shoved. The butler had to back-step fast to stay on his feet. Wren slammed the library door, and then walked briskly along the hall to push open double doors and enter the living room.

THE FIREPLACE was big enough to take the sofa that stood in front of it, but the man who lay at full length on the sofa would have overlapped a little. He put down a fine old illuminated volume of Dante on his sunken chest and looked at Wren from hollow eyes. Then he got up—a process which was not unlike the folding and unfolding of a carpenter's rule. He looked a little like Dante, Roman and esthetic with fine black hair that shagged over the tops of his close-set ears. He put out a hand that was like a bundle of lead pencils.

"You must be Wren. I'm Wilfred Doan."

"Right," Wren said.

"More power to you."

Wren cocked an eyebrow. "Meaning?"

"Meaning I hope you stand this table-tapper on her ear." He was pretty vehement about it. His long arms thrashed around a bit. "It gets me. Here I have in my pocket a down-to-earth money-making proposition for Urban Tavell. What does he do? He consults a fake soothsayer. A man of Tavell's wealth and supposed intelligence! It's disgusting!"

"Yet Freya backs you up. Recommends your proposition."

Doan nodded. "It's the idea of the thing."

"If I prove Freya is a fake, chances are Tavell won't agree to back your scheme. That's what he told me."

Wilfred Doan looked worried. His hollow eyes blinked. "In which case, we'd better make a deal. You'll be doing Tavell a left-handed favor." He reached to his hip pocket for his wallet, brought it out, laboriously counted bills. He had a hundred and ten dollars on him. He kept the ten, passed Wren the hundred.

Wren said: "I tell Tavell Freya is the McCoy?"

"That's the idea. After he signs the agreement I don't care what you do with Freya."

Wren took the money. "It's returnable if my conscience starts to bother me," he said. He turned, looked toward the end of the long living room. Florence Tavell was coming down the winding stairway. She had on a gray tweed skirt, a white blouse, neat brown shoes with walking-height heels that didn't spoil the curves of her calves. She carried a three-quarter length mink jacket over one arm and an alligator purse in her hand. The smile she had for Wren was somewhat warmer than he had expected.

"I take it you've found Freya," he said.

"Not exactly. But shortly after Mr. Tavell left to hunt for her in town, I found this." She put her jacket down on a chair, opened her purse and took out a slip of paper. On it was printed in pencil: WE WILL MEET AT THE OLD MALEY HOUSE AT THE APPOINTED TIME. SPIRITUALLY YOURS, FREYA.

"Sweet," Wren said. "You know why she prints instead of writing in longhand?"

Florence Tavell shook her head. She took a cigarette case and lighter from her purse. "Why?"

"She was married to an architect," Wren told her. "She used to help with the lettering. Where's Mr. Tavell?"

"He went after Mary Maley," she replied, pointing vaguely, palm upward. She went to a mahogany commode at the end of the sofa, opened it, took out a bottle of lighter fluid. She was ignoring Wilfred Doan beautifully. But then ignoring must have been something she had practiced plenty. She brought the lighter and fluid to Wren.

"Would you mind, Mr. Wren?" she asked, paying him in advance with a smile. "These victory packages of lighter fluid exasperate me. I asked Mr. Tavell to fill my lighter before dinner, but he must have forgotten."

Wren uncapped the bottle, held a lead pencil across the mouth of it, poured fluid along the pencil and into the small fill-hole at the bottom of the lighter. He replaced the plug, handed lighter and fluid back to her.

He said: "I'd like to telephone."

She nodded toward a Regency secretary that stood open against the wall. "Or if you want privacy, there's a phone in the library."

"This will do. You've heard about the murder of Robert Parkinson?"

She nodded shortly, her eyes steady.

From the sofa, Wilfred Doan asked: "What's that? Somebody killed?"

"Somebody," Wren said. "In Freya's apartment." He went bouncing to the phone to dial the number of the flat occupied by Horace, his clerk at the novelty shop. "Police want Freya," he told Doan. "Want a little man in a derby—Hello? Horace?"

Sitting very straight on the sofa, his face lengthening, Wilfred Doan ran fingers distractedly through his hair.

From the phone, Horace's voice asked: "Izat you, Boss?"

"Me. Horace, I'd like you to come out to the Tavell place. Immediately. Are you sober?"

"Sure, I'm sober onna day before payday. What else? Where'sa Tavell place?"

"North of town," Wren replied vaguely. "Remember the babe who dripped mink pelts? Use your instinct." He hung up.

THE FRONT door of the house had opened and Wren could hear a murmur of voices and then footsteps on the marble floor. Urban Malthus Tavell pushed open the double doors, connecting hall with living room, for Mary Maley. Tavell's out-of-the-corner glance touched Wren and caromed to Florence Tavell to dwell appreciatively on the grace of her as she advanced to greet Mary Maley.

"Good evening, my dear." Florence Tavell put out two hands to Mary Maley who dropped a knitting bag grasping them.

"Oh, hello Mis' Tavell. Mis' Tavell, it's so nice—"

What was so nice was lost in the confusion of recovering the knitting bag. Mary Maley was middle-aged. She wore a silly little brown pork-pie hat and a three-piece suit of hound's-tooth check material, the outer coat trimmed with unnamable fur. She was large through the hips and nowhere else, as though she spent a great deal of time sitting and knitting. She knitted her brows, too, and her eyes looked sleepless and tired.

Tavell recovered the knitting bag for her and the ball of gray yarn that had rolled from it.

"I declare, I been so nervous lately...." Mary Maley's sentenced trailed off into embarrassed silence as her tired eyes found Wren and Wilfred Doan, both strangers to her.

Florence Tavell kissed Tavell on the mouth. It was a good kiss, but, to Wren, slightly nauseating after the frank discussion he'd had with Mrs. Tavell that afternoon. Then Tavell shook Wren's hand briefly, accomplished an introduction that included Mary Maley, Wilfred Doan, and Wren. Mary Maley acknowledged with downcast eyes.

"We're going right away, aren't we?" Florence Tavell asked her husband.

"Why not? Unless Miss Maley feels too nervous."

"Oh, no, I'm not too nervous." Miss Maley's hands fluttered on the handles of the knitting bag. "It's just that this thing has been on my mind so long. Mis' Tavell, you don't know how it is. A loved one passes on and then people say you had something to do with it. Makes you grasp at straws, like this table-tipper. Of course, Freya isn't a straw exactly, I guess. If Mr. Tavell has faith in her, why that's good enough for me. And it would be such a comfort to know—"

She must have realized she alone was talking, and into an interested silence. Her lips closed tight and a deep flush spread upward across her wrinkled face.

Wren looked at Doan. The latter hadn't gone very far from the sofa, as though he expected to have to collapse on it any moment. He was worried. For that matter, so was Wren. There was something cooking on the back burner and the flame was turned up too high.

"You're going, Doan?" Tavell asked. "But I don't suppose you are."

Doan shook his head. "None of that spirit stuff for me."

Then Tavell rang for the butler, ordered him to bring Wren's coat and hat, then went to help Mrs. Tavell on with her jacket. There was no doubt about his being devoted to his beautiful young wife. His eyes tagged at the heels of her every movement like a pair of adoring puppies.

She said: "We're walking, aren't we, darling? It's only a little way straight back if we cut through the woods, and the path is clean."

"Walking?" Tavell said. "Dearest, you know I'm not much for walking."

She pouted. "But I'm dressed for it." And then the pout became a smile, and she patted his smooth cheek affectionately. "We'll ride if you want. It will be warm in the sedan."

Wren thought as they trooped out: *Yes, humor his little whims, lady, and later mourn luxuriously.*

CHAPTER FOUR

KILL-TRAP

THE TAVELL sedan was even longer than the convertible, and through the medium of its super-power it accomplished a mouse-into-man transformation over Urban Malthus Tavell. Tavell sent the car out of the drive like a rocket from a trough. The middle of the road was exclusively his and to hell with anything that got in his way. Wren found himself unaccountably in the back seat with Mrs. Tavell, and once, when the car swerved perilously, she caught his hand and held it tight for a moment. Her touch gave Wren a little chill.

It was a short, breathless trip. The big sedan simply executed three sides of a square across gently rolling countryside dotted with suburban homes and old farmhouses. Then Tavell turned off the road into frozen ruts that squirmed up to the old Maley house. It was one of those narrow, awkward houses, neither pleasing nor practical. Shutters were fastened across the windows. The roof was low-pitched, of sheet iron, that for tonight had regained its original gleam from frost and starlight. The wood that Florence Tavell had mentioned as separating the Maley place from the Tavell property began close upon the back door.

Tavell killed the motor. In the front seat, Mary Maley drew a shivering breath.

She said: "It's dark."

It was dark. Wren and Tavell got out on the same side and assisted the women. From the lane to the front door was a scant thirty feet through crackling weeds and matted grass. There was no porch on the place. A broken rocking chair was propped up against one end of the step and remained the only sign of attempted comfort. Wren got to wondering how anybody who had inhabited such a house had ever got to be worth three hundred thousand dollars. But, conversely, simply to live in such a house at least offered the opportunity of accumulating a fortune.

Tavell and Mary Maley were on the step, Wren and Florence Tavell just behind. Tavell knocked his timid knock. There was no answer.

"Odd, isn't it?" he said. "Freya should be here." He took hold of the knob, twisted, pushed the door open.

Out of the dark interior of the house came a bright lance of orange-red flame and simultaneously the nasty yap of a small-caliber gun. It was a single shot, fired low to angle up. Wren heard the whine of the spent bullet over his head.

Florence Tavell screamed and flung both arms around Wren.

"Here." Don't!" Wren broke the hysterical clinch, pushed Florence back from the door. He saw that Tavell had somehow accomplished the heroic. He had flattened Mary Maley across the doorstep and, not so heroic, he was cowering on top of her.

"Don't shoot!" Tavell's voice was high-pitched, spineless.

Nobody shot. From the house came nothing but the dim echo of Tavell's voice. Wren plucked a pencil-flashlight from an inner pocket, beamed it through the door. The spot of it caught a card table with a glass top, and on the table was some sort of a rigging composed of pine blocks, cabinet-makers' clamps, and a small hand gun—pistol or revolver, he couldn't tell which. A set-gun, a kill-trap that hadn't killed.

Tavell got on one knee above Mary Maley. He said: "Good Lord, Wren, it—it got her!"

"No, Urban!" gasped Florence.

"Couldn't have." Wren was gruff about it. He hated hysteria. He went to the step where Tavell crouched over Miss Maley. The woman lay partially on one side and there was blood on the step near her head. She uttered a faint moan, twisted convulsively onto her back, seized Tavell's arm with one hand, pulled herself to a sitting position. Wren got a supporting arm behind her back. Her eyes were rolling frantically, and there was quite a bit of blood flowing from a gash at her temple.

"Now then," Wren said gently. "You just hit yourself on that rocker. That's all. When Tavell threw you—"

"On—on that rocker," she whispered faintly. "I told Eben someone would fall on that rocker some day."

Wren slid his right arm under her knees. "Get back," he said to the Tavells. "Get her inside. Get a doctor."

"No. No! Don't take me in there. Not in that house!" She was kicking feebly at the air.

"There won't be any more shooting," Wren assured everybody. "People who plant set-guns don't stick around."

"Take—take me home," Miss Maley sobbed. *"Don't take me in that house."* Her head rolled sideways against Wren's shoulder and then back, her funny brown pork-pie hat going over her left ear.

She'd passed out cold.

THEY couldn't take Miss Maley home. As Urban Malthus Tavell pointed out, while Wren carried the unconscious woman toward the car, nobody could get near Miss Maley's house because of the dogs that guarded it. You couldn't summon Little Joe, Miss Maley's aged Negro servant, from the gate in Miss Maley's fence because the house was too far away. Therefore Little Joe couldn't corral the dogs. The only way to get the dogs tied up was to telephone Miss Maley's house and tell Little Joe to tie them up. Which meant finding a phone. Which meant taking Mary Maley to the Tavell house.

Wren, who was carrying Mary Maley while Florence Tavell pointed the way with the flashlight, had one foot inside the car door and was bracing up his burden with his knee, when Florence uttered a cry of dismay. Wren looked over his left shoulder at where the flashlight spotted the left front tire. It was as flat as it would ever be.

"Those damned ruts!" Tavell said.

"Your witless, reckless driving," said Florence Tavell coolly. The "darling" she added as an afterthought scarcely took the sting out of her words.

"Back to the house," Wren said, "where we should have put her in the first place. Must be some means of making a fire. Got to have heat—" He stopped talking. It took breath. He hadn't too much breath because Mary Maley seemed to be gaining weight.

He got her across the sill with Florence lighting the way. The slender beam from the flash pointed out stiff, friendless furnishings, finally found a downstairs bedroom where there was a small heating stove. There was a mattress on the bed, but no covers. Wren put Miss Maley down gently, peeled off his heavy coat, and threw it over her. Florence Tavell, in the meantime, had located an oil lamp, lighted it with her cigarette lighter, placed it on a marble-topped dresser.

"All right." Wren turned from the bed. "How long would it take you to get back through the woods to your place?"

"Five minutes, maybe ten," Tavell said.

"Seven, if we hurry," Florence thought.

"Then get going. Get a doctor out here as soon as you can. She's not in a bad way at all, but these scalp wounds bleed."

The Tavells went together. No sooner had they left than Wren was regretting that one of them hadn't stayed. There was a lot for one man to do, and since he had to carry the oil lamp with him, he had virtually only one arm.

Back in the kitchen he found cobs, paper and kindling in the woodbox behind the cook-stove. He brought some of each into the bedroom, laid a fire in the iron stove. When he struck a match to his handiwork, he discovered damps in the chimney. Either that, or he hadn't regulated the draft properly.

Choking, coughing, and shivering, he shook the grates, fiddled with the damper, and was finally rewarded with clean, roaring flame visible through the mica window of the stove door. He turned, looked back toward the bed. Mary Maley hadn't moved. The gash on her head was bleeding freely, but her breathing was regular.

He stripped off suitcoat and vest and then took off his white shirt which he tore into strips. With this he stanched the bleeding somewhat. But by that time the fire needed attention and he was damned near frozen. He put on his vest over undershirt and then added his suitcoat. He picked up the lamp, started back to the kitchen, but paused a moment in the front room to take a closer look at the set-gun.

It was a simple arrangement. A single-shot, twenty-two target pistol was wired to two wood blocks and the blocks were held to Freya's glass-topped table with clamps. Black linen thread was attached to the trigger, led back to a screw-eye in a block, then up to the ceiling, across to the side of the door, and thence to the corner of the door itself where it was anchored. There was just enough slack so that the door could swing nearly all the way open before the trigger tripped. If the gun elevation had been calculated a little better there was no doubt but what somebody would have taken on lead.

But who? Had the thing been designed for Tavell, for Florence, Miss Maley, or for Wren himself? He shook his head, then glanced at his watch. The Tavells had been gone about thirteen minutes.

HE HURRIED back to the kitchen, got more cobs, returned to the bedroom for a hasty look at his patient. His bandages hadn't done a whole lot of good. He was a better fireman than a doctor.

He was kneeling on the floor, feeding cobs through the stove door when the fireworks started. Outside the house, somebody shot through a chink in the shutter, shattering glass. Wren twisted around on one knee, stared open-mouthed at the window and then at Mary Maley on the bed. Three more shots, so close together as to create a prolonged and deafening roar. Wren saw the figure on the bed bounce under the impact of the heavy-caliber slugs. And then he shook off the fear that had hold of him.

He bounced to his feet and toward the dresser. The gun barrel in the chink of the shutter swiveled. He actually saw it turn, saw the cold hollow eye staring at him. He blew down the chimney of the lamp as the gun at the window roared. The lamp chimney exploded into fragments right under his nose. Needles of glass caught him in chin and cheeks. He bounced back from the dresser, dug into his trouser pocket for the automatic he had taken from the butler and lurched into the total darkness of the living room.

Of course he ran into Freya's table. The damned thing was right in front of the door and he'd forgotten about it. He kicked the table aside, got the door open, bounced over the step to turn to the left. Somewhere at the back of the house was a sound like somebody dropping a plank onto a pile of lumber. He skirted the side of the house, came to the rear where shadows from the woods encroached on the silver of the night. He didn't see anybody or hear anything. He was a perfect target for anybody who happened to be back among those trees, but there were no shots. He was feeling pretty futile when he noticed the acutely slanted doors of the cellar opening against the back of the house.

He tiptoed to the cellar entrance, stooped, felt across frost-glistening boards for the cold tongue of the hasp. The metal tongue hung down instead of bridging the twin doors to buttonhole the staple. He knew what the sound like piling lumber had been. Somebody had dropped the cellar doors.

Wren pulled back on the hasp tongue and the door swung open on creaking hinges. Moonlight showed him sagging skeleton stairs against a ramp of hard earth. He gripped the cold butt of the little automatic, took a deep breath, and started down the stairs. Ahead was darkness, but it was more welcome than the light. He skipped the last three steps, came pounding down on a rammed earth floor. He waited a moment, listening.

Somebody groaned.

Wren groped for matches, got one, scuffed the head with a thumbnail. The flare of light showed a brick-walled basement room, roughly twelve feet square, empty except for cobwebs. In one wall was a door of stained car-siding, and on a rusty nail hung a lantern. Wren reached the lantern, got it down onto the earthen floor before his match went out. He could detect a gurgle of oil in it.

The groaning came from behind the door.

Wren lighted another match, got the lantern going. While he was adjusting the wick he noticed a small piece of straight wood lying about six inches out from the foot of the door. It was a wood skewer, and attached to the blunt end of it was a yard-long length of black thread. This murder had more black thread attached to it than a magician would use in a dozen levitations.

He left the skewer where he found it, straightened. The door had a black porcelain knob and was locked by a key that had been left in place. He twisted the key, got the door open, entered with the lantern held high in his left hand and the automatic in his right.

IT WAS a vegetable cellar with no vegetables. On the bare earth floor was a long, hippy blonde. A mangy raccoon coat concealed some of her hour-glass contours. She wore large-sized, high-heeled pumps, but no stockings. Her nice legs at the moment were wearing a coat of makeup and goose pimples. There were handcuffs on her ankles and also on her wrists. The features of Gladys "Freya" Frye, Wren thought, were horsy, and her face showed hardening of the forties.

She sat up painfully, squinted at the light and at Wren.

"Heh," she grunted. "It's you, the magi."

"Me. What do you represent—America waiting to be discovered by Columbus?"

"Spare me that stuff." She groaned and pressed the palms of her manacled hands to her forehead. "I came over here late this afternoon to set up my table and look the spot over. Somebody slugged me. I got a taste in my mouth as if somebody poured dope down my throat. I just came to when I heard you fooling around out there."

"That's your story," he said. "You know about the shooting and you damn well think you've got an alibi. You haven't. On the floor outside the door is a wood skewer with a thread attached to it. You could be in here and lock the door on the outside with a skewer and a thread."

She looked daggers at him. Her lips were purple because the blue cold showed through the red rouge. She sneezed violently and wiped her nose on the furry sleeve of her coat.

"You get me the hell out of here, Wren. If I get pneumonia and die it's on your head."

Wren chuckled. He worked the slide of the automatic, throwing a cartridge into the firing chamber. He squeezed the trigger experimentally and got quite a jolt when the gun yapped and the bullet struck the brick wall to come whining back at him.

"It works," he said. "I'll count ten, Gladys. By that time you'll be out of those handcuffs, or I'll put you beyond the reach of the best medium in the business. One… two…."

She blinked at him. She named him foully.

"…three. You better get that gimmick out of your heel."

He meant it. She could see he meant it. She told him what he was again, with embellishment, but she got to work on the cuffs. She doubled over, got her hands on her right shoe, slipped it off. She hadn't a pretty foot. The joint of her big toe was enlarged.

She said: "What the hell if the gimmick isn't here?"

"…four. It'll be there."

She held the shoe by the counter, jerked on the heel, twisted. The heel swiveled around, off center, revealing its hollow construction. The medium shook a thin piece of steel a quarter of an inch wide and an inch and a quarter long from the heel. An inch-long channel was cut up the center of the piece of metal forming a flat, two-tined fork. She thrust the fork not into the keyhole of the bean-pattern cuffs but into that narrow space where the saw-tooth jaw enters the lock. She yanked and the jaws of the left cuff sprang open.

Wren said: "I'm up to seven. You're behind schedule. If you were doing this in a mediums' cabinet you'd be ready to wave the ectoplasm around by now."

SHE had the right cuff open, was working on the set that confined her ankles. She was free on the count of ten and threw both sets of cuffs at Wren's head. He didn't duck. She was chilled to the marrow and her aim was bad. He picked up the cuffs, dropped them into his pocket while Freya was getting into her shoe.

"Now," he said. "Out of here. Ladies first."

They went out and up the steps. Wren forced her into the house, past the set-gun, and back into the bedroom. For a moment it looked as though she were going to embrace the stove. And then she saw the poor, bloody thing on the bed.

"She—she's dead!"

Wren nodded. "Those shots. Only two of them missed. The one from the set-gun and the one intended for me. All the rest are…" and he shrugged.

"We found Robert—or Bobert—Parkinson in the closet of your flat in town. Three yards of best-grade ectoplasm strangled him. You're in a spot."

She said: "I haven't been in town all day."

"Bobert died last night," he insisted relentlessly.

"But I caught the ten o'clock bus for Carmel—"

He was shaking his head. "Bobert was strangled at about nine-thirty, according to the smashed watch on his wrist."

"But—but I left at nine. Listen, Wren, you've got to believe me. I left that apartment at nine o'clock. I—I can't prove it."

"You won't have to. They'll just show you the chair and tell you to sit in it. Tavell says Bobert was investigating you. To the police, it will look as though Bobert discovered you were out to rook Tavell, and you killed Bobert to shut him up. About the time you were doing that, Mary Maley showed up for her appointment—"

Freya goggled at him. "I never had an appointment with the Maley woman." She thumbed at the bed. "That's the first look I ever got at her."

He shrugged. "That appointment is noted on your date calendar in the flat. Nine-thirty last night. Cops will say Mary caught you killing Bobert. So Mary had to die. They'll say you tried with the set-gun, then tried again, direct method. They'll say you shot through the window, then dashed down the cellar to lock yourself up and frame a story about a big, bad Unknown who conked you and handcuffed you. But the conk and handcuff alibi won't hold because everything was at hand to prove you could have got out whenever you felt like it. You're in a jam."

Wild-eyed, she stared as though at the eight-ball that was rolling steadily in her direction.

"Wren, I—I didn't! I was out to rook Tavell, sure, but the sucker was practically asking for it. I didn't kill anybody!"

He picked up the lantern, motioned her toward the door with the automatic. "You know the path back through the woods to the Tavell mansion? Let's hit it. Exercise will do us good."

CHAPTER FIVE

THE RUNT OF THE LITTER

THEY MADE it in six minutes flat with the cold as a spur. Around in front of the Tavell house Wren saw that the big convertible was gone and in its place was a four-wheeled heap of junk with Varga girls pasted on what was left of the windshield. The jalopy could have belonged only to Horace.

He pushed Freya ahead of him through the front door and into the marble-floored hall where there was quite a to-do about something. The lanky Wilfred Doan was pacing back and forth like a distraught Hamlet to-being or not-to-being. In front of a closet door the butler crouched, washing his hands in the air and peeking through the keyhole. On the other side of the door small fists pounded and Florence Tavell's voice was pretty much in evidence.

"Get me out of here, Jason! Get me out at once or I'll discharge you!"

"But, madam, the key—"

"Get an ax!" madam cried.

That was how things were when Wren and Freya entered. Then Wilfred Doan saw Freya, stopped his pacing, said something short and dirty under his breath. Wren kicked the front door shut behind them, bounced over to the closet to nudge the butler out of the way. The butler saw the gun which was his and which was practically frozen in Wren's fist.

He said: "So you took it, sir."

Wren waved the gun. "And I'll use it. Who told you to waylay me at the door when I first came here, anyway?"

"Why—why...." The butler turned, looked at Wilfred Doan. "Why, it was Mr. Doan. He told me to put you in the libr'y and then—then tap you gently on the head."

"I did?" Doan shouted. "You're a dirty liar!"

"Everybody's a dirty liar," Wren said.

"Mr. Wren? Is it you? Can you get me out of this closet?" Florence Tavell wailed.

Wren looked at the lock. It wouldn't even require picking. He took out his key ring, employed a skeleton master and opened the door. Florence Tavell, flushed and beautiful, almost fell out of the closet and into his arms. Wren steadied her on her own two feet and backed off.

"Come on," he said. "Give."

She gave breathlessly. "A little man in a derby hat. He had a gun. I'd just telephoned—"

"Whom did you telephone?" Wren cut in.

"First I telephoned Dr. Bayne in Carmel," she told him. "My husband had already started for Carmel in the convertible to get Dr. Bayne because he's old and slow—the doctor, I mean—and I was to phone him to be ready. And then I had to call Mary Maley's house to get hold of Little Joe, her servant."

"What for?"

"To have Little Joe tie up the dogs. No one could take Mary Maley back to her house unless the dogs were tied up."

Wren said: "That does it. Go on. A man in a derby—"

"First," Florence went on, "there was that—that person of yours, that clerk. He came in while I was phoning about the dogs and asked where you were. And right after that the man in the derby came into the library where I was phoning, turned a gun on us, forced us into the closet."

"He'd heard what you were saying about the dogs over at Mary Maley's place," Wren said. "Where's Horace?"

Horace came out of the closet on all fours. He got to his feet somehow, leaned against the wall, and looked balefully at Wren. Horace had a beaut of a mouse and a bluish egg on his forehead.

"You don't look so hot yourself, Boss," he said.

Wren knew he didn't. He couldn't, being somewhat decolleté in suitcoat and vest, but no shirt. And then there were those places on his face where the glass from the lamp chimney had hit him.

"The man in the derby knocked you out, I suppose, when you were defending Mrs. Tavell?" Wren asked Horace.

Horace shook his head, jerked a thumb at Florence. "She defended herself inna closet." He sniffed miserably. "I don't have a way with women, do I?"

Wren took out one pair of handcuffs, tossed them to Horace. "I'm leaving you in charge. Shackle anybody who wants to go home. If Freya's too tempting, you might shackle yourself."

Then Wren reached into the closet, got the first overcoat he could lay his hands on, struggled into it. He turned to Florence Tavell.

"You'll have to go with me to show me the way to Mary Maley's house."

Florence Tavell preened herself momentarily from force of habit, drew her mink coat about her and took Wren's arm. As they went out the front door, a despondent Horace could be heard to mutter: "The boss always hadda way with women even if with the Army he's 1-AH."

WREN borrowed Horace's jalopy and with Florence on the front cushions beside him, he drove out onto the road to turn right following her instruction. The car was patriotic! Thirty miles-per-hour was its limit and you were stuck with it.

"Mary Maley's dead," Wren said shortly.

Florence was silent a moment. Then: "You mean she died before the doctor arrived? You mean from that scratch on the head?"

"I mean from four shots, none of them misses. Then I ran out of the house. Somebody banged the cellar door, which was bait for me. Down in the cellar was Freya, looking as if she had an alibi that wouldn't hold water. Freya's headed for the chair. Fast. Too bad to have to stop her. She didn't kill Bobert or Miss Maley. Freya's just a spook-crook trying to get along. And she made the perfect fall guy."

He sighed heavily, importantly. "Can't let justice down, can we? Freya didn't kill Bobert. Freya wouldn't have used three yards of luminous cheesecloth to strangle Bobert. Somebody who didn't know the cheesecloth was luminous did the killing. And, as I pointed out to the police, Bobert didn't die in Freya's closet. The actual murder probably took place in the bedroom or living room of Freya's flat. Then the corpse was carried to the closet and evidence of a struggle was staged. The time of Bobert's death was fixed exactly, a time when Freya was on her way to the bus station and therefore without an alibi.

"Then, to prepare a motive for Freya killing Mary Maley, the murderer printed a note on Freya's appointment calendar, indicating that Mary Maley had a date with Freya at the exact time of the murder.

It would appear to the police that Mary had caught Freya in the murder act and therefore knew too much. Since Freya has the habit of printing instead of writing, the forgery was simple. Clear?"

"No," Florence replied. Her voice was quiet but tensely controlled. "Of course I know nothing of—of what happened to Bobert except what Mr. Tavell told me, but—"

"Of course you don't."

"But you said Freya wouldn't have strangled Bobert with that piece of luminous cheesecloth. Why?"

"Oh, that. Merely that the cheesecloth sets up quite a glow in the dark—something the killer didn't know—and there was a window in the back of the closet. The glow might have been seen by somebody in the apartment across the alley, and the police would have been called to investigate prematurely. Bobert's body, according to the killer's plan, ought not to have been found until Mary Maley was dead. Because if the police got the chance to question Mary and learned that she did not have—and did not keep—that appointment at Freya's apartment, then Freya would have no conceivable motive for killing Mary Maley."

"And you simply asked Mary whether or not she had made or kept such an appointment?"

Wren shook his head. "I didn't ask. I knew that when your butler tried to railroad me into the library for a possible knockout that every effort would be made to prevent me from asking such a question. So I didn't ask. Liking to live as I do, I maintained complete silence on the matter. But then Mary told me. Inadvertently. She told me she had never kept an appointment with Freya when she referred to Freya as a table-tipper."

Wren chuckled. "Two schools of thought on what spirits do with tables. Some say spirits tip or tilt them. Others, like Freya, think the well-mannered spook should knock or tap. Yet it's a different technique the medium employs, and a table-tapper is not a table-tipper."

WREN braked the car suddenly and pointed to the left, to a high steel fence backed by straight row plantings of catalpas.

"This the place? Or is it something that belongs to the War Department?"

Florence said this was Mary Maley's. Wren had to back up a little to come abreast of a narrow gate in the barrier. He cut the ignition, took out the key.

"Maybe you'd better stay here," he suggested.

She uttered a short, strained laugh. "I intend to."

"Close up, murder's not too funny, is it?" She gave him a quick, gray-eyed glance. "If this is intended as an object lesson, Mr. Wren, because of the way I talked in your office this afternoon, save it, won't you? My opinion on the occasional necessity of murder hasn't changed."

Wren got out, stepped to the gate. Even before he had opened the latch the dogs began baying furiously. But then they were tied. They *had* to be tied, otherwise the killer could not have accomplished his point.

A well defined path of crushed limestone led through the grove of catalpa trees. The house, a good two hundred feet back from the road, was merely a modest frame cottage that couldn't have cost any more than the fence which surrounded the property. Lights burned at the windows, and as Wren stepped onto the porch he was aware of a steady, rhythmic *chink-chink-chink* sound coming from somewhere inside.

The door was not locked. Wren stepped into a tiny hall that gave into the living room. Lying full length on the red-tiled fireplace hearth was a middle-aged Negro about six feet and four inches tall—or, in this case, long. Little Joe, Mary Maley's keeper of the hounds, undoubtedly. The big man was out cold, and the conveniently near-at-hand poker must have been the weapon employed.

Wren stooped over the man briefly, assured himself that Little Joe wasn't in a bad way. Then he straightened, turned, his eyes traveling back toward the adjoining dining room. The *chink-chink* sound, coming from somewhere in the rear, had given way to the grinding of metal on metal and the high whine of an electric motor.

Wren took a quiet step toward the dining room, paused to stare down at a mahogany magazine stand that was laden with periodicals dealing with astrology as well as several paperbacked books of instruction devoted to the occult.

Back in the dining room, he stopped in front of a glass-fronted china cabinet. The door stood ajar, and there was some evidence of plundering. A Spode sugar-and-creamer set had been permanently ruined. The sugar bowl, of ample proportions, had been knocked off the shelf and a sizable chunk had been broken out of it on falling to the floor. He picked up the bowl and something rattled inside. He turned out of the bowl and into the palm of his hand a little heap of small change—dimes, pennies, quarters.

"I'll be damned!" he said distinctly, then poured the money back into the bowl, replaced it on the shelf beside the creamer.

From the dining room, two doors led into kitchen and bedroom respectively. He opened the latter, being very quiet about it, his right hand in the pocket of his borrowed overcoat and clenching the butt of the automatic.

INSIDE the bedroom, Mary Maley's closet door stood wide open. Crouching on the floor, the soles of his shoes and the seat of his pants toward Wren, was a man. He had a flashlight on the closet floor, and an electric cord leading from a baseboard outlet was connected with the power drill he was employing. Wren could just see the top of a safe over the rounded crown of the man's derby hat. And the safe expert was utterly oblivious to the fact that he was not alone.

Wren kicked the bedroom door shut. The man in the closet cut the power from his drill and turned around on his knees to look into Wren's gun.

It was the same little man who had turned up in Freya's apartment, the same narrow face with the same twitching nose. He said with some vehemence that he'd be damned, and stuck up his hands.

"You know what?" he moaned. "I case this damn joint for three lousy months, tryin' to figure a way to get past them dawgs. Tonight the Maley dame has a accident, the dogs is tied, I get a break, and now look at me!"

"No thanks," Wren said. "I've seen you." He stepped a little closer and looked over the man's shoulder. "How far along are you?"

The safeman had knocked the dial off with a lead mallet and was in the act of drilling out the lock.

Wren said: "Well, what's keeping you? Get on with it. You've no finesse with locks, but every man to his forte."

The little man in the derby goggled at Wren and waved his upraised hands in a sort of hopeless, helpless gesture.

"You mean—"

"I mean what I said. Get the safe open. I'm a dirty crook and I'll split fifty-fifty, down to the last penny."

The blank expression on the little safeman's face cracked into a broad grin. "Geez," he said. "Geez, I guess you're O.K."

"I guess so, too." Wren pulled a stool from in front of a vanity table and sat down to watch as the little man returned to his can-opening. It was a matter of five minutes before the last hole was drilled and the lock knocked out. Trembling fingers pulled the door open, and the man's light flooded the interior. Wren stood up, looked over the derby. Neither said anything for a moment, but you could see the little man's shoulders steadily drooping right along with his spirits.

"Three lousy damn months I case this joint!" It was close to a sob. "Tonight I get a break—"

"Uh-huh," Wren grunted. "And the safe is empty. Three hundred thousand kopeks sifted through our eager fingers. Tsk! But I'm not surprised."

The little man missed the jingle the pair of handcuffs made as Wren pulled them from his pocket. In his dazed condition, he couldn't have been aware that Wren had clamped one of the bracelets on his right wrist until Wren was tugging him out of the closet. And then he was sore about it. He scooped the sewers of his vocabulary for epithets to describe Wren. Boiled down and cleaned up for mailing, it all added up to a statement to the effect that Wren was no longer his pal.

"No," Wren admitted. "No profit in it. Besides, the police want to know how you happened to be in Freya's flat tonight."

"An' who's got a better right in her flat?" the little man raved. "Ain't I her brother? Ain't I Bud Frye?"

Wren cocked a chunky eyebrow at Bud Frye. "Her brother? The runt of the litter, I suppose."

CHAPTER SIX

TABLE TAPS

BECAUSE WREN was inconvenienced with Bud Frye, Florence Tavell had to drive them the mile back to the Tavell mansion. It was a good thing the heap was so well ventilated because Florence's haughty nose certainly would have had a lot of trouble sharing the same air with the likes of Bud Frye.

Jason, the butler, let them in, viewing Bud Frye with pardonable dismay. It did seem that guests at the mansion became progressively more peculiar with each new arrival. Florence Tavell went straight back to the living room without removing her jacket, but Wren lingered to superintend locking Bud Frye in the library. When that was done, Wren started back toward the double doors that opened onto the living room to find Horace coming toward him nursing a brandy sniffer in his hand. Only when it was brandy, Horace apparently didn't sniff. The bowl was more than half full.

Horace took a swallow of the brandy and said: "Gah! Think what these rich sons-a-whichs' livers must be like!"

Wren put a hand on Horace's arm and then turned to Jason who had just come from the library.

"Jason, if you'll set up a card table in the living room—some place on bare floor."

"Yes, sir. As for Miss Freya, sir." The servant inclined his head, went back into the living room.

Wren said: "Is Mr. Tavell back?"

"Yeah," Horace said. "An' just a minute before you came in a coupla city dicks were here. I got it they were lookin' for the horsy blonde, but when Tavell got through with them I think it was you they were after."

Wren pursed his lips, smacked. "Come again? And be more lucid."

"Two dicks at the door. Tavell talked to them, see? It seems some dame named Mary Maley got her head hurt inna accident and she was in your care while Tavell went after a doc. When the doc and Tavell got to where this was, you wasn't, and the Maley dame was dead from gun shots. So the coupla dicks went to view the remains and possibly pick you up if convenient."

Wren nodded. "They'll be back. We've got to work fast. I think in a few minutes somebody will try to dispose of a key." He scowled. "Must be a key to Freya's flat. And the killer wouldn't have disposed of it up to now. You mustn't let that happen, Horace."

Horace blinked. "I mustn't, huh?"

"No. Stand in the hall doorway and watch."

Wren went into the living room and toward the little group clustered about the fireplace. Freya was looking pretty regal in a wing chair. Wilfred Doan stood on the hearth and looked completely unattached. Florence and Urban Tavell made a nice family group on the sofa, holding hands.

As Wren approached, Tavell looked askance at him. "Why did you leave Mary Maley to the mercy of that gunman?"

Wren did not reply. He looked around, spotted the card table which

Jason had set up. He bounced over to the table and crooked a finger at the others.

"Might confine our questions to the spirits," he suggested. "Freya, if you please. And Mr. and Mrs. Tavell. We've a few things to settle before the police return to make themselves obnoxious with questions and searchings."

Wilfred Doan said: "Another one of those crazy seances? In just ten minutes, Mr. Tavell, I'm going home. I've showed you a good proposition, given you the chance to get in on the ground floor of a new enterprise. But there's an end even to my patience."

"You aren't going anywhere, Doan," Wren said. "Just collapse somewhere. Tavell will know whether he's backing you or not in a few minutes."

Freya came to the table and sat down in the chair Wren indicated. She was pale except for her nose. Her nose looked as though she had a bad cold. She sat opposite Wren while the Tavells sat on either side of him. As Freya set the example, all rested their fingertips lightly on the top of the card table.

"Be very quiet everyone, please," Freya said in a practiced Garbo contralto, though Freya herself looked as if she might break into hysterics any moment.

Wren looked at Florence Tavell. Her coloring was high, almost feverish, her gray eyes bright in anticipation. Urban Tavell, on the other hand, registered nothing at all.

A SILENT minute ticked by. Freya's eyes were closed, her lips compressed. If this was a trance, it was an unconvincing one. And then the tapping began. It was a little like the snapping of a toy gun, and if you had a fair imagination you might conclude that the sound came from the table itself. Wren's eyes narrowed purely for effect. He took a slow breath, then ducked his head to look beneath the table. The tapping went on uninterrupted, with no perceptible movement of Freya's feet. Wren straightened.

"Phenomenal!" he whispered, also for effect.

Freya's eyes popped open and she gave him a startled look across the table. Wren winked. Freya closed her eyes quickly. Across the room Wilfred Doan unfolded from his chair and tiptoed to the tapping table. He caught Wren's eyes and winked. Wren could feel a warm spot on his right cheek. That was Florence Tavell glaring at him. As for Urban Tavell, his eyes were downcast in the solemn attitude of prayer.

Wren said: "I shall ask a question—the acid test. I shall give a series of names, one of which was the first name of my great-grandmother. Should the tapping of the table choose the right one, I shall be convinced."

Another moment of silence and then Wren began, pronouncing the name *Clarissa.* From the table came a single tap for no. Wren kept on through *Alicia* and *Hannah.* On the fourth name, *Virginia,* there were two taps for *yes.* This was all news to Wren who hadn't the slightest idea what his great-grandmother had been called, but he accepted it as gospel.

"Well?" It was Tavell's voice, high-pitched, tremulous.

Wren drew a long breath. He inclined his head. "Yes, that is my great-grandmother's name. No one present except myself could know it. There is no explanation other than the supernatural."

Wilfred Doan rested a gaunt hand on the back of Freya's chair. "If Wren believes, who am I to doubt? Maybe I owe you an apology."

On Wren's right, Florence Tavell sat stiffly in her chair. Her nostrils flared slightly, and her long gray eyes had narrowed and were staring daggers at Wren.

Doan took from his coat pocket a long, legal-looking document which he plopped down on the table in front of Urban Tavell.

"Last chance, Mr. Tavell. Are you signing or aren't you?" Doan's fingers trembled across his vest-front, searching for a pen to offer.

"Something to write with?" Wren asked quickly, his hand coming out of his pocket. "Here's a pencil I found on the front lawn. Yours, isn't it, Tavell?"

Tavell's gnome-like eyes widened as he saw the pencil with the chased gold barrel. He reached for it, fingers clutching. His indrawn breath made a strangling sound.

"Yes. On the front lawn, you say? My—my pencil!" His laugh was a sickly thing with a sob in it.

"Better sign in ink," Doan suggested cheerfully. "Make it legal."

Florence Tavell raised her voice decisively. "He's not—" And that was when Wren kicked her ankle unmercifully. She pushed back from the table, more angry than hurt. Tavell pushed back, too.

"I'm not signing," Tavell said. "I—I…" his eyes went on a tour like a Prohibitionist looking for hip-flask bulges. "I strongly suspect that you are all in cahoots, plotting against me. In fact, I'm dropping the matter and I think I shall go to bed. I don't care if I never see Freya or Doan or Wren again."

He stood up, gave them each a reproachful look and went out of the room, a mite of a man stalking sedately on bow-legs.

FLORENCE TAVELL stood up, too. Wren looked at her, told her to sit down. He was curt about it. She did so, slowly, composing her beautiful hands in her lap. Her gray eyes watched him and a faint smile played at her red mouth.

Wilfred Doan said: "You fixed it—but good, Wren!" He dropped a hand on Freya's shoulder. "Come on, toots. Let's go pack our bags."

Wren said: "As a husband and wife team, you'd do better in vaudeville. Now that vaudeville's back, Freya, maybe you could put that double-jointed big toe of yours to better use than popping it to make like spirit taps. You know"—he chuckled—"you know, that's not the first time I met with a case like yours. Joint-cracking is one of the favorite methods. You hold your foot firmly against the floor and it makes quite a pop."

Freya's face was wooden, sulky. "How long have you known Doan and I were married?"

Wren shrugged. "Never met Doan before. But I'd heard that Gladys 'Freya' Frye had married an architect. And an architect was just the guy to proposition Tavell on a prefabricated housing scheme. Accent on the *fabricated.* But then you didn't fool Tavell, either. He knew all the time it was a rooking. I just played along with you two tonight to see if Tavell would follow through."

"Come on, toots," Doan said. "Let's start packing. The magi is too fast company." He led Freya from the room.

Florence Tavell put her elbows on the table and rested her chin on a bridge of slim, laced fingers. She was perfectly calm.

"If Urban knew that Freya was a fraud why did he pretend to believe in her?" she asked.

"He needed a fall guy," Wren said. "And he needed someone he could use as a decoy to get Mary Maley out of her stronghold. Mary was a believer in things occult and creepy and she trusted your husband. Urban Tavell's pretended belief in Freya was all build-up for tonight, for what took place at the old Maley house. You understand about the set-gun?"

She shook her head. Wren guessed that already she was mourning luxuriously.

He said: "The set-gun wasn't intended to kill anybody. Aimed too high, you see. But it gave Tavell an excuse to knock Mary Maley down and injure her as though by accident. Thus in seeming to have played the hero, he diverted suspicion. But the 'accident' was the thing. It provided the excuse for phoning Mary Maley's cottage and having Little Joe chain the dogs. You did the phoning, of course, while you thought Tavell was on the way to get the doctor. He wasn't. He had two things to do. He had to get back to the old Maley place and kill Mary. Then he had to swing over to Mary Maley's cottage and steal something out of a sugar bowl. After that, he went for the doctor."

"What did he steal?" Florence asked.

He shrugged. "I can only guess. Maybe it will come out at the trial. It might have been a receipt or a promissory note. A receipt, probably, which he promptly destroyed. You see, Mary Maley trusted him, even though she didn't trust banks. I think she handed her three hundred thousand dollar inheritance over to Tavell to invest for her—which was what Tavell had been working for. He was broke, or had been until he got his hands on Mary's money. Then, to keep the money, he had to kill Mary and destroy the receipt. Had to kill old Bobert, too, because Bobert knew of Tavell's financial condition. It would be difficult to explain to Bobert where Tavell got three hundred thousand to prime the pump."

"When," she asked, as though she found all this morbidly fascinating, "when did you discover all this?"

WREN'S gaze was remote, his brow furrowed. "It came a bit at a time, like olives out of a bottle. Little things. Something you said in my office this afternoon helped. You said Tavell's devotion *becomes* unbearable unless it is expressed in dollars. You said *becomes*—not *would become.* Indicating, possibly, that there was an interval when Tavell was broke.

"And other things. When I spoke figuratively about Mary Maley keeping her inheritance in a sugar bowl, Tavell nearly jumped out of his skin. Which meant nothing until I found a broken sugar bowl in Mary Maley's cottage. She must have kept the receipt for the money in the sugar bowl with her loose change, indicating how much trust she had in him. Didn't even bother to put the receipt in her safe. And Tavell knew where she had put it."

"What about the pencil?" Florence asked him.

"Oh, that? Simple. There was neither pencil nor pen on the desk in Freya's flat tonight. Nor last night, when Tavell took Bobert there to murder him. Tavell had to forge that note on Freya's appointment calendar as part of the machinery to frame both killings on Freya. He used his own pencil. Then some time tonight Tavell discovered the pencil was missing.

"He had a key to Freya's flat, you know. He'd necessarily have one to get Bobert there and to get Freya's handcuffs for the set-up in the cellar of the old Maley house. And when he found his pencil gone, his brain went back to the night before, and he thought he'd left it in Freya's flat. So he went back to look for the pencil, didn't need the key because the door was unlocked. I was there. He was afraid I'd found the pencil. I think he tried to nerve himself up to bashing my head in with a notary seal. And in the flat he found out I'd noticed the appointment with Mary Maley written on the calendar. Which accounts for his ordering Jason to waylay me if I came here tonight. Jason, the faithful retainer, tried to put the blame for that on Doan."

She said, and seemed worried about it: "But you haven't any material evidence."

"That's right—unless your husband still has that key to Freya's flat. I'm gambling that he kept it, thinking he'd take another look at Freya's flat to see if he could find the pencil. Now that he's got the pencil, and knows I found it on the lawn, he'll probably try to get rid of the key. But he won't get away with it. Not with Horace's eagle eye out for just such a move. Nobody will get away with anything, except you, my dear."

Florence took a short breath, held it a moment. "What do you mean by that?"

He turned his big white palms upward, shrugging with his hands. "That you're the real murderer. The untouchable murderer. Inadvertent? I don't know. But Tavell is the tool of the circumstances. Get the picture: Here's Urban Tavell, physically unattractive, an introvert, extremely shy. He's never earned anything, not excluding self-respect. Realizing his own inferiority, how does he express his inner yearnings? By batting around corners in powerful cars, borrowing personal power from a multi-cylinder engine.

"And, of course, the greatest satisfaction he got out of this world was possessing a beautiful woman for his wife. He'd bought you at a lavish price. No ceiling on you, is there? He bribed you to remain his wife, to stay with him in hope of inheriting a fortune someday. And then when he went broke, you were practically packing. He begged you to stay, said he'd get more money. And he got it from Mary. Had to kill to keep it. Had to kill to keep you!"

Florence hadn't moved. Her smile was fixed, satisfied, assured.

Wren said: "Tavell's pitiable. You're not. You're just beautiful. You'll find somebody else. But—" he shuddered slightly, "not me."

Her slim brows arched and her eyes cooled. "Oh? You flatter yourself, don't you?"

"I don't think so. I don't—"

HE BROKE off. Something bumped the floor hard on the second story of the house. And then there was the sound of water rushing swiftly through a pipe.

"Boss!"

It was Horace's voice, sounding faintly from the upper floor.

Wren bounded to his feet, looked toward the twisted stair at the end of the living room.

"The front stairway," Florence Tavell urged. "It's closer to the master bedroom." She was already leading into the front hall.

Wren passed her. Two police, one in uniform, came barging through the front door as Wren bounced for the stairs. They shouted at him, but he was halfway up the steps by then. In the hall upstairs were Gladys "Freya" Frye and Doan, hurrying toward the stairway, bags in hand. From the open door of the front bedroom came the sounds of a struggle.

Wren turned through the door, was vaguely aware of the presence of Jason, the butler. Wren got his gun out and dived for the adjoining bath, a modest little room about the size of the Aquacade. On the floor, thrashing it out, were Horace and Urban Tavell. A bright nickel door-key lay on the floor near the base of the toilet.

"All right. Break it up!"

That was when Tavell bounced Horace's head against the tile floor. At approximately the same time, Jason came through the bathroom door and neatly knocked the gun out of Wren's hand. It all happened very fast. There was Horace, inert upon the floor. There was Tavell with a heavy-caliber revolver in his hand. There were Wren and the cops looking pretty foolish, with Florence and the others somewhere in the background. Tavell had them all at bay, a bow-legged Puck with a big gun in his hand.

Tavell said: "Florence, we're getting out of here. You get the gun that Wren dropped while I hold them off."

From the background came Florence's rippling laughter. "Darling, I couldn't possibly. Not with a murderer, you dope!"

Which was what really shook Urban Tavell. He turned green, his gunhand trembled. And then Horace, who must have been doing a 'possum act, kicked at Tavell's shins.

Wren dived low to finish what Florence and Horace had started. Tavell's gun roared once, but the slug smashed into the wainscoting. He came down hard to strike the foot of the lavatory pedestal with his head. And it was over, with Wren and Horace standing up.

Horace pointed a shaky forefinger at the key on the floor.

"He was gonna flush it downa—" he gulped. "Flush it…."

"Uh-huh," Wren grunted. "We get the idea, Horace."

He walked back into the bedroom. Florence Tavell was waiting for him. He bounced to the door, and she dogged him, haunted him out into the hall.

"Even if I'm not appreciated," she said, "you ought to let me thank you."

"You're appreciated," he said. "You witch."

At least it sounded like "witch."

THE SPIRIT WAS WILLING

NOT EVEN ZOE OSBOURN, POLICEWOMAN EXTRAORDINARY AND THE BEST SPOOK-CROOK SNOOP ON THE FORCE, COULD PUT THE FINGER ON PETE STAHL AND HIS PHONY RELIGIOUS PITCH, "CHURCH OF THE LIFE EVERLASTING." BUT FINDING EDDIE BROWN, HIS SPIRIT-INVOKING ASSISTANT, CURLED UP IN A SIDEBOARD WITH AN ICE PICK THROUGH HIS EYE BOUNCED THE PHONY HOLY JOE RIGHT INTO THE BIG TIME—AND INTO JEFFERY WREN'S LAP, INCIDENTALLY—ALONG WITH THE SHUDDERING MR. HADLEY AND HIS BLUEBEARD WIFE AND OLD GRAMPS, THE ANCIENT SWING ADDICT WITH THE HOT HARMONICA AND THE ORCHID ROADSTER.

CHAPTER ONE

MRS. HADLEY'S BLUEBEARD ROOM

NOW THAT vaudeville is back, there are some members of the Indianapolis Police Department who wish Jeffery Wren were back in vaudeville. They hold that before Wren began discovering bodies with all the equanimity with which he had previously discovered rabbits in silk hats, homicide had followed fairly well defined patterns.

Not so the mad Hadley affair, in which the ninth life of Albertus Magnus was ignobly ended with an ice pick.

"I was in that," Wren will admit with hardly any provocation, "up to my neck. Paddling in gore again."

And then, if he has any sort of an audience, his deep voice will roll on to recall that morning of March 6th when an anonymous letter informed him of the nefarious activity of Reverend Peter Stahl. Or let's just call him "Pete," as Wren prefers, since Stahl was self-ordained by virtue of a diploma purchased from a mail-order house catering to spirit mediums. The letter read:

> Dear Friend:
>
> I saw your book, *The Dead Don't Talk*, and I know you don't take stock in spirit mediums, so I am writing about the Rev. Peter Stahl. I went to see him for the fun of it, and my left arm was killing me. Stahl summoned his control—which is a term for spirit, I guess you know—and the spirit was somebody dead named Albertus Magnus. It said I had angina pectoris, and I was supposed to return the next day for a psychic message, but I never did because my angina pectoris is only a Charley-horse from playing pool.
>
> Shouldn't something be done about this crook? You take my sister-in-law who goes to him and isn't in too good health—you can't tell he may do her more harm than good.
>
> A Well Wisher

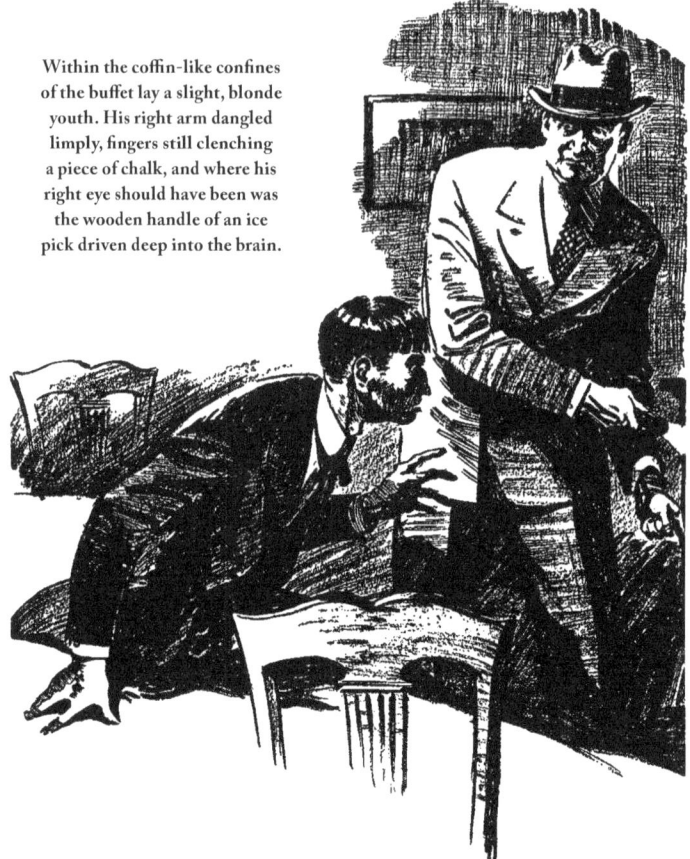

Within the coffin-like confines of the buffet lay a slight, blonde youth. His right arm dangled limply, fingers still clenching a piece of chalk, and where his right eye should have been was the wooden handle of an ice pick driven deep into the brain.

This disturbing missive arrived in the mail at Wren's bachelor quarters just as he was about to open his breakfast egg. In spite of the reference to the masculine sport of pool and the substitution of "fun" for "hell" the handwriting was feminine.

A sigh blew softly from Wren's lips and his fingers drummed in quiet fury on the breakfast table. Pete Stahl was not unknown to him. The crook medium had heretofore evaded the letter of the law by maintaining what he called "The Church of the Life Everlasting," by mixing sacred music with spirit materializations, by accepting "contributions" rather than charging fees. Not even the redoubtable Zoe Osbourn, policewoman assigned to snaring fortune tellers and fake mediums, could with impunity interfere with what was defined as

"the practice of a religion." However, the practice of medicine without a license was an entirely different matter.

Wren pushed back from the table, a frown troubling his usually serene brow. Slow, bouncing strides carried him across the room to the phone. As he looked up Zoe Osbourn's telephone number he observed to his own astute self that this time Pete Stahl had torn his pants. Quite!

AT NINE o'clock that morning, Jeffery Wren entered his novelty shop, located on West Ohio Street. Horace, the clerk, was draped over the joke counter, his thin, bloodless-looking face a smutty-story distance from that of a small, expensively dressed man. That portion of Horace's mouth unconcerned with his soggy cigar made sales talk while he demonstrated a bathroom-paper holder that included in its construction a Swiss music box.

"Cute, huh?" he said. "Annit's practical. Fellah says J.P. Morgan's got one inniz bathroom, on'y gold plated. How's about you?"

The reply, a forthright "No," was returned from Horace in the form of an unbelieving but disappointed echo. "I told you," said the customer, "I wanted to see Mr. Wren."

Horace sighed like an ill wind and indicated his employer with a limp wave of his faintly blue hand. The man at the counter turned. Eyebrows like fuzzy brown caterpillars crawled toward deeply incised wrinkles centering his forehead. Possibly he was aware of a certain sleek ostentation about Jeffery Wren which was reminiscent of Hollywood's Edward Arnold—a quality hardly expected in the proprietor of a shop dealing in itch powder, poo-poo cushions, explosive cigars, hanky-panties, and countless other items either inane or moderately obscene.

Wren's smile broke bright against his dark-complexioned face. The smile of the other man was small, as anxious as the wag of a dog's tail. He put a thin, strong hand into Wren's big palm and introduced himself as Walter Hadley. His voice, Wren thought, was carefully pleasant, a studied part of self-selling.

"If I were a magician, or a detective—you are both, Mr. Wren, I understand—I might be able to explain why my wife keeps one of the bedrooms locked at all times."

One of Wren's chunky black eyebrows lifted. "Moths," he suggested whimsically. "Or Mrs. Hadley is knitting small garments—"

He let that hang. A shudder convulsed Hadley's slim shoulders and moved up into his face where it was like the after-taste of bitter medicine.

"It isn't funny," he said.

"No," Wren agreed. "Obviously not. Not funny at all."

"Oh, I am aware of the absurdity of the situation—my modern young wife keeping a forbidden chamber like Bluebeard. But when you have lived with that locked room for two weeks, and you haven't the remotest idea *why* it is locked—" Hadley broke off, perhaps realizing that his voice was climbing like a fire siren.

Wren nodded. "Creeps up on you. Like a wool bathing suit." He led Hadley through a door at the rear of the store, up a stair, through a second door that bore the legend *Wren's Magic*. They paused in a small reception room, the walls of which were hung with photos of Jeffery Wren performing tricks and illusions he had featured on Keith's stages, and Wren unlocked the double glass doors of the magic shop beyond.

Here supplies and apparatus for amateur and professional conjurors were displayed to achieve "flash," in showmen's parlance. But if Hadley noticed any of the tricks and gimmicks it was in the preoccupied manner in which a bachelor might turn the pages of a child care magazine in some doctor's waiting room. He took prim steps in Wren's wake across the shop and into the thoughtful brown room that is Wren's office. There he sat in a proffered chair as though he had spoiled eggs in his pockets.

Hadley's mouth, Wren reflected, as he perched his big body on the edge of the desk top, spoke more eloquently of Hadley closed than it did open. It had a sullen droop at the extremities and a point of ruthless, unrelenting compression in the center. A small, violent man, this Hadley, with eyes like hoarhound drops dissolved to brittle, yellow-brown disks, translucent, revealing nothing.

He said: "Mr. Wren, I really must tell you at once that I have no money. That is, I have and I haven't."

"Ah?" Wren was faintly amused. "Remarkable feat. Does Morgenthau know how you do it?"

Hadley looked incapable of laughter. "Before the war knocked the props from my most recent business venture," he explained, "I settled a hundred thousand dollars on my wife, Joan. During certain judgment proceedings brought against me by creditors, the court ruled I was justified in thus protecting my wife. Legally, I am a pauper. I am worried about your fees, if you take my case."

Wren chuckled. "Look. You hand me an acorn. You ask me my price for felling the subsequent oak. Little mysteries sometimes grow—even grow to murder."

Wren gave the man a shrewd, heavy-lidded glance, noticed that Hadley had paled slightly and that on the verge of speaking he had changed his mind.

Wren said softly: "What about murder, Hadley?"

FOR AN instant the hoarhound eyes were startled from their blunt, brown stare. Hadley made an impatient negative gesture with his hand. "It was probably a car backfiring that night last week when Joan came back from the bus line. She swears someone fired a shot at her. But she's neurotic and imaginative."

"You think so?" Wren sounded disinterested. He picked up a newspaper clipping from the desk, turned it over and over in his large, deft fingers.

"Mrs. Hadley has a turbulent mind," said Hadley. "She is always seeking solace in some crank religion. Right now she seems to be interested in something called The Church of the Life Everlasting."

Peter Stahl's "church." Wren's black eyebrows lifted slightly, but he made no comment. He proceeded to mould the innocent bit of newspaper into a little cone. Then, without a single false move, he shook a scarlet silk handkerchief from the mouth of the cone.

Hadley's caterpillar eyebrows crawled toward a common center as he watched Wren deliberately tear the paper cone into confetti fragments to preclude any idea that it had been loaded with a "fake."

"You can be damned disconcerting!" Hadley's words popped like static electricity.

"Quite," Wren admitted mildly. "A disconcerted man will sometimes drop a card from his hand." He stepped around the desk, sat down in his swivel chair where he appeared solid and square and perfectly sure of Jeffery Wren.

He said: "Look. You've a nasty temper, Hadley. Inexplicable things anger you. Take this locked room business. First impulse must have been to choke the truth out of Mrs. Hadley—or use an axe on the door." He shook his head. "Only thing restraining you is the money. Your hundred thousand. You can't cross Mrs. Hadley because she might put that money where you'd never touch it."

"Go on, strip me!" Hadley defied him.

Wren chuckled shortly. "You'd catch cold.... But the money's the thing. Fear about what may happen to it is associated with two things in your mind: First, mumbo-jumbo about a locked room. Second, more tangible business about the murder attempt on Mrs. Hadley. Now, what's the connection?"

"I haven't the slightest damned notion!" Hadley ripped out. "What the hell do you think I'm hiring you for?"

"Hiring?" Wren reminded him quietly. "Hardly the word. You're asking favors." He watched Hadley subside contritely into the chair. "Where is this house with the Bluebeard room?"

"At 6028 Guilford Avenue. You see, I sold our big place in Williams Creek." Hadley seemed eager to impress Wren with former wealth. "Joan bought this house while I was out of town, using some of the money I had given her."

"You and your wife alone?" Wren asked. "No dangling relatives?"

"None. Mrs. Hadley is an orphan. Her only blood relative alive, to my knowledge, is an uncle. He became something of a parasite when Joan and I were married, but I put a stop to that." Hadley's fingers worked as though the only proper procedure to control parasitic uncles was strangulation. "The Claires spend a good deal of time with us. That's Molly, Joan's foster sister, and her worthless husband."

"Plays pool," Wren murmured, fishing out of season.

"Yes, he—" the twin caterpillars collided head-on. "How the devil do you know Elbert Claire fritters away time in pool halls?"

Wren seemed surprised. "Who mentioned it? Nothing to me if Elbert lives behind the eight ball. Never heard of him before. Go on about the locked room. Surely you've been inside it."

"Twice," Hadley said. "When my wife showed me through our new home, the door of the room was open. She said she thought the wallpaper in that particular room was hideous, and then closed and locked the door. We didn't need the room, and inasmuch as Joan is very sensitive to colors, I thought little about it until yesterday when I sent a decorator to the house with the idea of having that room done over."

"Mrs. Hadley wouldn't let the man in," Wren surmised. "Then it hit you. Hit you right between the eyes."

Hadley nodded. "I began to remember the odd looks Joan had given me every time I had referred to the room. How she had contrived flimsy excuses to follow me upstairs. How she watched me when I was around the house. I can tell you, Wren, when I went home last night, I had a nice case of blue shudders. Molly Claire was there, which gave me a chance to get upstairs without attracting Joan's immediate attention. I used a key from the linen closet on the door of the locked room."

HADLEY took a quavering breath. Wren waited with the patience of the Immovable Body anticipating the approach of the Irresistible Force.

"I couldn't find a damned thing wrong with that room!" Hadley exploded. "But while I was standing at one of the windows, Joan came to the door behind me. She was"—Hadley shook his head, bewildered—"she looked utterly terrified."

Wren's big body shifted. His chair spring squeaked in the quiet of the room, a small, startling sound like the death cry of a trapped mouse coming in the hush of night.

"Terrified of what?" he asked.

"God only knows!" Hadley threw out a helpless gesture. "I couldn't get a word out of Joan. She ran to her room, crying, and of course dear little Sister Molly intervened. I won't bore you with the details of the family row that followed. I would simply like you to find out what this is all about, if you will and if you can."

Wren said: "I see, I see," almost as though he did. And as Hadley rose to go, he added final words of caution. "Stay out of the Bluebeard room, Hadley."

The brown caterpillars went into conference. "You're serious?"

"Quite," Wren said gravely. "Never more so. Could be someone *wants* you to go in. To indulge in some grade A conclusion jumping, I'd say Mrs. Hadley is afraid of murder. But"—Wren shrugged heavy shoulders—"whose murder?"

Seconds after Hadley had left, Wren descended the stairs into the novelty shop, his hat and greatcoat on.

The enterprising Horace was standing at the street door, craning his neck as though Lady Godiva were putting on a repeat performance but with an upswept hairdo. He spoke to Wren without turning around.

"Boss, that guy with ants inniz pants that went out a min't ago—that Hadley gent—now he's got a tail. A guy inna ice cream hat."

Wren joined Horace at the door, looked down the street in the direction the clerk was pointing.

Standing in front of the cleaning establishment on the northeast corner of Illinois and Ohio Streets was a lank, loose-jointed figure of a man whose only claim to sartorial distinction was a pearl gray hat.

"Hadley," said Horace, "is inna drugstore across the street."

Wren frowned a thoughtful moment, then tapped Horace on the shoulder. "Get your coat. You shadow the shadow."

Horace turned. He swiveled his damp cigar around, encompassing the shop. "What about itch powder 'n stink bomb en'erprise?"

"Odd sense of values you have, my friend. Somebody's apt to get killed. Yet you're concerned with a dime's worth of itch powder. Get your coat."

"It's gonna look damn silly, that's all," Horace complained. "Three guys goin' In'ian file the hellover In'ianaplus. Now if one wuz a blonde with nice ponies anna cute wiggle—"

Wren walked out the door.

CHAPTER TWO

THE GHOST GIVES UP

JEFFERY WREN accomplished a majestic descent from a common carrier at Delaware and Sixteenth Streets. Locating Zoe Osbourn on the opposite corner became one of life's simpler chores. The policewoman's red-brown Chesterfield coat lent her a silhouette which resembled either end of a box car. Any description of the hat pinned to her hennaed curls would have amounted to utter gibberish.

"How's the public servant?" Wren touched his hat vaguely as he approached. "For that matter, how's the public?"

"Nothing I hear from the public proves Barnum was wrong," she declared in her husky bellow. "As for the public servant, she's a little tired of awaiting your pleasure, me lord!"

His smile twitched. "Look. I don't get paid for helping you catch your spook crooks. It's your job. My hobby."

The prominent pale blue eyes, which ordinarily gave a gullible expression to her heavy-featured face, regarded Wren now with frank suspicion. "I think, Jeff, you generally manage to pick up a penny here and there. Let's see that anonymous letter you phoned about."

Wren got out the letter from the "Well Wisher." Zoe scowled at the writing, and after a moment stuffed the letter into her purse. She pegged off down the sidewalk on heels too high and too slim for her piano props. Wren measured his stride to match.

Halfway down the next block they sighted the old residence which Stahl had leased, a two-story pile of red brick and crumbling mortar doubtfully reinforced with leafless ivy vines. Across the second story was a billboard with yard-high letters in red: THE CHURCH OF THE LIFE EVERLASTING.

Wren said: "Any particular strategy for entering that dread portal?"

Zoe shook her head. "I phoned Stahl for an appointment, but he said he had somebody else at this hour. We'll simply barge in. I'll suffer, if necessary, and develop symptoms. Otherwise, we'll just scout around."

Wren nodded, chuckling. They would descend upon Stahl as they had upon certain other mediums who no longer did business locally. From then on, the game was on the board. Joan Hadley's Bluebeard room, the attempt on that lady's life, Mr. Hadley's blue shudders, the shadow in the gray hat—these amounted to unknown factors X, Y, Z and so on. One thing was certain: Pete Stahl knew of Joan Hadley's hundred-thousand-dollar bankroll, and once Joan was enmeshed in his ectoplasmic web it was unlikely that she would escape with her money.

A privet hedge, grown tall and sturdy, surrounded the wide, deep lot of the Stahl place. Wren and Zoe Osbourn turned through brick gateposts and onto a limestone drive that drew a lazy scroll to a porte-cochere attached to the north side of the house. A 1939 vintage roadster, painted a true bathroom shade of orchid, with a squirrel tail drooping from its radio mast, was parked beneath the porte-cochere. Somebody in the car was playing *Pistol Packin' Mama* on a chromatic harmonica.

Wren said: "Isn't that your theme song, Zoe?"

She snorted. "I'm nobody's mama!" Her high heels dug into the loose stones like tractor lugs, and she hauled Wren to the porte-cochere. There she stood and goggled.

The harmonica virtuoso was old enough to know better—sixty, at least. His nose was so long and drooping he ought to have patented it for a bottle opener. He turned toward Wren and the policewoman without missing a single note. He had odd eyes, Wren thought, the sort you usually see in the face of a hunchback, yet the oldster sat erect, lean shoulders squared off against old age.

"Stop that!" Zoe Osbourn bellowed.

He didn't stop until he had brought *Mama* to her just deserts. Then he wiped puckered lips on the back of his gnarled hand and said, "Hot dawg!" in self-appreciation.

"Amen," Wren murmured.

Zoe Osbourn continued to stare and scowl. The old man's dark, sad eyes covered her deliberately. He said in a sharp, twanging voice: "See anythin' green? Know any good reason I shouldn't blow my mouth harp if I'm a mind to?"

Zoe Osbourn sniffed, "I guess not. Where's Reverend Stahl?"

The patent nose pointed to the house. "Inside, talkin' to Mis' Hadley."

Wren lifted an eyebrow. As he and Zoe Osbourn turned from the car, the oldster waved his harmonica and announced: *"Mairzy Doats."*

"All right, Jeff," Zoe Osbourn whispered. "I saw that eyebrow. Who's the Hadley woman?"

"A lady," he said. "Lady with a Bluebeard room. You can conclude she's a bearded lady, if you wish."

They rounded the house, and as they climbed stone steps to the unsheltered front door, Zoe Osbourn said: "You've got something up your sleeve. O.K. But if you louse up my arrest, I'll get your oily scalp!"

"Who's lousing up anything?" Wren looked serenely at her while he hammered the brass knocker on the door.

INSIDE the house a door opened and closed. Footsteps whispered. Zoe Osbourn managed to get on her sick-Pekingese expression before Peter Stahl opened the door. The medium was very tall, a raw-boned figure with the drooping carriage and shambling gait of the ragman's horse. His black suit had gone green with age. He wore a shoestring tie and a stiff collar. A porridge bowl haircut provided a fringe of black bangs across his shallow brow.

Zoe Osbourn said in what was, for her, a faint voice: "I'm that sick lady that phoned, Reverend Stahl."

"Uh—come in, come in," Stahl said in a vapid whisper that reminded Wren of half-dead flies stirring in a trap. And as soon as Wren and Zoe were across the sill, Stahl closed the door quickly as though, like a mummy, he had reason to fear light and air. There was little enough of either inside. Feeble fingers of gray morning penetrated the leaded glass transom and groped like blind things to the foot of a winding stair.

Zoe Osbourn seized the medium's hand, and for a moment it was a tossup whether she would lick the hand or try a Judo fall.

"Now I can hope!" she gushed. "I've heard how wonderful you are and you just don't know the agony I've suffered!"

"Her ankles swell," Wren said with malice. "Obviously."

The medium's vacuous gaze shifted to Wren. He waved a bony hand toward two chairs against the wall of the dim, lofty room. "Uh—but you will have to wait. I have a private sitting in progress at the moment. If you will excuse me, please."

In the wall opposite the chairs in which Wren and Zoe were seated, were two doors into separate rooms, both closed. Stahl went to the second of these two doors, and in the instant required for Stahl to enter, Wren got a camera-shutter glance at some gray-haired old lady within. This certainly wasn't Joan Hadley. Behind the other closed door, someone was moving about. Another woman. Her high heels *tack-tacked* across bare floor, then *tuck-tucked* on carpeting. A chair spring creaked.

Zoe Osbourn nudged Wren. "Stahl draws women like a corpse draws flies," she whispered. "Which is Mrs. Hadley?"

Wren shrugged. "High heels, presumably. I've never seen her." He glanced about the hall. Behind them and to his right were tall folding doors, also closed. On the knob hung a placard that read: *Chapel.* He thought there was a fourth door beyond the stairway at the rear of the room. The house had a distinctly unpleasant odor of old things and old people, like opening Grandfather's trunk in the attic on a rainy day. Above the distant drone of Stahl's voice, the thin trill of the harmonica rendition of *Mairzy Doats* penetrated the thick, damp walls. And from the shadowy rear of the hall came a distinct tap as of knuckles on a door panel.

Wren winked at Zoe. "Must be a signal," he whispered. "Probably from some confederate." He glanced at his wrist watch. It was seventeen minutes after ten. Outside the house, the harmonica virtuoso had deserted *Mairzy Doats* for *Shoo Shoo Baby.* Across the hall, high heels went *tack-tack* across bare floor again.

Two minutes ticked off. *Oh, shoo shoo, baby. Oh, don't cry, baby....* Gramps in the orchid roadster was swinging it. Footsteps sounded in the rear of the house, tapered off into silence. Across the hall, the second door opened. Peter Stahl came out, arm-in-arm with the thin, sickly looking old woman whom Wren had glimpsed before.

"Uh—I want it distinctly understood, Mrs. Cole, that I will accept no fees," Stahl was saying in his tired, tiresome voice. "Uh—my reward is the thought that I have been the medium through which the limitless knowledge of Albertus Magnus has brought comfort to the suffering. Yet the church for which I labor is a needy church, and I cannot discourage contributions from the grateful."

As Stahl and the ailing woman moved toward the rear of the hall, Jeffery Wren clenched his fists. It was a crime, one of the lowest on the book.

STAHL opened the door. The room beyond was dimly illuminated in that dull red light presumably favorable to spirits. The medium and his hopeful patient went on in and the door was closed.

"Who was this Albertus Magnus?" Zoe Osbourn whispered. "A doctor?"

"Of sorts," Wren replied. "Gets dragged from his thirteenth-century grave by all the medical mediums. Breaks the monotony for Albertus, anyway. May I quote his prescription for the gout?"

Zoe shook her head. "No, thanks!"

Wren managed to look lugubrious and quoted anyway. " 'Take the skull of a corpse, scrape bone dust from the cranium—' "

"Hell's fire!" Zoe Osbourn shuddered.

Perhaps five minutes dragged by in silence except for the distant trill of Gramps' harmonica. Wren wondered whimsically what Albertus Magnus thought of the *GI Stomp*. Then the door of the red-lighted room was opened by Stahl and he hurried the ailing old lady out into the hall.

"But—but I don't understand," the old woman said faintly.

"Simply that I find it impossible to become *en rapport* with the spirit of Albertus Magnus this morning," Stahl said. "Uh—conditions are unfavorable." There was about Stahl's pale face a slightly greenish cast. And as he hurried the aged woman to the front door, his left foot streaked moist, red-brown stains on the gray carpet. Blood?

Wren tapped Zoe Osbourn's shoulder, pointed to the tracks, glanced at Stahl's back. The medium was opening the front door for the old woman. Wren bounced to the rear of the hall, opened the door of the red-lighted room—a dining room, evidently, with all the usual pieces of furniture except that the center table had been replaced by a white-draped couch. Because of the red light, it would have been difficult to see blood dripping from your own fingers.

But you could hear it dripping somewhere in the room   *tap-tap-tap* like drops of water from a kitchen pump dripping on a wooden drainboard.

Feet scuffled in the hall. Wren glanced over his shoulder to see that Zoe Osbourn had laid hands on Peter Stahl. She had him by the coat collar and the seat of the pants, was giving him the bum's rush right into the red-lighted dining room. Her final shove sent him flying through the door and across the room to sprawl across the couch, legs and arms thrashing the air. He scrambled to his feet, made a futile effort to mend his tattered dignity.

"What—what is the meaning of this—this intrusion? Be gone, I say! Both of you. Must I call the police?"

Zoe Osbourn stepped into the room and slammed the door. She stood with arms akimbo and glowered at Peter Stahl.

"Brother, you've *got* the police!" She looked at Wren. "Where's that blood coming from, Jeff?"

Wren took a small flashlight from his pocket. Its beam cut through the murky red glow to spot brightly on the carpet. Stahl's gory tracks led from the buffet. There was a little puddle of blood on the carpet directly beneath the buffet front on the left side. Wren's light jumped up to the buffet top, centered on two ordinary school slates bound with red felt, the top slate larger than the lower. Both were tightly bound together with a strip of white linen, the knot in the cloth on the under side.

Wren said: "Something haywire with Albertus Magnus. Referring to his ninth life, of course. His spirit transmigrated into a body. Possibly a body in the uglier sense of the word."

Zoe Osbourn slaughtered him with a look.

"What are you babbling about?" she inquired testily.

The Reverend Peter Stahl sank slowly down on the couch.

"About Magnus," Wren said. "He couldn't do any slate writing. The spirit was willing, but the flesh—" Wren shrugged. He gripped what passed for a drawer pull in the front of the buffet, gave it a yank. All the drawer fronts were cleverly joined into a single panel that swung down on a hidden piano hinge at the bottom. A little stream of blood guttered down the inclined panel to splash at Wren's feet.

WITHIN the coffin-like confines directly beneath the buffet top, lay a slight, blonde youth in his late teens or early twenties. He wore neither suitcoat nor shoes. His right arm dropped limply through the opening, dangled. His fingers clenched a piece of chalk. The hollow-cheeked face was startling, grotesque in the manner of the ogle-eyed gent on an *Esquire* cover, because where you expected to see the right eye, you saw only the wooden ball handle of an ice pick driven deep into the brain.

"What—what's he doing in there?" This, from Pete Stahl, was not exactly convincing.

"Ah?" Wren raised an eyebrow. "You've no idea?"

Zoe Osbourn said hoarsely: "Well, he's not waiting for a buffet luncheon!" She scowled at Wren. "All right, master-wit. What is he doing in there?"

Wren was astounded. "My dear lady!" He pushed the slates some-what to one side, brought a heavy hand down on the buffet top. An oblong section of wood, neatly jig-sawed from the top, rattled under the force of the blow.

"A trap," he said. "Cut slightly smaller than the larger of the two slates. Held in place by movable lugs on the under side. Albertus, here, simply steals the smaller slate through the trap without disturbing the larger. He then writes on the inner surface of both slates, the small one in his hands, the larger one in plain sight on top of the buffet. He then replaces all as before, ties the linen binding again, puts the cut-out section of the buffet top in place. Very simple. Smooth enough for the gullible."

Zoe Osbourn snorted.

Wren said: "The trap in the top also explains how the mortal wound was struck. A direct jab straight down. Through the trap, of course. Couldn't possibly have been managed through the front opening of the buffet, because Albertus is tucked in too close to the top. Ought to be a big help to Homicide, since the killer had to know about the trap in the top."

Stahl took this last as a personal affront. He flung his loose-jointed body about, tried an end run around the couch. Zoe Osbourn was waiting for him. She lunged heavily. Stahl turned, evaded her grasping hands by inches.

Perhaps he had it in mind to try a way out through the swinging door that led into the kitchen. But Wren presented a solid looking obstacle in that direction. Stahl picked up a dining room chair, flung it at Wren. Wren, not constructed for convenient ducking, caught the chair and slammed it down onto the floor. He started for Pete Stahl.

The medium dashed to the south end of the room, straight toward a china closet. It was all so cockeyed that if he had jumped up on one of the shelves and attempted to impersonate a cracked teapot, Wren would not have been astonished. But as Wren and Zoe Osbourn closed in on him from two directions, Stahl whipped something from a drawer in the china closet and wheeled to face them. It was a nick-eled revolver.

CHAPTER THREE

SKELETON IN THE CLOSET

NOW, YOUR reverence," Wren said quietly, "keep it in character."

Stahl's eyes flicked from Zoe to Wren. "Don't touch me. I—I'll shoot myself!"

"Passive resistance," Wren said. "Don't know but what your cause could use a martyr. Go right ahead."

Stahl swiveled the gun around and shot Wren. Or tried to. Wren felt powder scorch on his left ear. As he crowded in close to the medium and got both hands on Stahl's chicken-bone wrist, he heard somebody scream in the front part of the house. On the other side of Stahl, Zoe Osbourn raised her big purse and slammed Stahl over the head with it. Stahl sat down hard on the floor, almost pulled Wren down on top of him. He was fully conscious, but the role of man-of-action had lost its appeal. Wren twisted the revolver from Stahl's limp fingers, passed it to Zoe Osbourn.

"Jeff, where's the phone? You—" Zoe had turned, looking for a phone. Her prominent eyes narrowed somewhat, and she elevated her voice to reach across the room, or even across the street. "Well, come in and plan to stay a while, miss."

In the hall door stood a tall, leggy woman, somewhere in her late twenties, Wren thought. She wore a three-piece suit in a lively shade of brown. Her hat was a darker brown to set off ash blonde hair, and its wide, rolling brim was good for her narrow face. A pretty, delicately featured face, but rouged too heavily, as though she had deliberately tried to mask something secret. Her eyes had a wide, wild look.

Wren raised inquiring eyebrows. "Mrs. Hadley?"

She took nervous, puppet steps into the room. Her glance was like a green dragonfly, darting, quivering, hanging now on Peter Stahl as she spoke.

"What's the matter? Was that a shot?" Then she saw the open buffet and the body in it. For a moment, it was all beyond her comprehension. Then she screamed, took faltering steps to the couch, collapsed onto it, screamed again.

Zoe Osbourn said: "Stop that! You can if you will." She went over to the woman and her attitude fairly defied further screaming. "You're Mrs. Hadley?"

"Yes." Mrs. Hadley nipped the word off.

The swinging door off the kitchen was stiff-armed open by the old man they had seen in the orchid roadster. He came in, his step brisk and steady, his sad eyes on the prowl.

"What's the carryin'-on?" he demanded nasally.

Mrs. Hadley turned. Her lovely green eyes appealed to Harmonica Gramps. "Uh—" She swallowed. "Mr. Rybolt, please, please take me home!"

Zoe Osbourn said: "Nobody's going home. I'm from the police. You can come with me, if you want, Mrs. Hadley." She took hold of Joan Hadley's arm, pulled her up from the couch. "Where's your phone, zombie?" Zoe asked of Stahl.

The medium waved toward the front of the house. "In the parlor. Mrs. Hadley can show you. That is where she was waiting." Stahl got to his feet as the two women left the room, and then sank into the nearest chair.

Harmonica Gramps came farther into the room, stared at the buffet. "Lord love a duck!" he gasped. "What's the boy doin' in that sideboard there?" And then he observed that the boy was beyond doing anything in the sideboard. He shuddered. "Lord *love* a duck! He's been frog-stuck!"

"Ice-picked," Wren growled. "Accurate, if less lyrical. Pete, who's the murder victim?"

"Eddie Brown," Stahl said faintly. "He does odd jobs around here."

"Odd in the extreme," Wren said dryly. He sat down on the edge of the couch, took out a cigarette and lighted it. "Any other confederates or servants in the house?"

STAHL shook his head miserably. Wren felt a little miserable himself. Because if you made this murder open-and-shut to include only Stahl, Joan Hadley, and this elderly Mr. Rybolt as your suspects, the crime just couldn't have been committed. Eddie Brown, the victim, had been alive at seventeen minutes past ten, presumably, since he had signaled to Stahl by tapping on the wall. The signal meant that Eddie was about to get into the buffet, to set the stage for some slate spirit messages for the doubtful benefit of the aged Mrs. Cole. Eddie had then gone to the buffet and got inside. Because he was in his stocking feet, he had made no noise about it.

Not later than twenty minutes after ten, Stahl and his aged "patient" had entered the dining room. During those three intervening minutes, the dirty work had been done.

Stahl would have an alibi in Mrs. Cole, and in Zoe Osbourn and Jeffery Wren, providing there was only the one door leading from that room in which Stahl and the ailing Mrs. Cole were closeted. During those same fatal three minutes, Harmonica Gramps Rybolt was playing *Shoo Shoo Baby* in the orchid roadster outside the house. And Joan Hadley was pacing the floor of the parlor, with Wren and Zoe Osbourn right outside her door.

But Wren distinctly recalled hearing footsteps in the dining room just before Stahl had entered that room with the sick woman. Not Eddie Brown who was in his stocking feet. Who?

A sigh blew softly from Wren's lips. He looked at Harmonica Gramps Rybolt. "You're Mrs. Hadley's chauffeur, Mr. Rybolt?"

Rybolt made the most of his six-foot height and at the same time drew down his eyebrows in a snowy glower. "Franklin P. Rybolt never fetched nor carried for nobody. Leastwise, not for hire. I'm Mis' Hadley's neighbor to the south. I give her a lift down here." He twitched his patent nose to cover a proud, boyish grin. "That's my car out there, I guess you noticed."

Wren nodded placidly. "Unavoidable."

Peter Stahl jerked upright in his chair as though on the verge of going into a trance. He pointed a skinny finger at Franklin P. Rybolt.

"How did you get in here? That side door was bolted on the inside."

Rybolt shook his silvery head. "Ain't the way I found it. Ain't the way the gas man found it, neither. He walked right in, same as me, and right out again after he read the meter."

Wren frowned. "When was that?"

"Little bit after you and the fat lady had gone in the front door. Right when I was playin' *Shoo Shoo Baby* on my mouth harp, as I recollect."

Wren took a deep breath. He removed his soft black hat and patted his expansive brow with his handkerchief.

Stahl said faintly: "There's no gas meter. I don't use gas."

Rybolt uttered a startled grunt. "You don't say! Sure looked like some sort of a meter reader. Flashlight, leather jacket, pencil in his cap, book under his arm—"

"And," Stahl interrupted, "the water meter is in a pit out in the front lawn near the street. The electric meter is attached to the rear of the house, outside. Don't you see, that was the killer! He was posing as a meter reader!"

Wren nodded. "So it seems." He heard Zoe Osbourn and Joan Hadley approaching down the hall. He stood up, took slow, bouncing steps to meet them. He was feeling quite amiable. He thumb-palmed his cigarette for the sheer hell of it and apparently reproduced the glowing butt from his left ear. Zoe Osbourn was not amused. As for the ash blonde Joan Hadley, she didn't even notice. Joan was doing a pocket trick of her own—nervously ripping a fine linen handkerchief to ribbons.

"Found Homicide at home, no doubt?" Wren's voice was actually palm-rubbing.

Zoe eyed him suspiciously. "You sound as if you'd cracked the murder already."

He shook his head, smiled. "But now it can be cracked. Not impossible, at least." And as he detoured the two women to go out into the hall, he noticed the bulldog set of Zoe Osbourn's face break into a wide grin.

The policewoman muttered: "You'll probably crack it, you slick-witted son of a witch!"

WREN entered the room in which Pete Stahl had been closeted with the ailing Mrs. Cole. It was an erstwhile library with empty book shelves, and small windows placed way up near the thirteen-foot ceiling. There was only the one door. He went out, moved toward the front of the hall, and into the parlor where Joan Hadley had waited. It was a dusty, plushy room, with a telephone on a small writing desk, three chairs, and potted Sansevieria plants on turned oak stands. This room also had only one door.

Wren stepped to the front window, found the sill and mullions layered with dust and the latch tightly closed. The other window looked out onto the side yard, and here he found wipe marks on the sill. The latch stood wide open.

He frowned, stared out of the window and to the ground. It wasn't more than a drop of a yard to the lawn outside. He went back through the door, crossed the hall, went through folding doors into the room designated as the "chapel." It was vast and barren except for a number of folding chairs arranged in rows to face what must have served as Stahl's altar—a white-draped packing case. On one side of this altar was an ancient radio console, ugly and massive. On the other was a wireless record player on top of a small cabinet, used no doubt to play sacred music through the radio as a prelude for public seances.

Wren walked softly around the radio console and to a door that opened into a large pantry. To the left, down three steps, was the side door leading to the porte-cochere. The door was unlocked, just as Harmonica Gramps Rybolt had said. Off the landing at the foot of the steps was a closet, its door slightly ajar. Some dead-black garment was hanging on a hook on the inner surface of the closet door, a leg or sleeve draped over the knob and in plain sight.

Wren opened the door, took the garment off the hook. It was of elastic-knit cotton, like long underwear, except that it was provided with feet, mitten hands, and had a hoodlike arrangement attached to the top for completely enveloping the head. Against the black cloth the complete skeleton of the human body was painted full size in white paint. A skeleton costume such as frequently turns up at Halloween parties and is seldom seen elsewhere. A label inside the neck band at the back said: *Hoosier Costumers, Inc.*

Wren hung the garment back on the hook, went on through the pantry into the kitchen, which was adjacent to the murder room. The kitchen had been modernized. There were built-in cabinets, tile wainscoting, a door of an automatic incinerator set in the wall, electric range and refrigerator. Stahl's breakfast dishes were piled in the sink.

He stood there a moment, looking back toward the pantry, wondering about that skeleton costume. Because the skeleton didn't belong in that particular closet. It didn't belong anywhere in the medium's house. It was as out of place as thirty days on a February calendar....

The men from Homicide arrived with their official photographer, and a bit later deputies from the coroner's and prosecutor's offices. Those among them who remembered Jeffery Wren from that other murder in which he had figured, nodded and gave him that so-it's-you-again look. Stahl's parlor was turned into an inquisitors' chamber to which all present repaired in turn and were subsequently released. The parade began with Joan Hadley who was tearing up her second hanky, marched on with old Rybolt, ended at long last with Wren himself.

Wren gave his theory about the time of the murder, and Homicide listened with pretty obvious patience. It seemed that Peter Stahl had already spoken of Eddie Brown's last important worldly act—the signal which he had tapped on the dining room wall. Homicide was as capable of putting two and two together to make four as Jeffery Wren. The whole thing was more or less tied and dried. This Eddie Brown had some enemy in whom he had confided the modus operandi of the slate trick. This enemy, for reasons which would eventually turn up, had wanted Eddie Brown dead, had entered, pretending to be a meter reader, had stabbed Eddie—as one plainclothesman put it—"in the buffet."

WREN, furious, but unruffled, had a damn good notion not to mention the skeleton costume at all. But there was the hope that official investigators would be as baffled as he was.

"Well, what about it?" asked the prosecutor's man, a dark, shrewish individual with horn-rimmed, nose-pincher glasses.

"Skeleton doesn't fit." Wren shrugged with his hands. "Obviously. No medium ever calls back the dear departed in the skeletal form. It's rotten for business. Who wants to picture sweet Aunt Jenny as a bunch of old bones? Too reminiscent of the conquering worm. Or don't you think so?"

He thrust big hands deep into the slash pockets of his fleece overcoat, and with all the dignity of a limousine rolling over the chuck holes in Hogan's Alley, he bounced from the room.

Ten minutes after he had left the Stahl house, he was in a drugstore on Sixteenth Street. He went back to the phone booth, looked up the number of Hoosier Costumers, Inc., spent a nickel, and dialed. From the proprietor of the shop, he learned a startling fact: The skeleton costume had been rented on the day before by someone named Eddie Brown. The description of Eddie Brown coincided perfectly with that of the youthful corpse of the same name.

"Eddie Brown was the name," the proprietor repeated. "For an address he gave The Church of the Life Everlasting, so I figured it was for a church entertainment."

"Undoubtedly," Wren agreed. "No end entertaining. Especially to Eddie." He hung up, slotted a second nickel, and called his novelty shop. Horace answered.

"Boss, you can always tell when we're onna case by the condition of my eyes. I got the most gorgeezus shiner I've had since the last time you went detecting."

Wren chuckled sympathetically, asked if Horace had collected the mouse for naught. Horace thought maybe he had.

"It's like this. I follow the guy inna ice cream hat, and I think he gets wise, because he stops tailing the Hadley gent. He ducks inna building lobby and goes inna phone booth. I bust in on him, see, just in time to hear him ask somebody: 'Bays there?'"

"Bays?" Wren repeated.

"So maybe it was 'Hays', I dunno. Anyhow, he resents my protrusion. He slams uppa receiver, and says: 'Tail me, willyah!' Hangs one on my eye then, and I'm down onna lobby floor. Some pip of a dame tries to help me up. When I'm through struggling with her, guy inna ice cream hat has got the hell out of there. That'sa picture, on'y these hazardous un'ertakings are sure tough on my lamps."

CHAPTER FOUR

WHITE HOUSE WITH BLUE SHUDDERS

AT SIXTIETH STREET, Builford Avenue extended into the old town of Broad Ripple which had been swallowed up by the northward growth of the city. Some of the original dwellings of the village were scattered in among the modern homes. One of these, a rambling gray frame house that had suffered from too many alterations, stood with its north wall a scant twelve feet from the spanking white clapboards of Joan Hadley's modern colonial.

Wren bounced up the short approach walk of the Hadley place, climbed the three steps to the door, and rattled the knocker. A dog uttered a short, disinterested bark. High heels tripped across a floor that sounded as though it might be tile. The door was opened, but not by Joan Hadley.

The woman was perhaps a year or two younger than Mrs. Hadley. She was a cuddlesome little thing with a girlish bow perched high in her dark red curls. She had large, pansy-blue eyes, a tip-tilted nose, eager red lips. She wore a fluffy white blouse and a short, green velveteen skirt.

Wren recalled Mr. Hadley's remark about "dear little Sister Molly," and came to a quick conclusion. He removed his hat, said, "Mrs. Claire," with scarcely any inflection.

"Why, yes." She was puzzled, and being puzzled did something to her eyes—made them look older and rather like high-grade amethyst quartz.

Wren's smile twisted. "How's Mr. Claire's Charley-horse? How's his pool game? How's well-wishing these days?"

Molly Claire reeled slightly on her four-inch heels. Blue-shadowed eyelids curtained confusion, but her recovery was quick.

"Ooh!" she said, and with her mouth it was a fine thing to say. Her pansy eyes looked at Wren as though he were a seven-layer cake adorned with no more than four lighted candles. "Why, *you're* Jeffery Wren!" She clapped her small hands. "I said to Elbert when we sent that letter: 'Honey, it won't make a teeny bit of difference if I *did* write it in my handwriting while you dictated and we didn't sign it. You know how wonderful Dunninger is on the radio, and this Jeffery Wren is probably just as good.'"

"Certainly," Wren admitted shamelessly. He stepped into the tiny central hall. A large, shaggy brown dog of indeterminable breed came out of the living room to sniff at the toes of Wren's oxfords. The dog raised wistful eyes and wagged its approval. Wren stooped to bestow a friendly pat on the animal's head.

"Yours?" he asked Molly Claire.

Molly shook her head. "Mrs. Talburn's Lad. Mrs. Talburn just dropped in this morning to return a cup of sugar she borrowed." Molly Claire was pointing, palm upward, toward the big house to the south of the Hadley place.

Mrs. Talburn herself came out of the living room carrying an empty china cup in her hand. She was an ample-bosomed woman with yellowed white hair done in a breakfast roll at the nape of her neck. She looked down at the dog, smiled, and clucked affectionately.

"Lad, you haven't been jumping up and getting the gentleman full of hair, have you?" she asked.

Wren said: "He hasn't. Very well mannered, aren't you, Lad?"

Lad looked pleased.

Mrs. Talburn said: "He's good because he's been such a sick puppy. Why, one minute he was frisking around, chewing something—it was that new crocheted basket, Mrs. Claire—and the next he was the sickest dog you ever saw." Mrs. Talburn's pleasant brown eyes moved from Molly Claire to Wren. "Poisoned, mind you! I tell you, there's nothing lower than a dog poisoner. Arsenic." She patted Lad's head. "But Mama and Mr. Rybolt got you to the veterinarian's in time, didn't we, Lad? You're going to be all right now, aren't you?"

Lad's tail thumped the floor. Mrs. Talburn walked to the door, and with one hand on the knob waved the tea cup at Mrs. Claire.

"You thank Mrs. Hadley for the sugar, won't you, Mrs. Claire?" she said, and opened the door. Lad trotted out ahead of her while she and Molly Claire exchanged good-by's.

AS SOON as the door was closed, Molly Claire extended her hand to Wren as though possibly she wanted to play ring-around-the-rosy. "Come into the living room, Mr. Wren. I know Elbert is just dying to meet you."

Wren followed Mrs. Claire into the Hadley living room. A large, soft, pink man in a gray Shetland suit, was doing all the slumping possible in an eighteenth-century wing chair. He came from behind a picture magazine, stood up, became rather formidable as he took pounding steps to meet them. He had pudgy, tuberous features. His small blue eyes were unpleasantly sharp, like chips of pop-bottle glass.

"Didn't catch the name, friend." He seized Wren's hand, and the game was to see if he couldn't convert Wren's knuckles into bone meal.

"This is Jeffery Wren," said Molly. "He knows we wrote that letter, honey."

"Well, I'll be damned!" Elbert Claire dropped Wren's hand. "Now, how the hell did you know, friend?"

"Elbert!" Molly was prettily shocked. Her husband's laugh was as phony as the flowers on a lady's hat. He flung a big arm around her possessively, said: "Well, honey, I will be damned, on account of how the hell did he know?"

Wren chuckled. "Where's Mrs. Hadley?"

The Claires exchanged glances. The female of the species then gave Wren a wondering baby stare.

"I just couldn't think of calling Joan, Mr. Wren. She's upstairs lying down, and just so upset about—about—"

"About a murder," Wren concluded. "Mr. Hadley at his office?"

Molly nodded her pretty head. "Waiting to pounce." And when Wren cocked a puzzled eyebrow, she added, "That's all he does—just waits to pounce on somebody who might have some money to put into some silly business. Like his peep shows."

"They were juke boxes," Elbert corrected. "Yessir, big-shot Hadley was going to make a million in juke boxes—he *said.*"

"They were both," Molly compromised. "The sort of juke box you put a nickel in and music comes out, but there was also a place to look in and see movies. That was what Walter Hadley started in before the war. He got people to back him with money, and then he went bankrupt."

"The old bucket-shop tactics," Elbert said and winked just as though he knew what he was talking about.

Wren asked: "What about this locked bedroom upstairs?"

"That's another thing." Molly did a little feline pouncing of her own. "Why shouldn't Joan keep the south bedroom locked if she wants to? She doesn't like yellow wallpaper. It makes her absolutely ill. And Walter Hadley just persecutes the poor darling so about that room, as though it were some sort of crime."

"I see, I see," Wren murmured. He turned back into the hall, started for the carpeted stairway. Elbert Claire took pounding steps after him, dropped a hand on Wren's shoulder. "See here, friend!" He tried to spin Wren around as heroes do in the movies, but Wren was no top.

"Something gnawing you?" Wren asked, his voice deep, cool. "Mr. Hadley asked me to have a look at the Bluebeard room. It will take someone named Hadley to stop me." He brushed Claire's hand from his shoulder like so much inferior lint, walked quietly up the steps. In the hall below, the doll and the dullard went into a whispered conference.

Wren tiptoed past one closed door to another at the south end of the upstairs hall. This door was locked. He took an ordinary skeleton passkey from his pocket, let himself in, closed the door quietly behind him.

It was a large, light room with two windows, one of which looked out onto the back yard and the other on the north wall of the rambling frame house next door. The wallpaper was brilliant yellow in the background with purple garlands splashed about—a little hard on the eyes, but not exactly frightening. The furniture consisted of a handsome three-piece suite in cherry wood.

Wren faced the south window. A scant four yards beyond the sash was a large window in some second-story room in the big Talburn house next door. He could see someone moving about—a man in shirt sleeves and suspenders. Wren watched a moment, then stepped to the door of the closet, opened it, turned his flashlight into the gloomy interior. The closet was barren except for some small gray object down on the floor in one corner. He stooped, picked the thing up. It was an ordinary blackboard eraser, with no sign of chalk dust on its felt base. Around its middle was a small rubber band.

HE CAME out of the closet, stood beside the bed looking at the eraser. Somewhere in the room a small clock ticked nervously. Out of the corner of his eye Wren caught a sudden flare of yellow light. He glanced toward the south window and beyond, through the window of the Talburn house. The man in shirt sleeves and suspenders had struck a match to light his pipe. The flame brought his features into sharp relief. There was no mistaking that hooked, bottle-opener nose. "Mis' Hadley's neighbor to the south," was Harmonica Gramps Franklin P. Rybolt.

The small clock ticked impatiently near at hand. Wren looked up and toward the chest-of-drawers. No clock there. No clock on the dressing table either. The ticking, now that he put his mind to it, came from beneath the bed. He dropped the eraser on top of the bed, got down onto hands and knees, raised the skirt of the spread. Wedged between the top and bottom frames of the spring was a wood box of the sort that formerly packaged Manila cigars by the hundred.

He thrust up on the top of the spring, got the box loose. It was heavier than he expected, almost slipped from his hand. Inside things metallic rattled like a plumber's tool kit. He brought the box from beneath the bed, rested it on the floor. Across the lid in crudely painted red letters was a single word: DEATH.

Inside, the clock ticked alarmingly.

Wren took a deep breath. He tipped up the lid of the box with a sudden motion of his big hand, looked down at the contents, frowned, and spoke a quiet, "Damn!"

Inside was the craziest collection of murderous junk he had ever seen. There was a piece of iron pipe with a shotgun shell fitted into one end of it. A small, all-metal hammer, of the sort supplied with a nut bowl, was also provided, either to bash in skulls or possibly to detonate the shotgun shell cannon. There was a long, slim-bladed knife that might have been ground down from a hack-saw blade, and a brad-awl to penetrate any heart too hard for the knife. Death by poison was ably represented by a pair of common household items—a bottle of paint remover and a thallium ant trap.

Beneath everything else was an ordinary alarm clock which didn't fit into the kill pattern at all unless it was supposed to scare a man to death. Letters clipped from a newspaper were glued to the face of the clock to spell out: *It's Later Than You Think.*

A faint metallic click in the silence, and then there was silence no longer. Two shots so close together that the sounds were welded into a single hammering roar came from the narrow opening in the door of the Bluebeard room. Wren fell flat on the floor beside the bed. His hat fell off in front of him. He swept the hat up, pushed it onto the edge of the bed, scrambled to the foot of the bed. He was on his knees when the third shot made the black hat jump like a nervous cat. He bounced to his feet, to the door, struck the panel with his shoulder. The door pinned a slim, bare arm above the wrist. Wren seized the blue steel automatic that had come close to fulfilling the prediction on the face of the clock, twisted it out of chill fingers.

Downstairs were pelting footsteps. Molly Claire screamed: "Joan! Joan, darling!"

Wren pulled the door fully open, caught Joan Hadley by the arm, jerked her into the room. She reeled back against the door frame, her green eyes staring wildly at Wren's face.

"You—you're not—"

"Not Mr. Hadley," he clipped. "No. You make me rather glad I'm not!" His squarish body blocked off the door as he turned to face the Claires, man and wife. Molly Claire was two yards ahead of her husband in the hall. She was still screaming: "Joan! Joan, darling!" Wren, unruffled, smiling slightly, was a good antidote for hysterics. The little redhead stopped short, and her oaf of a husband nearly fell over her.

"Joan?" Molly appealed to Wren.

"All right," Wren assured her. "Quite." And for just an instant, Wren thought, the pansy eyes were amethyst quartz again.

Elbert Claire said: "See here, friend, you can't go blowing off with a gun and then just say everything is all right."

"Think I can," Wren argued. "If I'm satisfied, you ought to be. The lady wasn't shooting at you." And his closing of the door was quietly insulting.

JOAN HADLEY sat down slowly on the edge of the bed. Her face, washed clean of makeup, showed pallor, nervous tension. Her green eyes mirrored screaming fear.

Wren touched the box of crude murder tools with his shoe toe. "These playthings yours?"

She shook her head positively. "I found them in here this morning, under the bed."

"Mr. Hadley's, you think?"

"Yes," she said tonelessly. Her eyes stopped their frantic darting, steadied, indicated decision. "He was in here last night. He—he's a maniac."

"Think so?" Wren showed the gun he had taken from her. "Whose? Where did you find it?"

"It's Mr. Hadley's. He keeps it in the bureau drawer in his room."

Wren kicked the box of murder junk. "Then this stuff isn't Hadley's since the collection doesn't include his automatic. Why did you open the south window in Stahl's parlor when you were in there this morning?"

"Because I was smoking. I didn't think Reverend Stahl would approve. So I opened the window"—she smiled slightly—"and removed the evidence of my cigarette."

"I see, I see. Moment ago you shot at me. Ruined my best hat." Wren smiled. "You thought that I was Mr. Hadley and that he'd slipped into this room as he did last night. You thought Mr. H. was choosing a murder weapon from this collection. You think Mr. H. knows the secret of this room." Wren shook his head. "He doesn't. I know, of course. The whole thing, my dear lady, is rather mad."

"It isn't," she contradicted. "You don't know my husband, how violent he can be. He threatened to kill—" She bit her lower lip hard.

Wren smiled. "I said I knew the secret. Mr. H. threatened to kill your uncle. That's the old man next door. Calls himself Rybolt. He's your uncle—your only blood relative."

Her indrawn breath was audible. "How did you know?"

"Remember at Stahl's? In the murder room when Rybolt came in? You started to say: 'Uncle, please take me home.' That's one indication. Another is the eraser on the bed. And, of course, the very existence of the Bluebeard room and its proximity to Rybolt's room next door. I gathered from something Mr. Hadley said to me that he had forbidden your uncle to enter his house."

"He threw uncle out," Joan Hadley said. Her fists clenched tightly, blanching her knuckles. "I mean that literally. He threw my uncle down the steps, said he'd kill him if Uncle ever set foot in the house again or made any attempt to see me."

Wren nodded. "But you maintained secret contact with your uncle. When you bought this house here, Rybolt rented a room in the house next door. You tossed notes back and forth. Notes fastened to the eraser. The eraser lent weight and its felt deadened the sound when it fell to the floor. But why, if you honestly believe your uncle is in danger from Mr. Hadley, why risk these contacts? Doesn't make sense."

Joan Hadley said nothing. She found a tuft of candlewicking on the bedspread and picked at it. Wren watched the pale, pretty face shrewdly.

"What's Uncle Rybolt's real name?" he asked.

Joan took a shallow breath. Her eyes searched Wren's face quickly. "Brown," she said faintly.

The chunky black eyebrows lifted. "Then Eddie Brown—"

"Was my brother—my own brother—and he was sick with tuberculosis. I wanted to do something for him with that money Walter gave me, but I knew Walter would stop at nothing to prevent me from using that money to help a member of my real family. When I learned I had a brother, I never mentioned it to Walter."

"You're quite sure Eddie Brown was your brother?" Wren asked. "Pete Stahl wouldn't be above panning off a substitute. Not if he scented money in the offing."

"Certain sure," she said. "Uncle and I traced Eddie through the orphanage records, employment offices, and finally through Selective Service. We found out that Eddie was living with and working for Reverend Stahl. But Reverend Stahl kept putting us off, saying that Eddie wasn't with him any more."

"I see. Trying to get you to put money across the board. Then he'd go into a trance and locate Eddie for you. That's Pete Stahl." Wren's smile twitched. "That's everybody. Everybody's out after that hundred thousand dollars Walter Hadley gave you to outwit his creditors. Even Walter Hadley."

Wren picked up the box of murder tools, tucked it under his arm. He put on his bullet-ventilated hat, looked down at the slim, wilted figure on the bed.

Joan said dully: "My own brother. And this morning was the first time I ever laid eyes on him."

Wren clucked sympathetically. He said: "Why not give Hadley back his hundred thousand and stop this thing? Stop it while you can."

She nodded. "Tomorrow." She smiled faintly as Wren left the room.

CHAPTER FIVE

ARSENIC AND OLD UNCLE

FROM THE front door of the Hadley house, Wren cut across the lawn to the porch of the rambling Talburn place next door. His knock brought a barking Lad, and, a few seconds later, Harmonica Gramps Rybolt himself.

"Well, if it ain't my partner in crime, so to speak!" Gramps extended a hard, wiry hand to Wren. "Saw you hikin' across the yard and figured you wanted to see me. Come on in. Come up to my diggin's." He waved his hand toward the stairway.

The shaggy brown dog jumped up, planted forepaws squarely in Wren's middle, caught Wren slightly off balance. Wren stepped back, bumped into the newel post of the stair rail. On the top of the newel post was a potted plant, the pot itself enclosed in one of those stiffened crocheted lace baskets which Wren considered an abomination. The plant toppled. Wren seized it, steadied it in place.

"Pretty thing," he said, referring to the plant.

Gramps chuckled nasally. "Thanks. Made it myself for Mis' Talburn." He unquestionably referred to the lace basket.

Wren was astounded. "You crochet?"

The old man drew down his snowy white eyebrows, thrust out his angular jaw a good inch beyond the top of his bottle-opener nose. "Now don't take that tone about it. Some old men twiddle their thumbs. I twiddle a crochet hook. Anything's better'n listenin' to your arteries harden. Oncet a feller kidded me about it, and I got out my old six-shooter and shot the ash right off his cigarette."

Wren chuckled as he followed the old man up the steps. They went along the upstairs hall to the halfway point, turned into the room which was directly opposite the window of Mrs. Hadley's Bluebeard room.

"Snug harbor," Wren commented, glancing about the room. Gramp's big bed was covered with a crocheted bedspread doubtless of his own handiwork. There was a dresser, a writing desk, a small radio. Above the radio was a war map pinned to the wall, and beside it a piece of brown butcher paper on which was written in black crayon a column of figures—small sums of money that totaled fifteen hundred and twenty-eight dollars.

"What's that?" Wren asked curiously. "Your share of the national debt?"

Gramps smiled slowly, a smile that didn't reach into his sad, hunchback's eyes. "That's money I don't have but ought to. I'd've won it if I'd been on all the radio quiz shows last week. I sort of like to keep track…. Here, you take the rocker, Mr. Wren. I'll set on the bed."

As Wren sat down, the door was nuzzled open by Mrs. Talburn's dog. Gramps flung out an arm toward the dog. "Here you, Lad, you get on downstairs. You know what happened this mornin', don't you?"

Lad didn't. His wistful brown eyes smiled. His tail thumped the door.

"What happened this morning?" Wren asked.

"Why," said the old man, "that fool dog got in here and got hold of a brand new crocheted basket I was stiffenin' for Mis' Talburn. He almost chewed it to pieces. A dog'll do that, you know, or even a kid. Like a sugar drop, which is just about what them baskets are. They're stiffened with sugar, you know."

Wren creaked forward in the rocker. He frowned. "That wasn't why Mrs. Talburn borrowed sugar from the Hadley house next door?"

The old man nodded. "Just so. Mis' Talburn, she's got the sugar diabetes and consequently don't seem to remember when she's runnin' low on sugar. Just I and her husband take the stuff, you know. I asked her for sugar to stiffen the new basket, and she said I'd used the last spoonful this morning in my coffee, and she run across to the Hadley house— Why, what's got into you, Mr. Wren?"

Wren was standing, staring down at the dog. He said: "That was the sugar that stiffened the basket. That was the basket that Lad chewed. Lad was the dog that was poisoned with arsenic after chewing the basket that was stiffened with sugar—" He broke off, looked at Gramps. Gramps' mouth was open. His sad, dark eyes stared at Wren as though he thought Wren had lost his mind.

Gramps said: "Sounds like 'This is the rat that ate the malt.'"

Wren shook his head. "It's no nursery rhyme. No. Not at all!"

Gramps got it suddenly. "You mean that sugar Mis' Talburn bor-rowed for me— You mean— Lord love a duck!" He stood up, paced to the end of the room, turned, ran fingers through his white hair. "There's somethin' I ought to tell you. Ought to have told the police this mornin', only I knew Mis' Hadley was dead set against it. That Eddie Brown that was frog-stuck, he was my nephew, Mis' Hadley's brother."

Wren nodded. "I know. Murder seems to run in some families. In others it's asthma, or twins."

HE LEFT the old man's room, went bounding down the steps with Lad at his heels. Outside the house he cut across lawns again to the Hadley door. He clacked the knocker once, found the door unlocked, walked right in. Elbert Claire was in the hall, evidently bent on an-swering Wren's knock. He rocked back on clatter-plate heels, blinked his sharp little eyes. His hands groped for trouser pockets he couldn't find and finally to his vest front where his thumbs hooked into pockets.

"You again, friend?" he was saying. "I thought you'd gone."

"Me again," Wren said. "Obviously. Where's Mrs. Hadley?"

Claire clawed pinkish, brush-cut hair. "I think she went for a walk. She's off her feed. Had a little tummy ache— Hey, Molly. Mol—lee!" he called toward the back of the house.

Molly Claire came tripping through a door at the rear of the hall. The redhead had a white postage-stamp size apron pasted on the front of her short green skirt.

"Oh, it's you again!" She sounded delighted. She linked arms with her husband and smiled at Wren. She had the nicest mouth. "Won't you stay for supper? I'm an awful punk cook, but—"

Claire said: "Don't apologize." He winked at Wren. "Mr. Hokus-Pokus can see I didn't marry you because I wanted a chef."

Wren said: "No, thanks. No supper here for me. Where did Mrs. Hadley go?"

Molly nodded north. "To the stores on Sixty-third Street. Her tummy was a little upset, and I thought the walk would do her good."

"Did you two eat lunch here?" Wren asked. "In this house?"

"We had a hamburger down at Sixty-third Street," Elbert said. "What's this all about, Mr. W.?"

"Did Mrs. Hadley eat anything this afternoon?" Wren persisted.

Elbert shook his head and Molly nodded. They looked at each other open-mouthed. Molly said: "I took her a cup of tea right after Mrs. Talburn dropped in. That was maybe three or four minutes before you arrived, Mr. Wren."

Elbert thumbed at Wren but looked at his wife. "He said eat. You don't eat tea. What's the matter with you?"

"You do so!" Molly argued. "In England you do, with cakes and toasted trumpets."

"Strumpets, you mean," said Elbert.

"Crumpets," Wren corrected. "And stop this. Mrs. Hadley had a cup of tea about thirty minutes ago. With sugar in it."

Molly gave him that bewildered baby stare. "Why, how did you know Joan takes sugar?"

Wren turned to the door. "By the symptoms." And he meant by the symptoms of having had tea the Borgia way.

He went striding down Guilford Avenue toward Sixty-third with the March wind tugging at his coat tails and blowing through the bullet hole in his hat. Under his arm was that box he had taken from the Bluebeard room. He felt like a one-man Murder, Inc. The tick of the clock within the box reminded him constantly, "It is later than you think." But not too late. Arsenic, from what he had heard, was a nasty poison and agonizing. But it was deliberate and not without antidote.

He had reached Paxton Place when it occurred to him that the proper procedure would have been to confiscate all the sugar in the Hadley house. Certainly he ought to have called the police. He slowed his pace, heard the ticking of the clock in the box. *It-Is-Later-Than-You-Think-It-Is-Later-Than-You-Think-It-Is-Later....*

Wren frowned. He shook his head and hurried on.

A lad with an Indianapolis Times sack over his shoulder was sitting on somebody's steps with his feet out on the sidewalk. He was folding papers. Wren stopped, nodded to the boy.

"Did a lady pass by here a while ago? A lady in brown, with ash blond hair. Trim. Nice looking—"

The boy's grin was more advanced than his years.

He said, "You bet!" and flushed. "You mean Mrs. Hadley? She's on my route."

"She walked straight on?" Wren pointed.

"Uh-huh." The boy folded a paper expertly into a neat, square-cornered pack that would break a plate glass window at twenty paces. "A man picked her up in a car."

"Ah? Just tooted his horn?"

"Uh-huh. He got out of the car and spoke to her, and then he helped her in."

"What kind of a car?"

The kid shrugged. "A jalopy. I didn't notice."

"The man. What did he look like?"

The kid looked sharply at Wren while his fingers mechanically folded a paper. "He was sort of tall. Sort of skinny. He wasn't dressed very good. Sort of down-at-the-heels, except his hat. He had on a new-looking light gray hat."

Wren lifted his eyebrows. It looked as though Horace's "guy inna ice cream hat" had fallen into place in the picture puzzle.

The kid asked: "Say, are you a G-man?"

Wren put a finger on his lips, rolled his eyes mysteriously. "Not so loud!" And then he hurried on to Sixty-third Street and across to the corner drugstore where he wedged himself into a telephone booth and called police headquarters.

JOAN HADLEY was missing. Also missing was an indetermin-able amount of white arsenic. Traces of the poison showed up in Joan Hadley's teacup, and quantities of it were found mixed with the top layer of sugar in the canister in the Hadley kitchen. Whether or not Joan had taken a lethal dose depended a great deal upon Joan's physical condition. She might be one of those rare persons who eliminate arsenic. Or then again she might die within seven to twen-ty-four hours. Nobody knew. It was purely a matter of trial and error with arsenic, and if you tried and erred you were too dead to talk about it.

The police hunt, Wren thought, was rather like the anxious process of digging out entombed miners. You couldn't tell until the very last whether you had Joan Hadley or Joan Hadley's body. The "guy inna ice cream hat" was a somewhat phantasmal figure, as badly wanted as the phony meter reader described by Harmonica Gramps Rybolt that morning at Stahl's murder seance. They were two of a kind, Wren concluded, which the law would have to possess in order to have a winning hand.

At six o'clock, Wren sat in that thoughtful brown room off his magic shop and felt enormously useless. He had just concluded a telephone conversation with Walter Hadley, who was at home. Hadley had exploded in Wren's face, like a short-fused firecracker. He had called Wren seven assorted kinds of a blundering idiot, any one of which would have melted type-metal. Asked if he knew anybody whose name sounded like *Bays* or *Hays,* Hadley delivered a succinct and unqualified "No!" that almost shattered the receiver diaphragm of Wren's phone.

At eleven o'clock, there was still no news. One radio commentator tried to make some, but his "it is believed that" and his "according to one authority" had the unconvincing ring of a Berlin broadcast. Jeffery Wren, worn out with doing nothing, his brain fagged from going around a circle that always began and ended with the skeleton costume in Peter Stahl's pantry closet, finally took two glasses of tawny port and went to bed.

It wasn't until the next morning while Wren was riding downtown on the bus, that he was struck with an original idea: Eddie Brown's murderer had had a confederate who had assisted in the perfect timing of the kill, who had slid open the bolt of the side door at the Stahl place, who had told the murderer exactly where Eddie Brown would be and how to get at him through the trap in the buffet top. That confederate was Eddie Brown himself!

Entering the novelty shop on West Ohio Street some minutes later, Wren found Walter Hadley there. Hadley was pacing the floor with Horace dogging his heels.

"You gimme the jim-jams," Horace was saying. "You gimme a coupla bucks and I'll go git us a pint a rum to settle our nerves—"

Hadley turned, saw Jeffery Wren in the door. He brushed Horace aside. Wren noticed that the yellow gleam predominated in Hadley's hoarhound eyes, that the eyes themselves nested in puffy blue-gray hammocks.

"I have to see you alone," he said to Wren. "Immediately, if it is at all possible."

WREN nodded, led the way up the stairs at the rear, across the magic shop, and into his office. He offered Hadley a chair which his guest ignored. Hadley's fluttering fingers were busy opening a folded sheet of paper to which was pinned a check.

"Read this," he said. "And for God's sake, tell me what to do."

The check was written in a shaky hand and made twenty thousand dollars payable to Walter Hadley. It was signed by Joan Hadley, dated March 6th. The accompanying note was printed in red pencil:

> Hadley:
> Cash the enclosed, small bills. Put the money in a shoebox and seal. Leave this box on top of the mailbox at the corner of Central and 59th at 3 A.M. March 8th. Walk east on 59th, and don't look back. Fail to do this and you'll never see Mrs. H again. Don't tell anyone and don't bring anyone with you either.

"Joan's been kidnaped!" Hadley said unnecessarily.

"Quite!" Wren pulled a piece of paper from a drawer in his desk, put it down in front of Hadley. He handed Hadley a pencil. "You still owe certain creditors some money, don't you? People who got trimmed when your juke box-peep show business went bust?"

Hadley nodded. "You—you think one of my creditors would try a stunt like this in order to collect? But it's impossible! The greatest amount I owe is ten thousand dollars."

Wren said gruffly: "You'd hardly expect the ransom to amount to the exact sum owed. That would identify the kidnaper." He gestured toward the paper. "Write, man! It's later than you think!"

Hadley wrote down five names: *Harry Mellish, Wright Canfield, Max W. Uhl, Paul Gardener, Basil Factor.*

Wren snatched the pencil from Harley's hand, underlined the last name.

"That's *Bays*—short for *Basil*. Some people pronounce the *a* in *Basil* like the *a* in *bad*. Others prefer *a* as in *ape*. Someone working for Basil Factor followed you yesterday. The idea might have been to kidnap you. But Horace shadowed your shadow, a man in a gray hat. Gray Hat no doubt reported to Basil that he was being watched. So tactics were altered. They'd snatch Mrs. Hadley, make her pay her own ransom through a check you could cash."

"Why—why that dirty damned—" Hadley wheeled toward the door. Wren caught him by the coat sleeve, jerked him back.

"Here. No barging in. You'd take an axe to a corn. This will take a bit of doing. Where can I find Basil Factor?"

"He has an office on Maryland Street. Basil T. Factor, Wholesale Wines and Liquors. I'm going—"

"You're going home," Wren said firmly. "You're a drawback on any team. If you had used your head last night when I asked if you knew anybody named *Bays*—" He broke off, added gently: "That's spilled milk. Water over the dam. Under the bridge." And he walked Walter Hadley out of the office, across the magic shop, and to the top of the stair. He refrained with difficulty from applying the toe of his shoe to the seat of Mr. Hadley's pants.

Back in the magic shop, Wren bounced from counter to counter loading his pockets with small, mysterious items which he thought might be useful in dealing with the likes of Basil T. Factor. Among them was an article known to spirit mediums as "the sponge." It was a round, opal glass jar with a quarter-turn cap of flesh-colored metal. At the top of the cap was a metal clip, also flesh colored, and constructed for easy palming. A sponge was attached to the inside of the cap, and the jar itself was filled with odorless wood alcohol. It was a nice thing to have around if you intended to snoop through somebody's mail.

CHAPTER SIX

HERE'S BLOOD IN YOUR EYE

SEVEN MINUTES later, a taxi put Jeffery Wren down in front of what must have been quite an imposing office building in the '90s. It was a three-story building of red brick, and, judging from the black- and gold-lettered sign across its front, was devoted entirely to Basil T. Factor's liquor business. Ground floor windows were plastered with advertisements for wines and whiskies. The center door had creaky spring hinges.

Inside, a turned oak rail kept three widely separated desks apart from salesmen, solicitors, and bill collectors. On the walls were more ads and blue and white cards bearing parsimonious platitudes such as: *A Penny Saved Is A Penny Earned. Time Is Money. Don't Waste It.* The gray-haired, hollow-chested goon pounding the typewriter looked as much a part of the building as the plumbing. Sharp black eyes behind rimless glasses pecked holes in Wren's placid face.

"Yes?" She didn't stop typing. In hot weather she must have been better than air conditioning.

Wren said, "Mr. Factor, please," and leaned against the forbidding rail.

The woman glanced at her wristwatch as she threw the carriage return on her machine, she was that efficient. "Mr. Factor will be in in six minutes. You may wait."

Wren unlatched the rail gate, opened it, walked into the sanctum and toward the desk on which rested a walnut block bearing the name *Basil T. Factor* in bronze letters. The typist twisted in her chair, tried freezing Wren with a look.

"You may wait outside." She indicated a straight oak chair beside the front door.

Wren smiled, shook his head. "I remember that chair. Something the Salvation Army gave away. Has slivers in it."

And then he proceeded to look over Basil Factor's mail. It was a bit more subtle than that, however. He managed to sweep the neat stack of letters to the floor with the sleeve of his fleece overcoat.

"How clumsy of me!" he said to the goon woman as she got up quickly from her desk and came over to straighten up the mess. Wren let her do most of the work, while his eyes noted the outside of each envelope. Unfortunately, Basil Factor's mail consisted of invoices, bills of lading, and direct mail advertising, with one notable exception. The fourth letter from the top of the new stack the woman formed, bore a local postmark, no return address, and was directed to the personal attention of Basil Factor.

The woman put the mail back onto the desk. Wren turned his back on the letters. His hands were behind him, ostensibly holding his hat.

The woman said: "Please go out and wait in that chair by the door." She was less icy. "Please, do. He'll only blame me for letting you come back here."

Wren was agreeable, especially since his moistened right forefinger had counted down the stack of letters and delicately filched the fourth from the top. He palmed the envelope, walked back to the rail, out the gate, sat down in the indicated chair. He put his hat in his lap, and the purloined letter rested on his thighs directly behind it, flap side up. A moment later, his right hand came from a suit-coat pocket and the alcohol sponge was palmed. A quick wipe of the sponge across the envelope and the opaque paper was instantly rendered transparent.

Inside was a card, the message partly printed with blanks filled in on a typewriter:

> Our recent survey indicates you have unoccupied property at…
> Route 1, Box 4, Ravenswood…. We urge that you make this available

for tenants at once. Help the man behind the man behind the gun find a home. Phone LI 4-5672 at once.

Defense Housing Committee,
The Radiohme Corporation

Wren's initial disappointment became an inspiration. Instead of making any attempt to get the letter back into Factor's mail, he dropped it into his pocket.

A FEW minutes later, the door of the building was opened by a short, fat individual whose breath wheezed through hairy nostrils, whose pockets jingled as he walked. He had a saddle-leather key case in a yellow-gloved hand, and the key exposed looked as though it belonged to the ignition lock of a car. His face was round, pale, and puffy, like a pan of raised dough with raisins dotted in for eyes, round nostrils and a Hitlerish mustache.

Wren stood up. "Mr. Factor, I presume?"

The fat man looked at him. His affirmative was halfway between a grunt and a growl. He showed Wren his back and plodded toward the rail and through the gate. Wren followed.

"This gentlemen wishes to see you, Mr. Factor," the girl at the typewriter said timidly.

"All right," Factor said. He still had his back toward Wren. He went to a clothes tree, took off hat and coat, dropped his keys into the righthand pocket of his coat. He turned, at last, to Wren.

Wren waltzed between Factor and the clothes tree, smiling pleasantly. Factor drew his mouth down at the corners and built up sales resistance.

Wren said: "I'm from the defense housing committee of the Radiohme Corporation. Our survey shows that you have a place out on the edge of Ravenswood which is vacant at the moment. We're hoping that you'll make it available to some defense worker in our plant."

Factor was shaking his head. He kept right on shaking it. "I'm not renting it. It's just a summer cottage anyway."

"We could get you a handsome rental for it," Wren persisted. "Say forty a month."

"Preposterous!"

"Not at all," Wren insisted, "if it's the place I have in mind. Suppose we run out and have a look at it right now."

"No!" Some color came into the doughy face. "And if I catch you snooping around there—" He broke off, swallowed, growled: "I won't rent it. That's final."

Now if Factor was as parsimonious as the mottos that adorned his walls indicated, there was some good reason why forty dollars a month for a river cottage wouldn't interest him. He colored angrily under Wren's shrewd gaze, flung back an arm as though he were going to bat Wren across the face.

"Get out!" he roared.

Wren ducked the blow that was never started, fell into the clothes tree, seized Factor's hanging coat apparently to steady himself. His left hand dipped lightly into the coat pocket, closed on Factor's keys, choked off their jingle as he brought them out concealed in his hand.

"If that's the way you feel about—" Wren shrugged and left.

Wren entered a tavern three doors west of Factor's wholesale house. He went back to the phone booth, looked up the Factor number in the directory, and dialed. The goon girl's voice answered, and Wren provided himself with a southern accent and asked for Mr. Factor.

"This heah's de janitah in de building across de street, Mistah Factah. Ah jest seen a traffic cop put a stickah on dat gray Chryslah of yourn."

"Preposterous!" Basil T. Factor exploded. "Why, my car's a green Packard, and I just this minute parked it half a block down the street. Who did you say you were?"

" 'Scuse me, boss!" Wren said, and had the satisfaction of hanging up rudely in Factor's ear.

Then he spent a second nickel, this one for life insurance. He dialed the number of Mrs. Talburn's house and asked for Franklin P. Rybolt.

"Wren," he said, as soon as Harmonica Gramps had answered. "Think you can still use that six-shooter you were telling me about?"

"Sure can, Mr. Wren. You take a guy like the one who's kidsnatched Mis' Hadley now—"

"Intend to take him," Wren cut in. "Listen." He glanced at his watch. "Take me forty minutes to drive across town. Give me fifty minutes. Then get in that orchid roadster of yours. You want a river cottage just the other side of Ravenswood. It's on Route 1, Box 4. Got that?"

"Sure have! You think— Lord love a duck, I'm so dang-busted excited—"

"Cool off," Wren said. "And don't forget the six-shooter."

He left the tavern, walked down Maryland Street where he found a dark green Packard sedan parked at the curb. He got in, thrust Basil Factor's key into the lock, started the car.

THE HOUSE was nearly square, one story, with a low, sloping roof. The shingle siding was painted green. It was built on high-water piles. Through naked willows and sycamores, Wren could see the brown turgid water with its tattered lace edging of white ice.

He gunned Basil Factor's green Packard into the lane, headed toward the house as though intent on knocking its stilt legs out from under it. He put the wheel hard to the left, slewed the car around on loose gravel at the foot of skeleton stairs leading up to a back porch. The idea was that if anyone was watching from the windows of the green house, that person should think Wren was Basil Factor, at least until the door was open. But it didn't work that way. Wren was on the porch, his fist raised to hammer on the solid door, when the door was opened by a man with a gun.

Wren noticed the gun first, since it was much more impressive than the man behind it. It was a revolver, possibly a .38, short-barreled and handy. The man was long and lank. His blue serge suit was shiny and didn't know what a crease was. His face was a narrow wedge, pale and yellowish, blue blotched like ripe Gorgonzola cheese. He wore a pale gray hat.

Wren said: "Factor sent me. You're to let the dame loose and scram. You see?"

Gray Hat nodded. "I see." His voice was soft and pitched high. "You'll come in out of the cold, won't you, mister? I don't think I caught your name."

"Jeff," Wren said.

"Well, that's a nice name. Mine's Mutt. How do you do? Come in, won't you? And put your hands up!"

Somebody inside the house said: "Mitch, you're a card!"

The gun gouged Wren's middle. He put up his hands and stepped across the sill. It was a large room with a fieldstone fireplace at one end. The furniture was maple with bright plaid upholstery on the chairs. The man who thought Mitch was a card sat at a square table. A revolver, whiskey bottle, and a glass two-thirds full were on the table in front of him. He was short, stocky, with coarse red hair. His left eye had a tight squint.

Mitch spoke to the man at the table. "Get on your hind legs and frisk this baby." The stocky man stood up, stuck his gun into his belt, and approached Wren. Mitch said to Wren: "We have to do things like this, Jeff. In the Secret Service you got to be suspicious of everybody. We're expecting a submarine loaded with Japs to come up White River any minute. You might be their inside man."

Wren chuckled. "Mitch, you're a card. About a two spot."

The squint-eyed man frisked Wren thoroughly. "He's clean," he said, and moved back to the table.

"Naturally," Wren said. "I wash." He cocked an eyebrow at Mitch. "May I blow my nose?"

"Please do," Mitch invited. "It needs it."

Wren took a handkerchief from his right hip pocket, wiped his nose, transferred the handkerchief to his left hand, put it into his left hip pocket.

Mitch said: "Can you tell us why the hell you came out here?"

Wren nodded. "Easily. We'll have a little talk. Probably become fast friends." He stepped over to the table. "What's the drink?"

"Scotch," the stocky man said.

"Pour him some, Charley," Mitch suggested.

Wren shook his head. "Tawny port is my drink. From New York State grapes. Whiskey?" He shuddered. "Horrible stuff!" His attitude suggested that he was already slightly tipsy. He brought his big right hand slamming down on the table squarely on top of the glass of whiskey. The slap was like a gun report. Then he turned up both hands, looked bewilderedly from empty palms to the table. Where the glass had stood there was only a ring of moisture to mark the spot.

"**SA—AY!**" Charley was baffled and belligerent. He looked at the table and then under the table. He looked around the table. Then his one good eye stared at Wren. Wren's smile quirked. Charley said: "How'n hell did you do that?"

Wren put a finger on his lips. "Sh-h. Magic!"

"Like hell! You can't work that stuff on me!"

"Can't I?"

"Hell no! You got that glass on you somewhere. In your pocket, maybe."

"See if his pants are wet," Mitch suggested.

Charley patted Wren's pockets. Wren's pants weren't wet. He walked all around Wren, came back to face him. He pulled his gun from his belt, rammed it into Wren's middle. "You gimme that glass, see?"

"Must I? With the whiskey in it?"

Standing on the other side of the table, Mitch chuckled. "Nobody could do that. Not with the whiskey in it."

Wren reached out with his right hand, snatched at empty air. It was misdirection. Charley stepped back, and he and Mitch both looked at Wren's right hand. The hand opened. It was empty. Wren's left hand brought the glass, still two-thirds full, from somewhere behind him.

"Here's blood in your eye," he said cheerfully, and dashed the entire contents of the glass into Charley's face. The Scotch caught Charley in the eye. Temporarily blind, he lurched toward Wren. Wren caught Charley's gun hand in his own right hand. His left arm looped around Charley's middle, twisted Charley to face Mitch across the table. Mitch looked too hard for a clear shot at Wren who was behind Charley. Wren's trigger finger levered on Charley's trigger finger. Charley's gun roared and Wren's luck rode the bullet. Mitch threw both arms up over his head and fell across the table. Wren released his hold on Charley, clouted Charley back of the ear with the thick bottom of the glass which was still gripped in his left hand. Charley went down with his face in a puddle of Scotch that glugged from the upset bottle on the table.

Mitch's face was bleeding. Possibly, Wren thought disinterestedly, Mitch was dying. He walked across the room toward three doors that were evenly spaced across the north wall of the big room. The first opened onto a kitchen. Wren merely looked into the room, closed the door, moved onto the next room.

This was it. He knew it as soon as he opened the door. You could tell by the smell of sickness. Blinds were pulled down over the windows. Wren walked in semi-darkness over to the bed, his eyes on the motionless bundle of bedclothes. Joan Hadley's body was wrapped from head to feet in a blanket. Wren worked a hand into the bundle, felt across the composed features. The flesh was cool, lifeless. She had died hours ago, but after dawn. Her kidnapers had been waiting for darkness to dump the body in the river. Wren wished suddenly that he had killed Charley, too.

The door of the river cottage opened. Wren turned, strode slowly out of the room. Three men had entered. There was fat Basil Factor, a hack driver, and Harmonica Gramps Rybolt. Factor and the taxi driver had their hands up and Gramps stood behind them with his six-shooter.

Gramps winked at Wren. "How'm I doin', Mr. Wren?"

"You're doing all right," Wren said.

"Listen, mister," the hack driver complained, "I don't know from nothing. Fats, here"—he thumbed at Factor—"hired me to bring him out here. This old coot tailed us into the lane—"

Wren nodded. "You're all right, cabbie. Victim of circumstance. You go find a phone. Get the police—or possibly the sheriff."

Gramps' sad eyes searched Wren's face anxiously. "Joan?"

Wren shook his head. "They let her die. Charley and Mitch and Fats Factor, here. They were afraid to call in a doctor. So they let her die."

Gramps' patent nose sniffled. "Why, you gol-danged—" And he booted Factor's rear hard enough to send Factor galloping toward the table. The six-shooter in Gramps' hand blared twice, once for each of Factor's legs. Basil Factor screamed, plunged heavily to the floor across the unconscious Charley.

Wren said: "That's about enough, Gramps."

CHAPTER SEVEN

OFF THE RECORD

"**YOU THINK** they'll put her in one of those baskets?" Gramps asked Wren. Gramps was sitting behind the wheel of the orchid roadster, waiting for Wren to get in. His eyes seemed to have sunk another inch back into his head.

Wren didn't think a reply was necessary. He took one last look at the house, at the sheriff's two cars and at the red ambulance from the City hospital. Then he slid into the seat beside Gramps. As he slammed the door, a rubber suction-cup coat hanger popped away from the window glass and fell to the floor of the car. He groped for it.

"Leave it go," Gramps said, as though nothing mattered now. He kicked at the starter. His eyes were misty and his bottle-opener nose bothered him. He drove slowly out of the lane and onto the road back to Ravenswood.

Wren noticed the radio on the instrument panel, saw that the dial pointer was set above fifteen hundred kilocycles, the limit of the broadcast band.

"Can you get the police radio?" he asked.

The old man shook his head. "It's ag'in the law, I heard, to have a radio that gets police calls except in a police car." He fiddled with the dial, then his arm dropped limply. "Don't think I could stand music right now."

"No," Wren said. "Not for me, either." His eyes were on the road ahead where he could make out the gas pumps of a filling station. "Stop up there. You mind? Have to make a phone call."

Gramps pulled up at the station. Wren got out, went into the office where he found a phone box. He dialed police headquarters and was lucky enough to get hold of Zoe Osbourn.

"My dear lady!" he greeted her cheerfully. "Can you tell me if the Stahl place has been under police surveillance since yesterday?"

Zoe Osbourn assured him that it had been.

Wren said: "Suggest you go there. Right now. You and the man on duty go down into the basement. There is an automatic gas incinerator in that house, but no gas. Remember? You might clean out the incinerator. If you find anything suspicious, bring it to the Hadley house. Possibly I'll hand you a killer."

Some minutes later, Gramps parked his orchid roadster near the front of the Hadley house. Two police cars stood in front of the place, and a good tenth of the population of Broad Ripple thronged the sidewalk.

"Now what?" Wren asked no one in particular. "Come on in, Gramps. Could be Walter Hadley cut his own throat while shaving. Always that possibility." And he elbowed his way through the crowd with the old man in his wake. The cop at the door stopped them until Wren identified himself. A harsh, metallic voice inside the house sang out: "Let Wren and the old gent in, Steve."

Steve let them in. In the living room Wren was greeted with unexpected cordiality by a lean, graying blonde man, a lieutenant of detectives. Wren had never heard the man's name, but he knew the underlings of Homicide always referred to him as "Loot." Loot's smile at the moment was the sort lavished on somebody who is about to be invited to eat crow.

"I guess we beat you to it this time, Mr. Wren. But mighty glad to see you in at the finish."

"Ah? This is the finish?" Wren's dark eyes compassed the living room. Pete Stahl, in a black overcoat of the same greenish cast as his black suit, was sitting on a hassock, hugging his bony knees. On the sofa were Molly and Elbert Claire. A couple of three-carat tears coursed down Molly's cheeks from pansy blue eyes. Big Elbert was holding her hand. There was a nice purple bruise on Elbert's jaw.

Walter Hadley sat in the wing chair beside the fireplace. He didn't see Harmonica Gramps at first, possibly because one of his eyes was closed—a shiner, Wren thought, worthy of Horace.

"Look," Wren said to Loot. "I'm new here. What gives?"

LOOT laughed dryly. He walked to a drop-leaf table that stood between two windows, pointed to a long, legal-looking envelope with one of its corners scorched brown. On the outside of the envelope was written: *Last Will and Testament of Joan Brown Hadley.*

Loot explained to Wren: "We were watching Peter Stahl, see? When he came out of his place and jumped in a taxi, we naturally tailed him. Gave him plenty of rope, see? He'd telephoned Mr. and Mrs. Claire, here. When Stahl got here, he and the Claires lit into Mr. Hadley and knocked him out. Then they went up to Mrs. Hadley's bedroom and found this will sewed up in her pillow. Stahl knew it was there, see? He claims he got a tip over the telephone, from whom we don't know and he doesn't either, he says. But before he'd tell the Claires where the will was, he made them sign an agreement whereby Stahl gets a tenth of John Hadley's estate, see?"

Wren shook his head. "Not entirely. How did they know Mrs. Hadley was dead?"

Loot's chuckle wasn't nice. "That's what's going to fry them!"

"Now, friend," Elbert Claire put in anxiously, "you've got that part bass ackwards. We just figured Joan would be dead by now if she had all that poison in her like you said."

Wren asked: "Who tried to burn the will?"

Loot pointed at Molly Claire. "The will don't favor her, see? But she's got an old one that does, one in which Mrs. Hadley left all her personal property to her foster sister, Molly Claire."

"That," Walter Hadley chimed in, "was when Joan's personal property just covered her clothing and a couple of diamond rings. But now that blanket bequest would cover Joan's bank account—my hundred thousand dollars."

"Tsk!" Wren cocked an eyebrow at Hadley. "You're all broken up, aren't you? Nearly lost your money."

"This will Mrs. Claire tried to burn," Loot continued, "was drawn up just a few weeks ago. The Claires are out."

"Who's in?" Wren asked. He started to pick up the will.

"Nix!" Loot said. "I got to get the prints off that. I'm waiting for the print man now."

Harmonica Gramps tugged at Wren's sleeve. Wren looked at him, saw Gramps nod at Elbert Claire. Gramps whispered: "That's him."

"I'll tell you about the will, Wren," Loot offered generously. "Mrs. Hadley left the hundred grand to her brother provided he could be properly identified. That brother was the Eddie Brown who was murdered yesterday in Stahl's place. The money was to be kept in trust for the Brown kid by some trust company downtown. But Mrs. Hadley had added a codicil to the effect that if Eddie didn't survive her, which he didn't, the money was to go to Mrs. Hadley's uncle, Frank Brown. That's the old gent behind you—the one who calls himself Rybolt."

"Who?" Gramps said faintly. "Me? Joan left some money to me?" He sat down limply in the nearest chair, tugged at his nose, shook his head. "I never had much. Never wanted much. What'd she go and do that for?"

Wren turned sharply toward the two Claires seated on the sofa. Molly was no longer weeping. Her eyes were amethyst quartz again. Elbert looked defiant, almost tearfully shy, like a small boy who is being teased.

"Greedy twosome," Wren murmured. "Loot, you know that box of murder tools I handed over to you? That collection of crude kill-gadgets? The Claires' work. They were trying to drive a wedge between Joan and Walter Hadley. Did it, too. The box of murder weapons they planted convinced Joan her husband was a homicidal maniac. They'd been building up to that. Building on the foundation of Hadley's violent temper."

"You're a dirty damned liar!" Molly Claire flung at Wren.

"Tsk, tsk! Such language!"

"ER—WREN," Loot said, "just one thing about that box of murder implements. Why the alarm clock?"

Wren shrugged. It was obvious. "Merely for the tick. If you hear a clock ticking in a room and can't find the clock, you look for it. In this case, Mrs. Hadley found the hidden murder tools. The gruesome quotation pasted on the face of the clock was a stroke of genius. Its purpose was to hide the true significance of the clock. Seeing the contents of the box, Mrs. Hadley immediately jumped to the conclusion that her husband had hidden the murder weapons in that room on the night before. But the collection couldn't have been Hadley's because it did not include an automatic which Hadley owned. Therefore, the Claires were responsible. Process of elimination. It couldn't have been Gramps, here, because Gramps didn't dare enter the Hadley house."

Gramps said: "Somethin' else, Mr. Wren."

Wren nodded. "You've never seen Elbert Claire up this close before. Right?"

The old man's eyes looked squarely at Elbert Claire. "Just oncet before," he said with firm conviction. "Yesterday mornin'. He walked in the side door of the Stahl house with a book and a flashlight, and I thought he was a meter reader!"

Elbert Claire sprang up from the sofa. A uniformed cop caught him by the collar and yanked him down.

"You're railroading me, damn you!" he shouted.

"Wait," Wren said gently. He turned to Gramps. "When you saw Claire enter the Stahl house, what were you playing on your harmonica? Wasn't it *Shoo Shoo Baby?*"

"Just so," declared Gramps.

"At what time?"

"Seventeen minutes after ten," Gramps said.

Wren shrugged. "There you are, Loot. I guess that clinches it. Walter Hadley's innocent. Gramps hasn't done any law-breaking, except that he carries a six-shooter, probably without a license."

Loot looked at Gramps. "You got a revolver on you?"

Gramps chuckled. "Guess so. Guess maybe you'll overlook my little crime, eh? Had this gun a long time. Can use it, too." He pulled out the gun and handed it to the lieutenant.

A door banged. High heels pegged on the tile floor of the central hall. Zoe Osbourn showed herself in the cased opening between hall and living room. She was flushed and out of breath. She had her big purse under one arm and a magazine under the other.

"Jeff," she panted, "I got it." She indicated the magazine. "It's in here."

Wren faced her squarely, shook his head, brushed his lips with a finger.

"Sit down, Zoe. Have a breath on me." Wren turned to the lieutenant. "Why don't you go through with the ritual of arresting the Claires, while I transact a bit of business with Walter Hadley?"

Hadley looked up in surprise. "Yes?"

Wren nodded. "We agreed to settle up when my job was done. My fee, remember? Shall we say twenty per cent of all you receive free and clear from your wife's estate?"

Hadley's laugh was nasty. "That's all right with me. You get twenty per cent of nothing. About what you earned!"

Wren cocked an eyebrow at Zoe Osbourn. "Witness the verbal agreement. Hadley pays twenty per cent of his wife's estate."

Zoe's mouth dropped open. She stared at Wren, pronounced slowly: "Why, you slick-witted son of the woman sawed in half!" She slapped her ample thigh. "Sure, I'm a witness!"

Loot was bewildered. "What goes on here?"

Wren said: "Indiana is a highly moral state. You agree, Loot? Dead set against murder. If Aunt Minnie wills Nephew George some money, but George kills Aunt Minnie to get it, the law won't let George benefit by the will. Right, Loot?"

"Right. But—"

Wren's smile was a trifle diabolical. "All I have to do to collect my fee is to prove that Gramps is the killer. Then, in due legal course, Hadley will inherit his wife's money."

GRAMPS blinked his deep-set eyes. "Wha—what you talkin' about? I didn't kill nobody."

"Just a couple of people," Wren said quietly.

"But—but you just said I hadn't broke no law."

"Misdirection," Wren said lightly. He turned to Loot. "Sorry. But I had to get him to hand over that six-shooter without a struggle. I've seen him use it. No more bloodshed today, thanks!"

Loot scowled at Wren. "You're serious?"

"Quite!" Wren sat down and placidly lighted a cigarette. "Gramps keeps a week-by-week chart of the money he could win on radio quiz shows if he were in each contest in person. That's the start of it. It indicates greed, avarice—even envy."

Loot slapped himself across the forehead. "Good Lord!" he laughed. "Suppose the police department figured things that way?"

Wren shrugged. "Might help. Who knows? But that started my suspicions moving toward Gramps. Then I wondered why Gramps should have said that the unknown meter reader was a 'gas man.' Perhaps a psychological association of ideas. After all, a gas operated automatic incinerator such as Pete Stahl has in his kitchen, could be used to get rid of evidence. And then why had Gramps acted so startled when Pete Stahl had said that he did not use gas? The answer, perhaps, was that Gramps had tossed some evidence he wanted consumed into the incinerator. Such evidence would not be burned. With a police guard on the premises, Gramps couldn't rectify his error. So he was startled."

Wren drew on his cigarette. He looked at Zoe Osbourn who started to open the magazine she had brought with her. He shook his head. He turned penetrating eyes on Pete Stahl.

"True, isn't it, Pete, that you kept Joan Hadley apart from her brother, Eddie Brown, even after you knew he was her brother? True that you said Eddie wasn't with you, but that you could locate him?"

Pete Stahl nodded his dark head sullenly. "But it was his idea." He looked at Gramps. "Old Brown's. He said if we stalled Joan off a while, she'd pay money to have me locate Eddie. Then we'd split the money."

Wren nodded. "But old Brown—I think I shall still call him Gramps—got acquainted with Eddie. Right? Not as Eddie's uncle, but just as a friend. Perhaps took Eddie out for spins in his roadster?"

"That's right," Stahl said.

"Gained Eddie's confidence, then," Wren continued. "Because he wanted Eddie to act as a confederate in a murder. A confederate to the murder of Eddie Brown himself."

Loot said: "By hell and by damn, Wren, that does it! You're nuts!"

Zoe Osbourn chuckled. "You'd better keep your mouth shut, Loot. The magician has a rabbit in his hat."

Wren smiled at Zoe. "Thanks. So I have. To continue: Eddie knew he was to be a confederate, but not to murder. Eddie thought it was a joke. To him the plot was merely one by which he and Gramps could scare the trousers off Pete Stahl. Eddie, on March 5th, rented a skeleton costume. This he was to hang in Stahl's pantry closet the next morning, just before Stahl had an appointment for a private seance. Next, Eddie was to unlock the side door of the house. Gramps would be parked under the porte-cochere in his roadster because he was chauffeuring Mrs. Hadley who also had an appointment with Stahl. Eddie's next job as confederate, was to go into Stahl's chapel and put a phonograph record on that wireless record player."

Wren glanced across at Gramps. The old man's face gave an excellent impersonation of that of a cigar-store Indian.

Wren asked: "Now you understand why I was interested in your radio, Gramps? It was tuned just above fifteen hundred kilocycles. Was tuned, in fact, to the wireless record player in Stahl's chapel. Thus *Shoo Shoo Baby*, a harmonica rendition, came from the radio in your car. It gave, you a three-minute alibi. You simply entered the Stahl house through the side door. You ignored the skeleton, costume which you were supposed to put on to scare Stahl into thinking he'd raised a real ghost. In one hand you had the fatal ice pick. In the other, I suppose, you carried that rubber suction-cup coat hanger from the window of your car. I might add that after one of those suction-cup hangers is removed once, it seldom sticks tightly to glass again."

"What the hell is the coat hanger for?" Loot wanted to know.

"To lift off the trap in the top of the buffet," Wren said. "So Gramps' right hand would be free to make a quick stab with the ice pick. After which he replaced the trap in the buffet top, went back to his car, turned off the radio, started playing the harmonica in person. The plan from Eddie's viewpoint was simply that both he and Gramps would have alibis for the time when the skeleton was to scare Stahl. Later, when Gramps again entered the house, he stepped into the chapel, got the phonograph record off the wireless player, and, in passing through the kitchen, dropped the record into the incinerator.... Now, Zoe."

ZOE OSBOURN opened the magazine, took out a white wax disk. "One of those home recordings," she said. "Gramps really recorded it, no doubt of that. Maybe he stepped into one of these demonstrations of home recording instruments which one of the local department stores has been putting on. Anybody who wanted to could cut a record for two bits."

"Which takes care of everything," Wren said. "The meter reader was a figment of Gramps' fertile imagination. Now we also know why Gramps knew he 'played' *Shoo Shoo Baby* at seventeen minutes past ten. Everything timed to a hair. Right, Gramps?"

Gramps was still a wooden Indian.

"What about the arsenic that got Mrs. Hadley?" Loot asked meekly. "That Gramps' work, too?"

"Of course. Only I don't think Gramps really wanted to kill Joan," Wren said. "The arsenic was too uncertain for Gramps' type of murder. The arsenic job was intended to convince Joan that someone in this house *was* trying to kill her. Just like the shot that missed Joan some weeks before. Gramps wanted his niece, Joan, to break away from Hadley and the Claires and go off with him somewhere. Then perhaps he could get the money without bloodshed. Wheedle it out of her. The point is, of course, that the arsenic did kill Joan and that Gramps poisoned her."

Gramps came to life. He creaked forward in his chair. "Why, I never heard of such a dang-blame bunch of hooey! I never set foot in this house before. How would I put poison in the sugar?"

"Simple," Wren said. "More expert timing on your part, Gramps. Yesterday morning you arranged that Mrs. Talburn should run out of sugar. Perhaps you poured her scant supply down the sink. You had a crocheted basket all ready to stiffen, complained to Mrs. Talburn that you needed sugar to stiffen it. Mrs. Talburn ran over to the Hadley's and borrowed a cup of sugar. Nothing else. Pure cane sugar. But when you mixed up the stiffening for the basket, you added arsenic. Then you left the basket where Mrs. Talburn's dog could get hold of it. The dog was taken with arsenic poisoning, and any investigation would indicate that the sugar borrowed from the Hadley house was the source of the poison.

"Actually to poison the sugar in the Hadley house, all you had to do, Gramps, was add arsenic to the cup of sugar Mrs. Talburn set out to return to the Hadley house. Police questioning of Mrs. Talburn will prove you had an opportunity to do just that. Mrs. Talburn handed the poisoned sugar to Molly Claire. Molly dumped it into the canister in the kitchen shortly before she made tea for Mrs. Hadley. Very simple. Very smooth. Very neighborly."

Gramps leaned back slowly in his chair. "And I thought I was so danged smart." His voice cracked a little. "Lord love a duck."

Wren stood up, glanced around the room at Stahl, at the Claires, at Gramps. "I know," he said softly. "He loves ducks. Only He knows why. Wonder what He thinks of snakes?"

A SLEIGHT CASE OF MURDER

TAKE THE HATBOX WHICH WAS DELIVERED TO JEFFERY WREN'S NOVELTY SHOP ONE MORNING—A FRIVOLOUS-LOOKING PARCEL CONTAINING, OF ALL THINGS, A PARAFFIN HAND. THEN THERE WAS THE PHONE CALL FROM MIRANDA LESTRARD, WHO DIDN'T KNOW WHICH WAY TO TURN FOR FEAR OF STUMBLING OVER A CORPSE. THAT'S HOW WREN AND HIS SIDEKICK SNOOP, ZOE OSBOURN, MET THE CREEPY MRS. KARPER AND HER HOUSE FULL OF HUMAN ODDITIES. SOME MURDERERS HANG THEMSELVES WITH ENOUGH ROPE—OTHERS HANG SOMEBODY ELSE!

CHAPTER ONE

THE CREEPY MRS. KARPER

JEFFERY WREN, who has repeatedly demonstrated his ability to cause anything to vanish, from an egg to an elephant, does not believe that the proverbial bad penny always turns up. To illustrate his argument, he frequently harks back to events revolving about Mrs. Karper. The revolving, be it known, was not entirely confined to the events, since Mr. Wren himself was observed to have shown signs of becoming a trifle dizzy before he got his hands on a certain kill-and-cover artist.

But take Mrs. Karper—take her far away, with best wishes for a gruesome evening. Let Mrs. Karper represent the bad penny.

"Or call her a lead quarter," Wren will suggest cheerfully to anyone willing to listen. "Mrs. Karper vanished. Utterly. Went *pffft!* You know, *pffft?*"

Which leads inevitably to his recounting of the entire bloody business which began one sunny June afternoon with the white thing in the hatbox.

It was a lady's hatbox, and why it should have been delivered to Wren's novelty store on West Ohio Street no one could have possibly imagined. No one, that is, except Horace, the thin, bloodless-looking clerk with the carnal mind. Horace's pale eyes were sly as he leaned across the joke counter and took a gander at the label: MISS MIRANDA LESTRARD, C/O JEFFERY WREN, BRILL BLDG., INDIANAPOLIS.

Horace's faintly blue hands molded Miss Lestrard's figure idealistically in thin air. He said, "Zowee!" in tribute to his own artistry.

Jeffery Wren returned from a late lunch at that precise moment. He crossed the threshold, his slow, bouncing gait reminiscent of an elegant hearse negotiating multiple railroad tracks, paused, and ele-

Wren flung the door open, turned on his flashlight. Over a jagged opening in the floor stood the man with the shovel.

vated one chunky black eyebrow.

"Ah," he said. "Mental lechery. Not to mention wishful thinking." The leer which Horace directed toward him was beyond all understanding until he approached the counter and looked down at the hatbox. He said: "H-m-m-m...."

"She'za blonde, huh?" Horace suggested.

Wren shrugged heavy shoulders. "How should I know? Never heard of the lady. Presuming she is a lady." While Horace snickered knowingly, Wren undid the bow-knot of the cross-strings of the hatbox.

INSIDE, reposing on a nest of pink tissue was something which he could not immediately identify. It appeared as though some Gargantua, given to chewing a couple of pounds of paraffin in lieu of gum, had spat his entire quid into the hatbox.

"Chic, isn't it?" Wren murmured.

Horace peered into the box. "For Crisakes, izat a hat?"

Wren's chuckle was deep and easy. "Who knows? Some women will wear anything."

He picked up the object, turned it over thoughtfully. On second glance, it grotesquely resembled a human hand, a right hand, and it was molded from paraffin. It was hollow like a glove and had a two-inch opening at the wrist.

"Ah. One of those." Wren's frown was slight, annoyed rather than

puzzled. His large, deft fingers drummed on the counter. "A spirit hand, Horace. The dear departed presumably leave such things behind at spirit seances. Inclined to prefer calling cards myself."

"Yeah?" Horace was frankly suspicious. "You're kinda off a subject of blondes, aren't-cha?"

Wren slid Horace a heavy-lidded glance. "Quite," he murmured. "Spirits like dabbling in paraffin. Nobody knows why. Probably a carry-over from making mud pies. Childish, but so is talking through a tin horn. Or tipping tables. Or—"

He broke off, his dark, discerning eyes reaching down into the hollow hand. Inside, between thumb and forefinger, were blue crystalline flecks imbedded in the white wax. Wren took off his Panama hat, fanned his sleek head briefly, put the hat down on the counter.

"My!" he said. He tilted the hand so that Horace could view the inside. Horace lipped his cigar around to the other side of his mouth.

"Well, well," he said disinterestedly. "It's a blue blight. What I wanna know, is it catching?"

Wren shook his head. "Hardly. But persons showing such symptoms are often quarantined. In jail, of course. Sometimes they even have to be put out of their misery in the electric chair."

Broad enough even without a hatbox under his arm, Wren was forced to sidle between counters to reach the door at the rear. He took buoyant steps up a flight of stairs, passed through a door that bore the legend, *Wren's Magic.* Beyond was a small reception room, the walls of which were adorned with photographs of his own sleekly ostentatious self as he had appeared on Keith's vaudeville circuit. He unlocked double glass doors, went into the magic shop to which amateur and professional conjurers were lured by the stock of tricks, gimmicks, and elaborate apparatus displayed in the counters and on the velvet-draped tiers.

The phone was ringing. Wren put the hatbox down on a counter alongside of one of Grant's talking skulls. He picked up the handset.

"Miss Lestrard?" he said with sufficient inflection to cover any margin of error. He was rewarded by a gasp of astonishment. Sure of himself, he said: "Jeffery Wren, Miss Lestrard."

"Why—why how did you know?" The voice had the pleasant lilt of youth plus something else that was excitement or fear.

He hadn't known, of course. Like most magicians and mentalists, he jumped to a conclusion now and then, took his triumphs where the law of averages provided them, pattered his way out of his mistakes.

"This thing in the hatbox," he said. "Takes a bit of explaining, Miss Lestrard."

"I just couldn't get it to you any other way," the girl replied anxiously. "I was afraid somebody had followed me, so I just put in on the delivery truck of the milliner for whom I work. I—I just don't know which way to turn for fear I'll stumble over a corpse!"

A sigh blew softly from Wren's lips. "Just any old corpse?"

"That," she said, "is just it. I don't know *who* it was. Just somebody lying there in the grass. I thought at first it was Mrs. Karper. She's the old lady I live with. She has a rooming house on Broadway below Sixteenth. She's a spirit medium for her own amazement, and on Tuesday night she materialized—I guess that's what you call it—that spirit hand I sent you. But that was *after* I thought I'd seen her lying dead in the back yard, so it wasn't her, if you can imagine that!"

"Wait," Wren checked her. "Ever try taking a breath? Surprising how much it helps." He heard the breath, shallow and tremulous.

Miss Lestrard said: "I just can't help it. Wouldn't you be breathless if you thought you found Mrs. Karper dead in the back yard, and she wasn't?"

"Quite," he admitted, elevating black brows. "No end upsetting. However—"

"If it wasn't Mrs. Karper, who was it?" Miss Lestrard's words came nipping at the heels of Wren's. "There's nothing there now but a patch of bare ground where somebody pulled up the grass. Everybody says I was dreaming, but I was wide awake, really. And I don't much care about staying in that old house with that creepy Mrs. Karper around— if she is around—and maybe find a corpse under my bed. You can't tell me something isn't going on!"

"Wouldn't think of it," Wren wedged in. "Something's going on. No doubt of it. Want me to see Mrs. Karper about it?"

"Oh, you can't do that," Miss Lestrard objected hastily. "Didn't I tell you? Mrs. Karper's vanished!"

"No!" He was incredulous.

"She did. Right out of the back seat of a cab belonging to the Duncan Taxi Service. That was Wednesday night. And she had my hat on, too. She went, *pffft!*"

"Not *pffft!*" He was amazed. "With your hat on."

"So I'd like to see you about five o'clock," Miss Lestrard concluded. " 'By now." And she hung up with very little consideration for Wren's eardrums.

HE PUT the handset down deliberately, frowned at it. *"Pffft!"* he said, and grunted. Then he lifted the phone, dialed police headquarters, and asked for Zoe Osbourn, the policewoman assigned to snaring fortune tellers and fake spirit mediums. Together, Wren and Zoe Osbourn had fixed the wagon of many a spook crook. Why not the creepy Mrs. Karper?

A couple of minutes later, Wren descended into the novelty shop where he discovered Horace draped across the joke counter demonstrating a trick necktie to a man and woman. The tie was provided with a concealed thread and spring for secret manipulation.

"Say you're walkin' downa avenoo," Horace was saying, "an' you meeta swell lookin' babe of a opposite sex, you wave your tie atter. Like yoo-hoo, on'y classier, see?"

The woman said: "I'm afraid we're not interested," as though Horace were offering her a nice case of smallpox. She was rather tall, a honey blonde, her well-proportioned figure rigged out in an expensive-looking sheer black dress. Long, sleek legs were painted a coppery tint and a red-lacquered toenail peeped through the open toe of her high-heeled pump. Wren thought it was too bad about the toenail. Too bad about the lady's upper lip, also, for it was short and curled slightly toward her nose, giving the impression that she smelled something disagreeable. Otherwise, she was something to turn and look at.

The man was tall and no rather about it. All his tailor had done in the way of padding his gray-green tweed sports jacket couldn't conceal the fact that he was exceptionally thin. Dark wrinkles lined his hollow cheeks. He was short on chin, long on nose, while his eyes were stony-gray and peering. He wore his straw sailor at a tipsy angle.

"Some other day, sport," he said to Horace in regard to the necktie. He turned, discovered Jeffery Wren, which was no great feat. He plunged toward Wren, his right hand outstretched.

"Well, hello there! We're Jake and Martha." The thin man seized Wren's hand, and the effect was somewhat like that of an electric shock because he had one of those jokers' devices known as a "joy buzzer" concealed in his palm.

Wren looked from the man to the woman. "Which is Jake and which is Martha? Ever since *Frankie and Johnny* I've gone out of my way to make sure about such things."

The man took a foul-smelling briar pipe from his mouth, pointed to himself with the bit of it. "I'm Jake. Can you handle the rest of it by the process of elimination?"

"If," said the woman, "we had said Jake and Martha's Number One and Jake and Martha's Number Two, Mr. Wren would have realized who we are. Or as it were. I never know." Martha had a pleasant, throaty laugh.

"Sure," Jake said. "You know, Mr. Wren. 'The Hamburger of Mouth-Melting Goodness.' Jake and Martha's at Sixteenth and College and Sixteenth and Central." He smacked his lips.

"No," said Wren. "I'm a vegetarian—as of right now."

He turned on his heel, would have walked out of the store if Jake hadn't dropped a slim hand on his thick shoulder and flashed a roll of bills under Wren's nose.

"Money talks, sport, money talks."

It did at that. Wren turned slowly. "Ah? What about?"

Jake raised his straw hat to scratch meditatively at the exact center of his high, hairless dome. "Put it this way," he began. "Martha's father, name of Martin Owen, is an old goat."

Martha said: "Jake Wister!" She sniffed reproachfully. "He isn't anything of the kind. Dad is simply in his dotage and susceptible to women. Look, Mr. Wren. You know Miss Eudora Crowley, don't you?"

Oddly enough, Wren did know Miss Crowley. She was an aged spinster, carriage trade and carriage dated, remarkable for her money and for the tenacity with which she clung to the fashions of yesterday—or day-before-yesterday, since Miss Crowley was all of three score and ten.

"What about Miss Crowley?" he asked Martha.

"She and Dad are in love," Martha explained. "They have been for years and years. Yesterday, that's Wednesday, Dad got a letter mailed the previous day. It was from Miss Crowley. She said she was leaving for French Lick and would he meet her down there? She didn't come out and say so, but it was pretty evident the object was matrimony."

Wren shrugged. "Well? Any objections?"

"Objections?" Jake slapped his lean thigh. "That's good, that is, with Miss Crowley worth all kinds of dough and both her and Martha's old man on their last legs!"

Wren looked coolly at Jake, said to Martha: "Blunt, isn't he?"

"Disgusting!" Martha sniffed.

"You've got to be blunt," Jake insisted. "That's the only way to get any place. Call a spade a spade, is my motto…. Look, sport, we'd like to hire you. Martha's old man went down to French Lick yesterday and wired us right back that his girl friend had stood him up. She wasn't at the hotel and nobody had seen her. We wired back to the old man, and we get a reply from Western Union that Martin Owen isn't in French Lick. What he's done is go tottering off looking for Miss Crowley. So we'd like to hire you—" He paused, looked incredulously at Wren who was shaking his head.

"What's wrong, sport?"

"Wrong?" Wren cocked an eyebrow. "Not a thing. Simply not interested. Good day. Happy hunting for the old love-birds." And he bounced back through the door at the rear of the store before Jake could lay a predatory hand on him.

PROMPTLY at five o'clock, just as Wren had got rid of his last customer for the day, the double doors of the magic shop were opened gustily by Policewoman Zoe Osbourn. She had a white cartwheel hat plastered on the back of her hennaed curls. Her dress was a flowery thing, predominantly lavender, with pre-O.P.A. ruffling. Had there been an inscription in gold, "To a Pal from Al," worked diagonally across the front, Zoe Osbourn would have resembled one of those magnificent floral tributes that show up at gangster funerals. She pegged across the shop on heels too high and slim for a woman of her weight.

"What's this nonsense about a spirit hand that packs a pistol, Jeff Wren?" her strident voice demanded.

Wren slid a heavy-lidded glance toward Zoe Osbourn and then toward the doors. Entering the shop in the wake of the policewoman, was a girl—small, scarcely twenty, brunette, and pretty. Across the threshold, she stood primly, her dark eyes seeing spooks in corners.

"How's the ghost squad?" Wren wanted to know of Zoe Osbourn as he bounced around from behind a counter. "For that matter, how're the ghosts? Who's haunted now?"

"Me." This in a small voice from the girl in the doorway. "I'm Miranda Lestrard."

"Ah?" He raised his eyebrows. Noting Miss Lestrard's delicious coloring, her delicate features, he decided that poignant was the word for her. "You're haunted? Werewolves, no doubt."

Miranda Lestrard flushed, lifted a spunky chin. "And I don't think that's very funny, Mr. Wren."

Zoe Osbourn turned, her prominent, gullible-appearing blue eyes narrowed a trifle as she appraised Miss Lestrard. The girl wore a short black skirt that flared from a slim waist and flaunted a saucy edging of white petticoat lace at the hem. Her white blouse had a revealing neckline that barely capped her shoulders. Lowering her eyelids under Zoe's penetrating stare, Miss Lestrard's lashes were like soot against rich cream.

"You keep your hair braided, dearie," said Zoe Osbourn. "I was here first. Jeff, where's that spirit hand?"

He waved toward the hatbox on the counter. "No admission. Have a look. Don't miss the big show on the inside." He stepped across to Miss Lestrard who had opened her purse and was digging in it like a terrier at a gopher hole.

"Here, Mr. Wren." Miranda Lestrard took from her purse a crumpled piece of notepaper. "I found this in the bathroom wastepaper basket this morning. I don't know whether it has anything to do with the spirit hand or not, but it's pretty funny and I do mean queer!"

As Wren spread out the paper, Zoe Osbourn came from behind the counter, carrying the spirit hand as though she had a dead mouse by the tail. "Jeff—" she began, and then looked over his shoulder at what he was reading.

It was a penciled scrawl, the false start of a letter. It read:

> Dear Mr. Merwin:
> Last year I had fingers and toes, but I shur don't want any this season, so....

That was all. That, for Zoe Osbourn, was quite enough. She slapped herself across the forehead, gave forth an exasperated snort.

"Last year he had fingers and toes, and this year he don't want any! The driveling idiot! And don't you look at me that way, Jeffery Wren!"

He was, he presumed, looking a trifle smug. "Gruesome, isn't it? But illuminating. Considering somebody's been murdered."

"Ha!" Zoe Osbourn looked quite capable of biting a crowbar in two and then welding it together again with the heat of her glance. "Illuminating, he says! It is like hell!"

CHAPTER TWO

MR. HITCH'S FINGERS AND TOES

ZOE OSBOURN stared down inside the hollow paraffin hand. Then she looked suspiciously at Jeffery Wren.

"Did you treat this with Lunge's reagent?"

"That what it's called? Knew it was the paraffin test the police use to see if somebody's fired a gun." He shook his head. "No, not I. Hardly. Where would I obtain Lunge's reagent?"

"Those—those blue specks were in there when I found it," Miss Lestrard said. "That was this morning. I was snooping around to see if I could find Mrs. Karper or even my hat. I noticed one of the treads on the basement stairs was loose. I lifted the front edge of it, and beneath was a little hidy-hole, and the hand was in it. I thought if I got it to Mr. Wren, he'd be interested. I'm"—she smiled, rolled her eyes—"I'm provocative like that."

She was, at that. Wren took the paraffin hand from Zoe Osbourn and put it back inside the hatbox.

Zoe asked: "Who's Mrs. Karper?"

"A medium," Wren said. "For her own amazement. Let's try and make head and tail of this, shall we?" And he led the way back into the thoughtful brown room that was his office.

He placed two chairs for the ladies, noticed that Miss Lestrard tried to see on all sides of herself before she sat down.

"Oh, come, Miss Lestrard!" Wren's chuckle was reassuring. "No spooks here. They can't stand me."

"You just relax, dearie," Zoe Osbourn suggested kindly, "and tell us about it."

Miranda drew a shivering breath. She crossed nice knees, quirked her right ankle to examine the toe of her pump.

"Tuesday night about ten o'clock, I went out into Mrs. Karper's back yard where there's an incinerator. I had a waste basket full of scraps to burn. There was quite a breeze, you'll remember, and some of my scraps got away from me. I went across the back yard, chasing a piece of white ribbon, and that's when I fell over the body. But actually!"

Wren observed that Miss Lestrard's eye rolling was extremely effective. He said: "You thought it was Mrs. Karper. But why?"

"Because it had on long skirts," she said. "It—the body—was part way under a lilac bush. I said: 'Why, Mrs. Karper, what on earth,' and shook her, but she didn't say anything. So I ran right back to the house."

Zoe Osbourn snorted. "Why didn't you call the police, dearie?"

"Oh, I couldn't. I was too scared. I just went up into my room and sat there shuddering." Miss Lestrard's nearly bare shoulders shivered exquisitely. "I don't know for how long. But after a while, there was a tap at my door, and I finally got up nerve enough to answer it. You don't know how it is with Mrs. Karper. She's the creepiest thing! You don't see much of her for days and days, and then she'll shuffle in on you in her bedroom slippers when you least expect it. And this was when I least expected it."

Wren nodded. "Mrs. Karper was at your door. Hale and hearty!"

Miss Lestrard nodded her head, yes. "I nearly died!"

Zoe Osbourn snorted. "What about the corpse in the back yard?"

"I don't know what about the corpse," the girl replied. "I said to Mrs. Karper, 'You're dead!' just like that, and she said that was nonsense, nobody was dead around there. And she wanted me to come down to the parlor for a spirit seance."

"Ah?" Wren said. "You alone?"

"No, all the other roomers were there except Herbert Sharrod, who was out for the evening. Oh, Fred Duncan wasn't there, either, but you never see much of him. He's not exactly a roomer. He rents Mrs. Karper's garage, lives in it, and runs his taxi business."

"All right," Zoe Osbourn said testily. "Who was there?"

"Old Mr. Hitch, who works for a safe company that's making war stuff, and Mr. McFee, and Jake and Martha Wister."

Wren stared, a trifle incredulous. "The hamburger king and queen? Jake and Martha live in a rooming house?"

Miranda nodded vigorously. "I guess it's the housing shortage. But you take Herbert Sharrod—he's got oodles and oodles of money and a great big car, and he lives there, too. It's funny, isn't it?"

"It's fishy, dearie," Zoe Osbourn said, lighting a king-sized cigarette. "But go right on. You went down to the parlor for a seance."

"Well, it wasn't the first time," continued Miss Lestrard. "Mrs. Karper keeps everybody hopped up about her supernatural powers. She's given us living-or-dead tests, table-rappings, and what-not. But tonight it was different. She had an old crazy-quilt suspended across a wire so as to screen off one corner of the room."

Wren's smile broke bright against his tanned skin. "Crazy-quilt. There, Zoe, is a medium with a sense of humor."

"Ha!" Zoe glowered at him. "If you'd stop tossing in your witty asides, Jeff, maybe we'd get somewhere. What about this spirit hand?"

"There was some melted paraffin in a double boiler on a table in front of the quilt," Miss Lestrard continued. "And also a lard pail full of cold water. Back of the quilt was a chair, and Mrs. Karper asked us to handcuff her into it. She had the handcuffs and they seemed real enough. She looked awful, sitting there, going into her trance. She had on her ugly yellow wig and one of those funny dresses. Her dresses look as if they came out of the Ark. They're cast-offs from some aged eccentric—"

MISS LESTRARD broke off, rolling big black eyes at Wren who had lifted an eyebrow significantly. Wren made a negative gesture with his large hand, smiled.

"Go right on. Just ignore me."

"That's about all," she said. "The lights went out and Mrs. Karper was in her trance, handcuffed to her chair. There were what she calls manifestations—drafts of cold air and whispering. Something planted a kiss right on top of my head, and I think I screamed a little. And then we could hear something splashing around in the paraffin and then in the cold water. And when the lights were on again, there was that cast of the spirit hand."

Zoe Osbourn gave her cigarette ash an exasperated flip. "Well, Jeff, if you ask me, Mrs. Karper made the hand herself. Most of the mediums can work out of handcuffs. And she'd been gunning somebody. She gave herself away when she put her hand in the paraffin."

"You think so?" he asked quietly. "Then treated the cast of her hand with Lunge's reagent to see if she had shot the gun? Undoubtedly. Shoots people in her sleep and wants to catch herself. Thoughtful of her. Very considerate of the police department, is Mrs. Karper." He turned to Miranda Lestrard. "What about this vanishing stunt? From a taxi, you said. With your hat on."

"That was last night," said Miss Lestrard. "I saw her go out and get into one of Fred Duncan's cars. She got in the back seat and she had on my very best hat. I ran across the hall to Herbert Sharrod's room, and Herbert and I followed Fred Duncan's cab in Herbert's car. We could see Mrs. Karper sitting there in the middle of the back seat. And then suddenly"—Miss Lestrard tossed up black-gloved hands expressively—"*pffft*, she was gone!"

"Horsefeathers!" Zoe Osbourn commented. "Plain and unadulterated horsefeathers! *Pffft*, she was gone, my hat!"

"Her hat," Wren said, chuckling. "Miss Lestrard's hat."

Miranda pouted prettily. "Well, you just ask Fred Duncan or Herbert Sharrod! She vanished, and nobody's seen her since."

Zoe Osbourn got heavily to her feet. She glared at Wren who was sitting on top of the desk.

"Give me that unfinished letter you said was so illuminating, master-wit!"

He shrugged, gave her the letter Miss Lestrard had filched from the bathroom waste-basket. "Any idea who wrote this?" he wanted to know.

Miranda's eyes widened, surprised. "Oh, didn't I mention that?"

"You mentioned everything else," Zoe growled, "and mixed it to hell-and-gone."

"Nahum Hitch wrote it," Miss Lestrard said. "He's one of the roomers, and he always writes in that cramped, spidery scrawl."

"Last year he had fingers and toes, and this year he doesn't want any!" Zoe said. "Fry me a banana, what's illuminating about that, Jeff?"

He shrugged heavy shoulders, looked quizzically at Miss Lestrard. "Can we reach Mr. Hitch via the phone? At Mrs. Karper's?"

She nodded vigorously. "If he's not out in his victory garden." And she gave him the number. Wren twisted around on the desk, dialed, and eventually drew a pleasant masculine voice that did not belong to Mr. Hitch. While waiting, he looked at Miranda. His smile was whimsical.

"Mrs. Karper vanished. From a taxi. Most convenient. Avoided paying her fare that way, no doubt."

Miranda crinkled her nose at him. "This isn't funny. It's murder, and—" She broke off because it was evident that Wren was listening to the phone.

It was a crabbed, old man's voice that came from the receiver. Wren identified himself, his voice a smooth, deep purr, well calculated to soothe the savage beast.

"We haven't met," he said. "Not yet, Mr. Hitch. But we've something in common." Then he whispered, as though repeating a password. "Fingers and toes!"

"Well, sure now!" Mr. Hitch became more cordial. "Them damn things! How'd you know I had 'em? It ain't been in the papers yet."

Wren looked at Zoe Osbourn, appeared satisfied that she was approaching the boiling point. "Most people have them, Mr. Hitch. But what to do about it?"

"That does it!" Zoe bellowed. She squared off in front of Wren, her bulk blotting Miss Lestrard from view. "Give me that phone!"

Wren slid behind the desk, keeping Zoe off, listening to what Mr. Hitch was saying. "You get some quicklime and spread it on thick. That'll take care of your fingers and toes."

"Should think so. Quite!" Wren dropped the phone handset on its cradle, severing the connection. He looked at the fuming Zoe Osbourn, and a sigh blew softly from his lips.

Zoe stood with arms akimbo. "Go on, stun us, master-wit!"

"All the ingredients of murder," he murmured. "Take evidence of gun-play. That's the Lunge's reagent in the spirit hand. Add Mr. Hitch's fingers and toes. Spread quicklime on thick. The thing's done. A dish fit for the coroner!"

MIRANDA LESTRARD moved forward to the edge of her chair where she perched daintily, birdlike in her alertness.

"I told you there was a body somewhere."

"So you did, dearie," Zoe Osbourn admitted, nasty-nice about it. She watched what Jeffery Wren was doing with a half-dollar. The coin moved in and out of his big, deft fingers as though minted from quicksilver. "Look at the man! He's happy about the whole thing!"

"Happy?" He raised his eyebrows. "Who's happy about it? On the other hand, why hang crape for perfect strangers? Runs into too much money." The coin vanished, and he said: *"Pfft,* like Mrs. Karper."

Zoe Osbourn pegged to the door, stood with one hand on the knob. "When it's quicklime, you don't go *Pfft.* Homicide better hear of this." She slammed out of the office and into the magic shop.

"An intelligent woman," Wren commented to Miss Lestrard. "Easily misled. In a nice way, of course…. But about Mrs. Karper's vanishing act. Let's simplify that. You and one Herbert Sharrod followed Mrs. Karper's cab because Mrs. Karper had stolen your hat."

Miranda bobbed her pretty head affirmatively. Wren chuckled. "Try it this way," he suggested. "Mrs. Karper stole your hat because she wanted to be followed. Wouldn't vanish without an audience. Who would? No applause. No astonished gasps."

Miranda's eyes widened. "Why, I never thought—" She stopped, mouth open, her small body rigid. Because from the magic shop had come a sound. Wren recalls regretfully that it was a thud, though he has always been thankful that it was neither dull nor sickening. The floor trembled and there was a clatter of things on shelves.

Wren and the girl reached the door simultaneously, got it open. The first thing that met the eye was Zoe Osbourn's big white hat rolling like a lazy hoop to settle to the floor with a soft *pat-pat* sound. Near the double glass doors of the magic shop, a short, small-boned figure of a man in a dapper white suit stood jittering. His teeth were chattering. His sharp, knowing face was pallid. Upstanding red hair added something to his terrified appearance, but why he was afraid, Wren didn't know. Because the man in the white suit had the whip hand. He had a nickle-plated revolver in his right hand, and this was unsteadily pointed at Policewoman Zoe Osbourn.

Zoe sat on the floor, her legs out straight and her back against a counter. She was pressing both hands against her temples as though to keep her head from splitting, and her prominent eyes were slightly glazed.

"Jeff! Jeff!" she was shouting hoarsely, hopelessly, as though pursued by a nightmare.

"Stop her, Jeff. She'd got the hand!"

The "her" shuffled toward the doorway and toward the jittering little puppet in white. Under her arm was the hatbox which presumably contained the spirit hand. Except for her hideously frizzed yellow wig, she might have come out of anybody's family album. The hat perched on top of the wig was strictly Queen Mary and tied on with a gray veil. She was shapeless, dumpy. Her black skirts swished the floor, showed nothing of her extremities except a soiled pair of dark felt bedroom slippers.

Wren might have stopped the apparition—he had trapped a few in his day—if it hadn't been for Miranda Lestrard. That little lady screamed blue murder as though she had been wanting to get it off her chest for days and days.

"Mrs. Karper!" And Miranda keeled toward Wren, draped herself considerately into the crook of his arm, went limp.

Mrs. Karper turned around without any apparent muscular effort, like a weathercock in a changing wind. Her right hand was occupied with an automatic pistol, blunt-bodied and ugly, like an angry blowsnake. Even without the gun, she was enough to frighten little children. She hadn't any teeth, which had led to the collapse of the lower part of her face. Her skin was warty. A bulbous red nose suggested an intimacy with spirits of another sort. In spite of the yards of restraining veil, her yellow wig had slipped forward over one eye. She was, on all counts, the hardest looking female Wren had ever seen.

"Here," she said, and passed the hatbox back to the man in white. "Here, McFee, carry this. And stop that shaking. I'm just reclaiming my own property, the hand the spirit give me."

The little man in white took the box and skipped through the door into the reception room.

Zoe Osbourn got heavily to one knee, but no farther. Her glance bored Mrs. Karper through and through, but was no match for the old gal's gun.

"The old bat socked me!" Zoe said venomously.

Mrs. Karper backed through the double glass doors. She swung one of the panels shut, got the key from the inside of the lock. Wren, divining her intention, said: "Look, Mrs. K. What's a lock to me?"

Mrs. Karper's one visible eye glinted diabolically. She swung the second door into place, locked the two together while her gun stared at them through plate glass. Just before she scooted with the man in white, she thumbed her raspberry nose at Wren.

CHAPTER THREE

DIG A GRAVE FOR A LADY

ZOE OSBOURN got to her feet, steadied herself by clutching the edge of the counter. She looked from the locked doors to Wren. She glared at Wren and at the limp figure in his arms.

"Don't just stand there!" she bellowed. "Get those doors unlocked fast. Put the girl down on the floor."

He had already started to lower Miss Lestrard, but the girl's legs suddenly stiffened and her dark eyes popped open.

She said: "I guess you'd better not. I might soil my blouse." She stood on her own small but adequate feet and began nervously patting her black hair. Zoe Osbourn stood at the counter, goggling.

"Why, why, you—you twerp!" She stalked heavily toward Miranda. "You dirty, unprincipled little twerp!"

Miranda lowered her eyes, raised them effectively to Wren. Like a child in a school play who has forgotten her lines, she teetered on her toes and picked at the waist-band of her skirt.

"I just didn't want to get mixed up in anything," she said limply, "so—so I passed out."

Wren gave his head a grave half-shake. "Miss See-No-Evil. Afraid you can't just shut your eyes—not to murder!"

"You bet you can't!" Zoe echoed. "You don't want to get mixed up in anything, huh? Well, you're mixed up plenty, my girl!"

Miranda backed a step from Wren and Zoe Osbourn. "That's just the trouble," she pouted. "Try to help the police, and they suspect you."

Zoe snorted, turned to the phone on Wren's counter. "Don't they, though, dearie…. Jeff, get that door open. I'll phone the radio dispatcher."

It took Wren, all told, about twelve seconds to manipulate the key which Mrs. Karper had left in the other side of the lock. As soon as she had talked with the radio car dispatcher at Headquarters, Zoe Osbourn took Miranda Lestrard by the wrist and towed her out into the reception room and down the stairs.

Wren followed at a leisurely bounce, came into the novelty store below. Horace was alone, draped over the joke counter. He had been playing solitaire, but with a pack of reader-back cards so he could make sure of winning. His pale eyes stared at the front door through which Miss Lestrard had unwillingly departed.

"Has she gotta build!" he sighed. "Or when it'sa babe it'sa shape."

"Quite," Wren agreed. "I might even suggest 'figger.' However, a moment ago two persons passed this way. A man in white. Also an old lady in a yellow wig—presumably a lady. Did they get into a car?"

Horace stared coldly at Wren. "Crisakes, what kinda taste you think I got I should notice that frowzy old bosco with warts? I'm a gen'leman of discrimination."

Wren sighed. "Lock up shop, Horace. We've got to find the body. I suppose it's inevitable. Miss Eudora Crowley's body. Must be Miss Crowley, since Mrs. Karper wears Miss Crowley's cast-off garments."

He took a cigarette out of nowhere and lighted it meditatively. "Where would you be, Horace, if you were a body? If you'd been a body for three days and if you were supposed to be in French Lick?"

Horace pondered a moment, then snapped limp fingers. "I gotcha! Unner a table inna beer joint."

MISS EUDORA CROWLEY'S house was one of those grand mansions of another era, situated well back from North Illinois Street. Shortly after dusk, Jeffery Wren stood on the sidewalk that edged a weed-choked lawn and stared at the wrought-iron rail that crowned the roof and was silhouetted against the neon-tinged night sky.

"There's paradox," he remarked quietly to Horace. "Miss Eudora Crowley, spinster, has a widow's-walk on her roof."

Horace pointed out in some detail that you could never tell about these prudish old maids. He asked uneasily: "Whatcha gonna do?"

"Probably break and enter. Something criminal." And Wren moved up a moss-grown brick walk that approached the house, Horace dogging his heels. There was no visible sign of life in the place, which made it all the more peculiar that Wren found the front door unlocked. He pushed it open, stepped into musty gloom, and waited for Horace. As Horace stumbled across the sill, Wren caught him by the arm.

"Listen," he whispered.

It was a teeth-on-edge sound, as if someone were carving initials on stone with a pocket knife. That stopped and was followed by a rock-on-rock bumble.

"Mice inna basement," Horace said faintly, "playin' witha coal. Le's get outta here."

"Who's afraid?" Wren scoffed.

"Me, if you wanna get personal about it!"

Wren took out a flashlight, covered the glass bulb with his hand before turning it on. He let the light seep through his fingers to point around a large reception hall with a stairway wide enough for a hearse leading to the second story. At the foot of the steps stood a Boston bag and an old valise, ancient pieces of luggage that had been places and seen things. Wren took quiet steps to the foot of the stair, stooped over the baggage. There was a thin, unmarred film of dust covering the bags and their handles.

"Probably been standing here since last Tuesday," Wren commented. "She was leaving for French Lick. What comes after bags, Horace?"

"Bag-worms," Horace said, with no enthusiasm. "You mean baggage men?"

"Also taxi drivers. Illuminating, isn't it?" Wren straightened, listened to that teeth-on-edge sound. After that, he could distinctly hear the steel blade of a shovel biting into loose gravel. His flashlight pointed to the rear of the hall. He followed the beam to a door, opened it onto a large, old-fashioned kitchen. Finding the door that led to the basement was a matter of trial and error. He beckoned to Horace with his flashlight, and Horace came forward reluctantly, his teeth mushing the end of his cold cigar.

"If you think I'm gonna establish a beachhead—" he started to protest, but Wren was shaking his head.

"Wait here. Stop anything coming out." Wren opened the door fully and sniffed at the dank air of the cellar. His light flickered on and off, gave him a camera-shutter glance of skeleton stairs. The wood treads, he reflected, would probably creak.

"Too bad we're not armed."

Horace whispered limply: "Uh-huh."

Wren sighed to himself and began the descent. The sound of digging went on endlessly, desperate in its haste. Wren's groping foot finally moved from the last creaking step to an uneven brick floor. To his left, a thread of light marked the lower edge of a closed door. He put his right hand into his jacket pocket, forefinger extended like a gun barrel, moved toward the light. Fingertips of his left hand touched rough boards delicately, wandered down to reach a knob. The knob rattled, and abruptly the digging stopped and the light went out. It was, Wren decided, somewhat too late to begin to worry. He twisted the knob, flung the door open, pulled out his flashlight, and turned it on.

OVER a jagged opening in the floor of the furnace room stood the man with the shovel. He was tall and lean, coatless but wearing gray flannels that in spite of earth stains and coal smudges retained the mark of good tailoring. The bright beam highlighted an angular face with close-set eyes of deep blue, a thin, straight nose, and a Hapsburg jaw. If you wanted to be generous about it, you could say he had an extremely high forehead, but any kill-joy would have told the man he was losing his chestnut hair. He was in his early thirties, yet his breath came short, asthmatic, sawing across the teeth of his protruding lower jaw.

Wren said: "Here. What goes on? Have you a burial permit? A grave-digger's union card?"

The ink-blue eyes focused sharply on Wren's pocket. "Let's see it," he suggested, his voice flat, cold.

Wren took his right hand out of his pocket, cocked his thumb. He made a *clok* sound with his tongue. "Lie down. You're dead."

"That's what I thought," said the man, referring to Wren's empty hand. He leaned easily on his shovel.

Wren glanced at the floor. Beside the jagged opening was a mound of gravel, brick, and some white, powdery substance.

"Quicklime!" he gasped. "Sometimes I astound myself. Amazing, isn't it? And I was really pulling Zoe Osbourn's leg."

Into the shallow grave, the earthly remains of Miss Eudora Crowley and a hundred or so pounds of quicklime had been unceremoniously dumped. Her lower extremities were partially covered with earth. She was dressed in once-white muslin, a gown that had been fashionable decades ago, with a high, boned net collar, and long, tight sleeves. Bullets had ripped into the spinster's meager breast, and the resulting blood contributed an unlovely stain to the dress front. She had, Wren thought, been dead for some time—probably since Tuesday. In spite of the grave stains and the pinch of death, there was still a quality of sweetness about her features, particularly around the mouth where true beauty lingers last of all.

Wren raised his eyes. The man had shifted his shovel to his right hand, and in his left was a small blue automatic. Wren frowned slightly.

"No fair. I wasn't looking."

The man uttered a short, dry laugh. "That's your hard luck. What are you doing here?"

Wren cocked an eyebrow. "Thought that was clear. I represent the Association of Mushroom Growers. On the lookout for dank, dark sites—"

"Stop that," the tall man said, and meant it. "Who told you the body was here?"

"My own astute self. Come to think of it, what are you doing here?"

"Hell, I own the place," the man said. "Now I do.... You get over to the wall, turn around, and count to a hundred slowly."

"Delighted," Wren said, and looked at it. He stepped toward the wall, turned suddenly toward the man, flung his lighted flash across the room. The lightbeam whirligigged, struck the opposite wall, and conked out. Three shots jabbed the dark, the reports welding into a single roar that reverberated from walls and furnace pipes. Wren lunged, ran squarely into what must have been the handle of the tall man's shovel. It gouged an "Ooph!" out of him, and he sat down hard. A blind kick caught him in the shoulder. He went back, his head slamming against the floor. Then the dark was full of pelting footsteps, a sound effect that was like a cow kicking over a milk bucket, then Horace's, "Crisakes!" After which, the silence was little short of thunderous.

Horace turned on a dangling droplight. He lifted his left foot, shook water from shoe and trouser leg.

"Stepped inna bucket," he explained unnecessarily.

Wren sat up, stared coldly at Horace. "Check me. There was some casual mention of your guarding the door at the top of the stairs. Remember?"

Horace said: "Hell, I'm not twins."

"Thank God!"

"And there's a coupla ways outta this basement."

Wren stood up unsteadily and was momentarily convinced that the man who held that life began at forty had done very little meddling in murder. He noticed that Horace was staring down into Miss Crowley's grave. Horace looked a little green. Wren murmured something about imperishable beauty.

"Every guy to hizown taste," Horace said. "I'll take mine with a little more life, like that Lestrard babe. Or a big girl like Hamburger Martha." He cast a pale-eyed glance toward the mound of brick and earth, and his slim shoulders twisted. "Good thing he didn't get her buried. I'da hadda dig her up again."

Wren lighted a cigarette, sent an oblique glance at Horace. "Off on the wrong foot. This was exhumation, not burial. The cold fish we just encountered was a ghoul. Two schools of thought on what ought to be done with Miss Crowley. Some would bury her. Others want the matter public. Shall we join the ghouls or undertakers?"

Horace spat a bit of cigar leaf from one side of his mouth. "I'll tear offa breakfas' food box-top an' join a Junior G-men."

"Think not," Wren contradicted. "Think you'll fill in the grave and re-lay the floor. We'll play along with Mrs Karper. She wants the body hidden. Blackmail, of course. Nothing else explains the spirit hand and the Lunge's reagent. Get the shovel, Horace. The evening is all yours when the job is done."

Horace took his cigar out of his mouth and his lips curled bitterly. "You nuts? You got any idea whatcha doin'?"

"Hurry," Wren urged. "Miss Crowley won't care. Not now."

Horace stumbled out of the furnace room to find the shovel. He flung over his shoulder: "I hope to hell you know whatcha doin'!"

Wren's nod was cocksure. "Only worry we have is what will the killer do with all the rope. Some murderers hang themselves. Others hang somebody else."

WREN was really sorry about the quicklime. He stood in somebody's tomato patch in a vacant lot situated directly behind Eudora Crowley's old house. Beside him, Zoe Osbourn smoked cigarettes and watched two paunchy policemen toil with spades as they turned the good earth and the quicklime. It was about ten o'clock, and the police worked by torchlight. A sergeant of detectives by the name of Hogan, assigned to the Homicide Bureau, directed the proceedings. The sergeant, it seemed, was considered fair game for any number of mosquitoes, and the more he was bitten the more inclined was he to do some biting of his own.

Hogan tramped over to Zoe Osbourn, his long, Irish face covered with welts. He spat at a tomato vine.

"By the time we plow up this whole damned community victory garden," he said to Zoe, "and have half of Indianapolis on our necks, I'll begin to get a stinking notion it was a bum steer."

Zoe squared off in front of Hogan, her fists tightly clenched. "Did I say there was a body here? All I said was that there was a killing on Tuesday that's somehow connected with Mrs. Karper's rooming house. I also went to considerable pains to discover that Nahum Hitch, one of the roomers, purchased a quantity of quicklime."

"For his fingers and toes," Wren added.

Zoe wheeled to Wren. "And you can stop that patter, master-wit. It's *finger and toe,* a fungus disease that attacks the roots of cabbage and other vegetables of the order—" Zoe cleared her throat—"of the order *Cruciferae.*"

"My!" Wren smiled brightly. "You've been reading. A walking five-foot shelf."

Sergeant Hogan pointed toward where the cops were digging. "That's where Hitch admits he put the quicklime to get rid of that fungus in his soil."

Zoe's snort was derisive. "Fry me a banana! You don't expect him to tell you where he buried the body, do you? A man with his record?"

Wren's splitting head reminded him not to do any eyebrow raising. "Mr. Hitch has a police record?"

"As long as your arm," Hogan informed him. "Hitch is just one of his several aliases. We wanted him five years back for questioning on a safe job, but he disappeared behind that hedge of whiskers he's wearing, I guess."

Wren regarded with renewed interest the stooped, gray-haired man who stood on the other side of the patch in the full glare of a police light. Hitch's rosy face was framed in a clipped beard that resembled a pre-war pot-scraper. From beneath John L. Lewis eyebrows, his tiny eyes dealt murderous glances to all and sundry who wore the blue and brass. He was securely handcuffed to a stolid-looking plainclothesman.

Wren walked down a row of tomatoes and around to where Hitch was standing. He said: "How're you? Hope Mr. Merwin of the *Times* prints your letter about combating finger and toe disease with quicklime. Doubtless will. After a little editing."

Hitch spat hopefully to the windward. "Go to hell."

Wren shook his head. "No, thanks. You've sent too many cops there to suit me. They've ruined the place."

"You're not a cop?" Hitch asked.

Wren just managed to look sinister. "I've cut a few throats in my time." Which drew a fishy stare from the detective.

Hitch uttered a cracked laugh. "I'm just actin' suspicious so as these damn fools'll spade up this patch for me. Aim to put out late cabbage there next week."

Wren nodded. "One way of getting your tax money back.… By the way, where do you keep your quicklime?"

Hitch jerked a horny thumb in the direction of Miss Crowley's house. "Lady back there let me have the stuff delivered to her garage."

CHAPTER FOUR

HERBERT'S AUNT

WREN MOVED away, out onto Capitol Avenue. He turned left at the next corner, walked east to North Meridian where he caught a southbound bus. At Sixteenth he alighted, walked east to Broadway. Halfway down the block was a faintly illuminated signboard mounted on two turned posts that must have originally supported a porch roof. It read, MRS. KARPER'S FURNISHED ROOMS.

The house stood well back from its neighbors, as though ashamed of something, possibly its own front porch which was faced with stucco in a shade of green which Wren had previously associated only with a certain kind of perfumed candy sold in dime stores. The rest of the structure was red brick with a sort of brewery tower standing front and center. A neon arrow pointed up a gravel drive, lighting a second sign: DUNCAN'S TAXI SERVICE.

Wren walked up the drive in the glare of the floodlight which was bracketed to the north wall of the house. A fire burned brightly in a steel mesh incinerator, the ruddy flame showing the entire back yard with its drooping willow, its lilac bushes, and the grape arbor that stretched from the rear of the house to the two-story garage at the back. Jake Wister stood before the bonfire, his tall, thin body silhouetted against the flames. He had his fingers wedged into the tight slots of his hip pockets, and Wren could have hung his Panama hat on either one of Jake's elbows.

"Hi," Jake said, his stony gray eyes peering into Wren's impassive face.

Wren nodded. He sniffed at an odor that was sulphurous, walked slowly around the fire and back to Jake.

"Disappointing," he remarked. "Thought Mrs. Karper was tied to a stake in the middle of that inferno."

Jake's mouth quirked at the corners. "It's the vulcanite of my pipe bit. Martha burnt it. She says it stinks."

"Quite," Wren agreed.

"That's married life for you." And having disposed of that philosophically, Jake brought back his dynamic personality and clapped Wren on the back with it. "What d'yah know, Joe?"

"Very little. Have you seen Mrs. Karper this evening?"

Jake shook his head. His eyes took all, gave nothing in return. "But she came in just after dusk with McFee. Herbert Sharrod saw her. Martha and I were at Jake and Martha's Number One until about an hour ago to see what the warm weather was doing to the hamburger business."

Wren frowned. "She came back here? With the police looking for her?"

Jake nodded his hairless head. "She came back. She asked Fred Duncan to drive her to Crown Hill Cemetery. And damned if she didn't vanish again!"

"Incredible."

"Well, you can't prove it by me. I didn't see her vanish the first time. If I had, I'd have figured how it was done. You can't fool Jake Wister with hocus-pocus…. But Fred Duncan swears she vanished out of the back seat of his car, and he's got a bad case of shakes over it."

Wren gave Jake a sly glance. "Would you? Suppose we go have a talk with shaky Fred."

Jake left the bonfire, took gangling steps toward the garage. Wren followed through wide open doors where two identical black sedans were parked. As they crossed in front of the cars, Wren swept a hand across the radiator grill of each. They climbed steep steps through a trap in the ceiling and on into the loft. There Jake knocked at a door.

"Who is it?" The challenge was stage-whispered.

Jake winked at Wren. "See what I mean?" Louder he replied: "The password is 'The Hamburger of Mouth-Melting Goodness.' How's about a little hospitality, Fred?"

There were heavy, plunging footsteps and the door was opened by a short, thick-set man whose stringy black hair fell parenthetically on either side of his round face. Fred Duncan had a button nose, eyes that would have looked good in a stuffed squirrel. His teeth were so large, so obviously porcelain as to recall the show window of a plumbing shop. He had a heavy-caliber revolver in his right hand and a fifth of rum in his left.

Wren gave his head a sober half-shake. "Got to stop opening doors. There's always a gun behind them." This gun pointed impolitely at Wren's tummy.

"Who's he?" Fred Duncan asked. He still whispered.

"Jeffery Wren," Jake told him. "He's a magician. He'll tell you what gives with Mrs. K."

BEYOND the door was a surprisingly comfortable living room which also served Duncan as an office for his taxi business. He tossed his gun onto a rolltop desk that stood near the door, nodded Wren and Jake into chairs, dropped into the most comfortable seat himself. The phone on the desk rang, and Fred merely stared at it.

"Ring yourself dry," he whispered. "I'm not going out in a car again tonight."

"Ah? What's the secret?" Wren asked. "Or is it laryngitis?"

Fred cocked large feet onto an ottoman, began moodily paring his fingernails. "I always talk like this," he whispered. "The damn butcher who yanked out my tonsils really had himself a time."

Jake said: "Tell Wren about Mrs. Creepy Karper, Fred."

Fred put down the knife, recovered the rum bottle, drank out of it. He gagged. "Hell, she vanished. Last night when she did it, I didn't believe it. I figured she could have slipped out of the cab when I got stopped by a light, or maybe when I was looking at a nice pair of gams crossing the street in front of me. That was my theory, in spite of what Herb Sharrod and the Lestrard kid said. They were right behind me last night, and they said they didn't see Mrs. K. leave the cab. But tonight—"

He broke off, got some Dutch courage out of the bottle. "Hell, she came up the steps here, shuffling in her bedroom slippers, knocked at my door, asked if I'd take her to the cemetery, of all places."

Wren said, "I see, I see," just as though he did. "Mrs. Karper always wears bedroom slippers?"

Duncan's beady eyes crawled over Wren's impassive face. He nodded. "Her feet hurt…. Anyway, I took her out in the car, and after last night's vanishing act, I was really on my toes. I didn't stop once on the way, timed the lights just right, and every time I had a chance, I was watching her in the rear-view mirror."

"Astute of you," Wren commented.

"I might just as well have been blindfolded," Fred went on. "Just across Washington Boulevard, I took another gander into the mirror, and—hell, she wasn't there!"

Wren's fingers drummed on the chair arm. "When was that?"

"About an hour ago, I guess. Soon as I saw she was gone, I lit out for home as fast as I could make it!"

Jake said: "I bet!" He looked at Wren. "What would you have done, sport?"

Wren sighed. "Wouldn't spread it on so thick. You've overdone a good thing, Duncan. Neither of your cars has been out all evening. Because the radiators are cold." He made a tsk sound with tongue and teeth. "Such a warm night, too."

He stood up suddenly, started toward the door, his eye on the revolver on Duncan's desk. Jake dogged him, dropped a hand on Wren's thick shoulder. Wren permitted himself to be turned around, and backed to the desk. His left hand stole around behind him.

"Well?" he said, annoyed.

"Now listen, sport," Jake said, stony eyes peering, "what gives? You mean Fred's lying?"

Wren had the gun. He got it up under his coat tails, thrust it butt first into his hip pocket. His oblique glance caught Fred Duncan's sharp eyes stabbing at him.

"Conclusions might be drawn," he said quietly. "Suggest you draw some." Then he turned, bounced through the door and down the steps.

On the verge of leaving the garage, he turned abruptly to the two parked cars. The first yielded nothing of interest, but the second held a different story. In the glove compartment he found a carpenters' rule—one of those zigzag folding affairs—and a pint-sized strawberry box with a sliver-edged slot about half an inch long cut in the center of the wood bottom. A six-foot length of strong black thread was attached to one end of the carpenter's rule.

He said, "My!" audibly, then listened intently for a moment to footsteps on the floor above and the rumble of voices. He got out of the front seat of the car, left the door ajar rather than risk the noise of closing it. He got into the rear seat, discovered that the cushions were equipped with seat covers that had a smell of newness about them. He used his flashlight sparingly, located the snaps that permitted removal of the covers from the back of the seat, pulled the cover down to reveal the original upholstery. The center section of the back could be folded down to form an armrest in the center, but there was nothing remarkable about that. What really had Wren sharpening his wits was the rust-colored stain that blotched the gray upholstery fabric—that and the two holes that bored somewhat above the center of the stain.

"Bullets and gore," he murmured, and then snapped out his flashlight to crouch in the compartment.

Jake's gangling footsteps sounded on the stairway, crossed the concrete floor, crunched out onto the drive, and diminished into silence. Above, Fred Duncan paced the floor with nervous, choppy steps.

Wren scrambled heavily out of the car, out of the garage, and toward the back porch of the house. Odd, he thought, how suddenly he could see through all the darkness that shrouded Mrs. Karper.

"Must be vitamin A," he mused whimsically, as he climbed the steps of the porch and opened the kitchen door.

MARTHA, of Jake and Martha's Numbers One and Two, took her honey-blonde head out of Mrs. Karper's refrigerator. She had confiscated a cold bottle of beer and a wiener. Her curling upper lip accounted for that look she gave Wren, as though he had entered driving a team of goats. She waved the bottle of beer gaily, said: "Have you met our Mr. McFee, Mr. Wren?"

Wren looked at the small, dapper figure on the south side of the room and nodded.

"Met over a gun. Wasn't it, McFee?"

The little man in the white suit was the same who had accompanied Mrs. Karper to Wren's magic shop. He was plastered up against the white cabinet sink as though trying to employ the principles of protective coloration.

"Oh, come," Wren said. "You're no snow rabbit. That red hair is a dead giveaway. Why the jitters? The police are working Mr. Hitch's victory garden. Crime takes a holiday."

McFee stopped his jittering. "Geez," he said, "I didn't know Mrs. Karper was going to bust into your shop with guns. Honest. She just said we would drop by and pick up something that belonged to her."

"Bygones," Wren said, "have gone by. Forget it." He turned abruptly to Martha Wister who was dipping her wiener into a pot of mustard. "Where's Miss Lestrard?"

Martha put the end of the sausage into her mouth, bit at it, made a face. She took the wiener out, threw it onto the floor, where it bounced. She made gagging sounds.

"Rubber," she explained unnecessarily. "That Jake! Next time I marry a man, he's going to be somebody who has never seen the inside of that novelty store of yours, Mr. Wren. It's always something like that. Once, even, it was itch powder in the bed."

"Jake's a card, isn't he? Where's Miss Lestrard?"

"Toots is upstairs," McFee said. "She had a little run-in with the bulls. I'll show you where her room is, Mr. Wren."

McFee took brisk steps to the swinging door, which he politely held open for Wren. Wren went into the dining room. He wasn't sure whether it was the draft of the closing door or whether McFee had tugged at his coat tails. Halfway across the gloomy old dining room, he felt his left hip pocket, and was certain it had not been a draft from the swinging door. McFee stepped ahead of him, taking pecking steps on hard heels across the floor of the central hall toward the foot of the oak stairway. Wren's long stride caught up with McFee. He grabbed the little man's left wrist in both his hands.

McFee turned a sharp, scared face toward Wren. "What's eatin' you?"

Wren glanced down at McFee's wristwatch. "What time is it?" he murmured. "My watch has stopped."

"Oh," said McFee, and breathed again.

Wren jerked the sleeve of McFee's white coat down over his left wrist, dropped McFee's arm. McFee started up the steps, but Wren stopped him a second time. He dangled McFee's wristwatch in front of the little man's astonished face and smiled broadly.

"Don't know which is worth more, but we'll trade," he insisted. "Your watch for my wallet."

McFee blinked. He looked down at his own naked left wrist. He fingered one lop ear bewilderedly. "Cripes!" he said, then: "Wow! Are you a fast worker!"

"Unquestionably," Wren returned coolly. "Quite! My wallet, please."

McFee wiped off a sheepish smile, returned Wren's wallet. "On second thought, I guess I won't show you Toots's room. It's the fourth door back to the north side of the hall. I don't want you should snatch my pants on the way."

Wren chuckled. "Thanks. Veritable den of thieves Mrs. Karper has here. Hitch is a safecracker. You're a fingersmith. Makes one wonder about the Wisters and Miss Lestrard. About the Sharrod person, too."

MISS MIRANDA LESTRARD told Wren sweetly to come in. He opened the door, removed his hat, stepped across the sill to find Miranda seated on a footstool beside the old chair in the room. She had on a pink housecoat, with a pink bow in her black hair, and the entire effect reminded Wren of one of those dolls that children contrive from a hollyhock blossom and a rosebud.

In the chair was a man, and the last time Wren had seen this lanky individual was in the basement of Miss Eudora Crowley's house.

"Have you met Mr. Sharrod yet, Mr. Wren?" Miranda asked.

Wren nodded. "We've chewed the fat a bit. Over an old grave somewhere. Had many a ghoulish laugh together."

Sharrod extended himself from the chair to his full six feet. His close-set, ink-blue eyes bored into Wren. His breathing was once more audible and asthmatic.

Miranda was prettily puzzled. "Whatever are you talking about?"

"Mr. Sharrod isn't talking about anything." Wren's smile was not quite as pleasant as usual. In fact, Herbert Sharrod found something in it to bring the beads of sweat out on his high forehead.

Wren said: "Could be a rumor among roomers, of course. It's whispered, Sharrod, that you were at Mrs. Karper's spirit seance on Tuesday night. Somebody was. Somebody whose hands were neither tied nor fettered."

Sharrod shook his head slowly. "Not I." He stepped away from the chair and toward Wren.

"And you didn't dabble in paraffin? You didn't plant a discreet kiss on Miss Lestrard's head?"

Miranda giggled, but that didn't get very far because Herbert Sharrod swung with his left, caught Wren in the middle with a lean left fist.

Wren considered that one tummy-punch was enough to take from one man in an evening. His own swinging right came a long way but connected somehow with Sharrod's Hapsburg jaw. Sharrod's eyes flickered white even before he crashed to the floor between the chair and Miss Lestrard's footstool.

Wren looked sharply at Miranda. "No. Don't scream."

"No," she said, and took her hand away from her pretty mouth. "I'm not going to. Gosh, what was that, Judo?"

He shook his head. "Don't think so. Not positive, of course, but it could be Wren starting to roll." He picked up Sharrod bodily, lugged him to Miranda's bed, and dumped him there. He was feeling pretty good about everything. He turned to Miranda.

"Herbert wanted me to run off with him tonight and get married," she said. "I was trying to decide. Now I've got more deciding to do than ever." Her dark eyes regarded Wren with renewed interest, certainly a different kind of interest. He cleared his throat uneasily.

"Look," he said.

"I'm looking," she admitted. "You're not as old as I thought."

"Don't look, then. Not like that." He had started to sit in Herbert Sharrod's chair, but thought better of it. Instead, he took bounding strides up and down the room. "We've a murder on our hands, re-member?"

She remembered. She would not, she said, forget to her dying day. "But if it wasn't Mrs. Karper I saw in the back yard Tuesday night, who was it?"

"Miss Eudora Crowley," he said. "But don't mention it to anyone. Not yet."

Her eyes widened. "Why—why that's Herbert's aunt!"

CHAPTER FIVE

ROPE TO SPARE

WREN TURNED, stared at the unconscious Herbert Sharrod on the bed. "Mammon rears its ugly head." He frowned. "And I'd about decided it was a matter of mistaken identity. Concluded that somebody was gunning for Mrs. Karper and shot Miss Crowley in error. Conceivable, isn't it, if Mrs. Karper wears Miss Crowley's cast-off garments? And, Mrs. Karper has enemies, hasn't she?"

"I'm not sure," she said, "but Tuesday night at the seance Mr. McFee said that some time when Mrs. Karper was handcuffed in that chair, throwing a trance, she'd wake up with a knife in her"—she frowned— "in her kitchen, was the way he put it."

Wren chuckled. "That's quite a threat. Believe 'kitchen' is slang for tummy. Bad place to find a knife. Especially in oneself…. But Mrs. Karper's a blackmailer, wouldn't you say? And if she knew somebody was out to shoot her and had got Miss Crowley instead, Mrs. Karper would have good reason to vanish. Law of self-preservation."

"Who's Mrs. Karper blackmailing?" Miranda asked innocently.

Wren shrugged. "Who isn't she blackmailing? More to the point. Veritable den of thieves here. Why should they congregate under one roof? Why should Mrs. K. have them all under her thumb? My guess is she brought them all here. Like a herdsman, fattening steers for slaughter. Her flair for spirit mediumship is tongue-in-cheek. She uses her supposed supernatural powers to tighten her stranglehold on the roomers. Has to have some way to explain where she gets her information, so she blames it on the spooks. Actually, she's something of a detective or has an ex-detective working for her. Otherwise, how could her use of Lunge's reagent in the paraffin hand be explained?"

Wren paced to the other end of the room, turned, looked obliquely at Miranda. "She may even be blackmailing you."

Miranda didn't rise to the bait. "That's silly. I haven't done anything."

He shrugged. "Then you're a lamb among wolves…. But let's go back to this morning. You smuggled the hatbox containing the so-called spirit hand out of this house. You said you thought you were being watched or followed. By whom?"

She shook her head. "It was just a feeling. Maybe because I saw Mrs. Karper vanish, and I didn't know but what she was watching me unseen. Like the Invisible Man. I even spent some of my hard-earned money to have Fred Duncan take me downtown in his cab."

Wren lifted his eyebrows. "Ah. That's illuminating. Explains Mrs. Karper's raid on my shop."

"It does?" Miranda stared at him. "You mean Mrs. Karper and Fred Duncan are in cahoots?"

"Obviously. Close as two peas. Another thing, Fred Duncan's re-volver happens to be a thirty-eight police positive. Fred could be an ex-cop, which would explain where Mrs. Karper's blackmail evidence comes from. More convincing than giving spirits the credit."

He walked to Miranda's north window and looked down onto the gravel drive, which was illuminated by the floodlight bracketed to the wall of the house. "This your vantage point when you saw Mrs. Karper get into the back seat of Duncan's car last night?"

She nodded.

"And you couldn't see through the rear window of the car from here?"

She tugged thoughtfully at her lower lip. "No. I guess the light glared on the rear window so I couldn't see into the car. Not actually. At first, I just heard Mrs. Karper shouting at Fred Duncan. I got up to look out the window to see what it was all about. That's when Mrs. Karper got into the car. She had my hat on top of that ugly yellow wig. So I ran out across the hall to get Herbert Sharrod. He was the only one in the house at the time, and I knew he'd take me in his car to follow her."

He nodded. "But you didn't see Fred Duncan get into the car?"

"No. But he must have been there, under the wheel. Otherwise"—she rolled her dark eyes—"who could have driven the cab away?"

"It was Fred driving," he agreed. "Also, it was Fred getting into the back seat, wearing Mrs. Karper's dress and wig. Not to mention your hat. And Fred had rigged up quite a thing. Wedged into one side of that center arm section of the back of the rear seat was the folded portion of a carpenters' rule. One end of the rule was unfolded, say twenty-four inches of it, and sticking up. On top of this was a berry box. Fred put the yellow wig and your hat on top of the berry box, probably while you were across the hall with Sharrod.

"Then Fred crawled over the back of the front seat, put on his chauffeurs' cap, and drove off. He had previously tied a length of black thread to the extended leg of the rule. The thread reached to the driver's seat."

MIRANDA stared, round-eyed. "You—you're wonderful!"

He smiled. "Thanks. So are you, in a way…. But there isn't any other way the disappearance could be worked. Duncan couldn't palm Mrs. Karper. There couldn't be trap doors in the cab floor. Actually, when you and Sharrod caught up with Fred's cab, all you saw of Mrs. Karper was her wig through the rear window. Her wig and your hat. While Fred was driving, he removed Mrs. Karper's dress from himself. Probably ripped it off. Could have hastened the process by using a razor blade. To effect the disappearance he merely pulled the black thread. The extended section of the rule folded down, taking Mrs. Karper's wig out of sight. But before Fred actually stopped the cab so you and Sharrod could catch up and witness that Mrs. K. had vanished, he disposed of the rule and berry box in the glove compartment. Probably kicked the rags of the dress and your hat under the seat. Fred himself appeared in masculine attire, utterly baffled. Pretended to be baffled, anyway."

"But what's the reason behind the vanishing act?"

He shrugged. "Either to cover Mrs. Karper's disappearance, supposing that she thought it wise to step out of the picture until somebody stopped gunning for her. Or simply to lure you and Sharrod from the house. Inclined to prefer the latter line of thought. With you and Sharrod out of the house, she could freely search all the rooms for further blackmail evidence. Evidence of the murder of Miss Crowley on the night before. Possibly hoped to find the weapon."

"She would have had plenty of time to do that," Miranda added, in support of his theory. "Because when Herbert and I talked to Fred Duncan, Fred insisted that Mrs. Karper couldn't have just vanished and that she must have slipped out when he had pulled up at a stop light. Herbert and I were sure we would have seen her if she had, but then it didn't seem logical she could have just gone *pffft.*"

Wren nodded. "Highly improbable. So you went back to the traffic signal and scouted around for traces of Mrs. Karper."

Herbert Sharrod was stirring on the bed. His eyes flickered open, and he groaned.

"There's your Herbert," Wren said cheerfully. He walked to the door, took hold of the knob.

"Well, he's not my Herbert!" The black eyes were indignant about it.

Wren chuckled. "You can have him if you want him." He left the room, crossed directly to the closed door of Herbert Sharrod's room, found it unlocked. He was on the point of entering the room when he heard Zoe Osbourn's familiar strident voice in the hall below.

"I'm looking for Mr. Jeffery Wren," she said, and sounded peeved about something.

Wren stepped into Sharrod's room as Hamburger Martha replied to Zoe that Mr. Wren was upstairs talking to Miss Lestrard.

"Oh, he is!" Zoe bellowed. "Never mind showing me the way. I can find that slick-witted son-of-the-woman-sawed-in-half without any assistance from you, my girl."

Wren was halfway through the drawers of Herbert Sharrod's bureau when Zoe Osbourn stepped through the open door. "Ha!" she said. "Meddling again."

Wren didn't turn around. He tossed a savings account bankbook onto the top of the bureau. "Our Mr. Sharrod has a healthy balance. Forty-three thousand dollars and some odd cents. Or aren't you interested?"

"You're darned tootin' I'm interested!" Zoe came up behind him, and her prominent eyes glared out at him from the mirror on the wall. "Sergeant Hogan found the body of Miss Eudora Crowley."

"Did he?" Wren was so preoccupied that he forgot to sound surprised. "Oh, *did* he? Is that so? Miss Crowley, you say?" He turned to face the policewoman.

She snorted. "You were a little late with the patter that time, Jeff. You damn well knew it was Miss Crowley."

"Who else could be mistaken for Mrs. Karper?" he wanted to know, and then moved to the closet to search the pockets of Sharrod's seven summer suits. "How did Hogan get wind of it?"

"A telephone tip to Headquarters," Zoe told him. "The man didn't identify himself." She followed Wren to the closet. "What are you looking for?"

"Haven't the faintest idea. Probably the same thing Mrs. Karper was looking for when she lured Sharrod and Miss Lestrard away from here last night. Sharrod's Miss Crowley's nephew."

"Right," she said. "And a lawyer. He's 'and Sharrod' at the tail end of a long list of mouthpieces on a door in Circle Tower. And Sergeant

Hogan found Miss Crowley's will tucked away in a drawer at the old lady's house. My guess is that he'll be over here shortly."

Wren came out of the closet. He scratched delicately at the top of his sleek head. "We'll have to move. Rather fast, too. Can't have Homicide beating us to a solution. Deplorable thought."

She eyed him suspiciously. "*You'll* have to move fast, that's sure. Cops don't like digging in victory gardens after dark, especially with the mosquito situation what it is. Headquarters won't stand for withholding evidence."

"Now who's withholding anything?" He bounced to the bed and attacked it with considerable vigor, poking the mattress and pillows, pulling down the sheets. Finally, he got down on his hands and knees and looked under the bed. There, Herbert Sharrod had stashed a fine leather suitcase. One of those mossy gray cobwebs that accumulate under beds in even the best regulated households connected the handle of the suitcase with the bed-spring. Caught in the fragile web was a tiny bit of red paper.

"**CONFETTI?**" he murmured. "No. Hardly that."

Zoe Osbourn got down heavily beside him, knocked off her big white hat trying to see under the bed. "What's so damned remarkable about a piece of confetti?"

"Not confetti," he contradicted. "That's out of season."

The bit of paper, less than half an inch across, had a jagged, black-edged hole burned in the center.

"It's a cap," he said. "The sort small boys fire in cap pistols."

Zoe's hennaed curls brushed Wren's cheek as she turned her big-featured face toward him. "What gives?"

He shook his head. "Nothing gives. You've got to take. But don't take that exploded cap. Mustn't touch that. Homicide will be interested." He straightened, stood up.

Zoe snorted. "Hell's fire! Why so ethical all of a sudden?"

He sat down on the edge of the bed, his chunky black brows drawn together. "Couldn't be a cap pistol. Loud book? That's a possibility. Bingo?"

"Bingo, he says!" Zoe stamped to her feet.

"Improbable that it was Bingo." Wren thoughtfully removed his fountain pen from the inner pocket of his coat. With great deliberation, he grasped the cap of the pen in his right hand and the barrel in his left. He unscrewed the cap, screwed it back on. His smile broke, lingered a moment, and was gone.

"A pen," he said. "That's the best bet. Hurry, Zoe. See if we can find a fountain pen around here. That's the one subtle move."

Zoe rubbed the ball of her thumb with the tip of a forefinger, the old "gimme" gesture. "You come across with the truth or I'll subtle move you right down to Headquarters!"

He said: "On second thought, we won't look for the pen. He wouldn't leave such damning evidence about. Only oversight on his part that we found the paper cap." He looked up at Zoe's scowling face, smiled. "My dear lady, we've got him."

"Ha! I hate to admit it, but all I've got is an all but uncontrollable desire to bat your brains out!"

He appeared anxious for himself. "Not that! No rubber hose. I'll talk. The motive part is simple. If Miss Crowley was mistaken for Mrs. Karper because of their similar attire, the motive might be hate or escape—providing Mrs. Karper is running a blackmail business. If there was no mistake, Miss Crowley's money is behind it. There's Herbert Sharrod, a nephew, who might inherit. And Jake Wister frankly stated he wished Martha's father would marry old Miss Crowley because of her money. Yes, we've got to consider greed as a possible motive."

Wren lighted a cigarette, waved it like a wand. "Turn back time. Turn it back to Tuesday night. Tuesday night is famous for its murder and for Mrs. Karper's seance. The seance is famous because its only purpose was to perform the paraffin test for nitrates on the hand of the person Mrs. Karper believed to be the murderer. You've got that, Zoe? The seance was simply a subtle excuse to get the paraffin impression of somebody's right hand."

Zoe nodded. "Sure. I got that right off the bat. Get back to Miss Crowley."

"Miss Crowley intended to leave for French Lick Tuesday night, there to meet Martin Owen. Martin Owen happens to be Hamburger Martha's father. Object of the meeting—matrimony."

"Yeah? Who says so?"

Wren shrugged. "Jake and Martha. They wanted to hire me to find Miss Crowley after Miss Crowley had failed to show up in French Lick. They wanted the marriage to take place because Miss Crowley was a rich old lady. Jake was quite frank about that.

"Miss Crowley's bags were packed and waiting in the hall. She had called Fred Duncan of the Duncan Taxi Service. Might point out that Fred is the Duncan Taxi Service. Think we'll find that Miss Crowley habitually patronized Duncan. Could be that Duncan got Miss Crowley's cast-off garments for Mrs. Karper."

"Never mind the conjectures, Jeff," Zoe said impatiently.

"Fred drove up in front of Miss Crowley's house," Wren continued. "Miss Crowley came out, got in the back seat of the cab. She left her front door open, told Fred to go get her bags, pull the door shut after him. She trusted him, which leads me to believe Miss Crowley had employed Fred frequently before. But Fred never even touched Miss Crowley's baggage. Because while he was in the house, the murderer shot Miss Crowley in the cab. Bullet holes and gory stains prove the point. The killer then jumped in under the wheel of the idling cab and drove off. Fred Duncan, of course, just didn't stand there when he heard the shots. He must have run from the house. It was night, but Fred must have got close enough to get some clue as to the killer's identity. Otherwise"—Wren shrugged—"no blackmail for Mrs. Karper."

"Duncan and Mrs. Karper are in cahoots?"

"Oh, quite. Thought I'd mentioned that."

"All right." Zoe goggled at him. "You mean to tell me the killer drove off in that cab with Miss Crowley, his victim, bobbing around in the back seat?"

"Yes. Certainly. The cab offered a quick get-away. Then if the killer could dump Miss Crowley's body in Mrs. Karper's back yard, it might appear as though the whole thing were a mistake. As though someone gunning for Mrs. Karper had accidentally killed Miss Crowley."

Zoe nodded. "He'd do that to build up a false motive. The real motive must be Miss Crowley's money." Her puzzled frown returned. "We know that Miss Lestrard saw the body in Mrs. Karper's back yard. But who moved it to Miss Crowley's basement?"

Wren, on the alert this time, asked: "That where it was finally found? Mrs. Karper must have hidden it there—obviously. Protecting her blackmail victim, of course. Can't blackmail a person slated for the electric chair. Hardly. No money in it."

WREN walked over to the bureau and snuffed out his cigarette in Herbert Sharrod's ashtray. He turned to find Zoe Osbourn with a pussy-cat grin on her face.

She said: "Wait a minute, Jeff. Wait just a minute!" She opened her big purse, took out a king-sized cigarette and lighted it. "You wait until Zoe gets some fire under her boiler, and she'll blow that smug look right off your handsome puss!"

"Thanks," he said, smiling. "No idea it was handsome."

"Like hell!" she growled. "Now, look here. If Mrs. Karper concealed the body, and the killer's motive is Miss Crowley's money, how can the killer profit by the murder? He can't—not until Miss Crowley is declared dead legally. And if the killer can't collect, how can Mrs. Karper blackmail him?"

Wren shrugged. He turned to the bureau, picked up Herbert Sharrod's bankbook. "This, dear lady. Forty and more thousand dollars. Not to be sneezed at by Mrs. Karper. Better than nothing. And she'd get nothing if Herbert Sharrod went to the chair for his aunt's murder. Eventually, if the body wasn't found, Miss Crowley would be declared legally dead and Sharrod would still be safe. Safe and probably rich. More blood-money for Mrs. Karper.

"Don't you see, Sharrod was the man Mrs. Karper trapped into putting his right hand into the paraffin at the spirit seance she staged an hour or so after the killing. Remember Miss Lestrard's statement? She said all the roomers were present *except* Sharrod. They were all present and accounted for, holding each other's hands. All but Sharrod. Sharrod was the spook in the dark. It was Sharrod who kissed Miss Lestrard. And it was Sharrod who made the spirit hand, acting on Mrs. Karper's instructions. Why he would agree to do such a thing isn't obvious. Maybe just the idea of playing pranks. Maybe he liked the notion of being in the dark with Miss Lestrard. One thing is certain—he didn't know about the paraffin test for nitrates."

Zoe Osbourn pegged for the door. "Where's this Sharrod man?"

Wren, cool enough about it, said that he'd put Sharrod to sleep in the room across the hall. He went loping to Miss Lestrard's room. Zoe already had the door open and was confronting Miranda across the sill.

"He's not my boy friend and he isn't here!" Miranda denied hotly. "Herbert went out of here at least fifteen minutes ago, and—"

Downstairs, a screen door slammed and Martha Wister screamed. "McFee! Mr. Wren! Help, somebody. He's killing Jake!"

Wren turned in his tracks, tore down the hall, down the stairs, with Zoe Osbourn and Miranda behind him. In the hall was Martha Wister. She had little Mr. McFee by the collar of his coat and the seat of his pants.

"You get out there and help Jake, you nasty little yellow cur!" Martha cried.

McFee protested that he was not a well man and didn't want to get mixed up in anything. Martha glimpsed Wren, dived for him.

He said: "Where?"

"Duncan's!" Martha gasped.

Zoe was close behind Wren as he rounded the house and ducked under the grape arbor. In the back yard, the steel wire incinerator blazed high with fresh fuel—something that smelled like rags and feathers.

"Smell a witch burning somewhere," Wren commented to Zoe as they pelted through the open garage doors.

Zoe didn't say anything, because the noise from the loft certainly suggested that somebody was getting murdered.

Wren beat the policewoman to the foot of the steps only because he knew where to look for them in the gloom. He had Fred Duncan's gun out. He went on up, hit Duncan's door with his shoulder and broke into the room.

There were three men in the room. One of them, Fred Duncan himself, was swaying and spinning in the approximate center. His dumpy figure was somewhat elongated and his disproportionately large feet stretched down hopelessly toward the floor some twelve inches below. There was nothing about this marvelous levitation which wasn't lucidly explained by a length of sash cord stretched tautly from a beam above to Fred's strangled throat.

The reason that Duncan was spinning was that Jake Wister and Herbert Sharrod were fighting all over the place and a few of their spent blows were landing on Duncan's body. Herbert Sharrod was using both fists and anything he could pick up. Jake was using his long left, and when it seemed advantageous, he'd get in a kick. Jake's right arm was occupied with Miss Lestrard's hatbox.

Zoe Osbourn said loudly, "Boys! Boys!" like a schoolteacher trying to break up a free-for-all in the playground. And when that didn't make any impression, she began to swing her big purse which contained practically everything from a compact to handcuffs. She bopped Jake on top of his bald head with it. Jake backed, staggering but not out. Herbert Sharrod, who had learned about kicking from Jake, booted the hatbox under Jake's arm. The box crumpled. Tissue and the spirit hand went flying, practically into Wren's waiting fingers. He bounded back with his prize, trained Fred Duncan's revolver on the skinny combatants, and the war was immediately over.

"He—he—" Jake panted, pointing a crooked finger at the gasping Sharrod, "he was up here snooping. Martha and I came out to see Fred. Fred was— Hell, sport, he still is!" And he elevated gray eyes to the swaying corpse.

Wren said: "Obviously. He still is."

CHAPTER SIX

THE TIMELY END
OF MRS. KARPER

IT WAS crowded in Mrs. Karper's dusty, plushy parlor with all of Mrs. Karper's roomers assembled under the watchful eyes of the police. The entire case had resolved itself into a routine fingerprint comparison, with the paraffin spirit hand the object of the undivided attention of experts in Mrs. Karper's dining room.

"Well, it certainly isn't my hand, and anybody can see that without a spyglass," Miranda Lestrard announced. She was seated on a Turkey-red plush sofa, her arms straight out in front of her, ink-stained fingers widespread. Her big black eyes were on the hands of Martha Wister, who was sitting next to her. "Anybody can see *my* hands are too small."

Martha Wister smelled of Miranda and found her inexplicably unpleasant. "My deah," she said, laying it on with a shovel, "you wouldn't imply that because my hands aren't like sparrows' claws—"

"Now see here, you two," her husband Jake interrupted, to assume the role of peacemaker, "cut out that catty stuff. We're all in the same boat. Only maybe friend Herbert is sitting where most of the leaks are."

Herbert Sharrod said nothing. He stood as near the door as Police-woman Zoe Osbourn and a uniformed cop would permit. His ink-blue eyes stared hard at Miranda Lestrard—stared, Wren thought, somewhat like the fox at the sour grapes.

Nahum Hitch was squatting on a stool beside the green Dutch tile hearth. He scrubbed his left palm with his pot-scraper whiskers and uttered a cracked laugh. "Don't count me in on the boat trip, Jake. It's a holy cinch I couldn't've hung Fred Duncan with all them coppers on my neck. First time I ever was glad to be in the company of a copper!"

"I mean," Jake explained, "we're all in Mrs. Karper's boat. It'll come out now. Those of us who are owing any time to the big house up-state will have to serve it. The cops are wise to you, Hitch, already. And they'll dig up your record, McFee—"

"Geez, keep your mush shut!" Little McFee's sharp face was almost as pale as his white suit. "I haven't pulled a stick-up nor lifted a leather in three years." His beady eyes shifted to Wren, remembering, no doubt the episode of Wren's wallet. His lips curled up in a sickish smile.

Jake said: "We can't keep it quiet. Look how it is with Martha. She's served time. It's all water under the bridge. But Martha and I got a kid, a little girl. Prettiest little girl you ever saw. She's away East at a fancy school. Suppose it gets into the papers that her mother made a mistake once and had to pay for it in prison? What do you think that's going to do to our kid's life? Here we been paying Mrs. Karper eighty hard-earned bucks a month for a lousy two-by-four room, just so the old harpy wouldn't broadcast to the kid about Martha's record. Now it all comes out in the papers—" Jake broke off, his stony eyes peering sharply at Wren. "What did you say just then, sport?"

Wren shook his head. He glanced at Martha and her blue eyes were glinting with tears. "Nothing. Scarcely anything, Jake. A mere murmur of sympathy." And Wren moved along the wall, edged his way over to where Zoe was standing. He had an eyebrow elevated, saying as clearly as a neon sign: "I told you so." Zoe winked at him.

"Jeff, it begins to percolate. Why, you slick-witted limb of Satan, I get that crack about a loud book and Bingo. I—"

Wren put a finger to his lips, shook his head. The oak door of the parlor was opened and Detective Sergeant Hogan came in briskly.

"Now, folks, we'll get this over as quickly and as painlessly as possible," he announced.

"When we were searching Miss Eudora Crowley's house, we came across her will tucked away in a writing desk. It's nothing fancy—just one she drew up herself—but duly witnessed. I'm going to read it."

HOGAN drew the document from his coat with a flourish, cleared his throat, read the first paragraph hurriedly.

" 'I, Eudora Emonds Crowley, being of sound mind, do declare this to be my last will and testament, revoking all previous wills.'

"Now," Hogan injected, "here it comes. 'To Martin Crofts Owen—' "

Martha Wister screamed: "That's Dad!"

Jake said: "Well, your old man always said she was going to leave him her money, didn't he?"

Hogan scowled at the Wisters. "Don't get too excited, folks. Here we go again: 'To Martin Crofts Owen, my beloved sweetheart of yesterday, today, and in the Hereafter, I bequeath the sum of seven hundred thousand dollars in securities of the United States Government reposing in my safety deposit vault at the Fletcher Trust Company.'

"That," Hogan added, "is about everything she had, isn't it, Sharrod?"

Herbert Sharrod inclined his head. "Except her house, perhaps. This isn't any news to me. Aunty always felt I could stand on my own feet."

Hogan nodded. "Sure. Well, there's another little paragraph here, and then that's all." His eyes returned to the will.

" 'To my nephew, Herbert Vincent Sharrod, I leave all property, real and personal.' And," Hogan concluded, "that's all." He looked around the room, his eyes narrow, discerning. Nobody said anything.

"Don't you get it?" he asked finally. "Mrs. Osbourn, don't you? Doesn't anybody get it except Mr. Sharrod over there? You get it, don't you, Sharrod?"

Sharrod stared coolly at Hogan, and kept his mouth shut.

Wren said: "Oh, come now, Sergeant. Suspense is all right. But you're overdoing it."

Hogan's smile widened, triumphant. "I sure didn't think it would slip by you, Mr. Wren."

Wren frowned. "You mean about the 'other' being left out in the last paragraph? It ought to read: 'I leave all *other* property, real and personal.' Right?"

"You bet that's what I mean!" Hogan crowed. "It's a flaw big enough to drive a truck through. Sharrod can break this will by blowing his breath on it. A codicil couldn't revoke the first bequest any better than that last paragraph. The old lady left out the word 'other.' What it says, as written, is that Herbert Sharrod gets every damn thing she had!"

Herbert Sharrod said: "But I have no intention of contesting the will, I assure you."

"Sure, you assure me. You would, now that we got you over a barrel with your pants down!" Hogan sprang in close to Herbert Sharrod, shouting in Sharrod's face: "That wax impression Mrs. Karper tricked you into making—that so-called spirit hand—it's your right hand. It proves you shot a gun the night your aunt was killed."

"Quite." This from Wren was scarcely audible. He sighed softly. "A wax impression of Sharrod's right hand. There's the rub, Sergeant. Sorry, of course. There's the flaw you can drive a truck through, as you aptly put it. Sharrod is left-handed. I should know. Bitter experience. When he took three shots at me tonight, the gun was in his left hand. Mrs. Karper didn't know, otherwise she wouldn't have given him specific instructions to use his right hand when he was playing spook and dabbling in the melted paraffin. Mrs. Karper didn't know until too late that she was getting the goods on the wrong man."

Hogan wheeled on Wren. "Now listen here, Mr. Wren, let's not get into an argument about this. Lunge's reagent don't lie, and by heaven and hell, Sharrod shot a gun with his *right* hand and Mrs. Karper proved it."

Wren shook his head. "Sorry. Sorry as anything. Tuesday night, Herbert Sharrod shot a cap. Just a little firework cap such as children use in toy pistols. Nothing more. Anything ever printed on Lunge's reagent and the paraffin test for nitrates, always cautions that investigators make sure the nitrates found on the suspect's hands came from a gun. In this instance, the nitrate came from the flash of an exploding paper cap, fired in a"—he glanced at Herbert Sharrod—"fired in an exploding fountain pen."

SHARROD ran a hand across his high forehead. "God!" he said hoarsely. "How did you know? Can you prove it, Wren?"

"Yes. Think so. With some help from you, Sharrod. Might tell us about how you played spook at Mrs. Karper's seance. Not omitting the detail about the pen."

"Well," Sharrod began, "when Mrs. Karper enlisted my services for her seance late Tuesday night, I had no idea anyone had been murdered. The way Mrs. Karper approached me on the subject, it sounded like a very good joke, and I readily agreed to her plan."

"And then," Wren put in, "there was Miss Miranda Lestrard. You could kiss her in the dark. Even if only on top of the head."

Sharrod flushed, admitted as much with a nod. "I might as well confess that I came here and got a room at Mrs. Karper's only because Miss Lestrard lived here…. But to get back to the seance. It was arranged that I should pretend to go out to a movie, announcing my intentions to everybody. Then I was to slip in by the back door, go quietly to my room, and await Mrs. Karper's signal. When I got to my room, I found a small package on the floor just inside the door. It was wrapped in tissue paper, and there was a little gift card attached with my name on it. I opened the package, took out what appeared to be a fountain pen. But when I took the cap of the pen off, there was a small, sharp explosion."

"The cap," Wren said. "The exploding device is right where the nib of a regular pen is. Sell the things in my novelty store, along with other cap-firing jokes, such as loud books and Bingo shooting devices. Felt certain it had to be a pen, though, to get you in the right hand. A left-handed person grasps the barrel of a fountain pen in his left hand, naturally, unscrews the cap with his right…. I can take it from here, Sharrod. The paper cap was discharged from the trick pen after the explosion. It fluttered down, finally lodging in a cobweb just under the edge of your bed. Imagine you'll welcome cobwebs under your bed the rest of your life. Because the murderer thoughtfully retrieved the pen so that you'd have no proof."

Sharrod nodded. "That's it. I was worried because I couldn't find the pen."

Hogan said: "Yeah, but—"

Wren said: "It's simple. The real killer merely found paraffin melting on the back burner of Mrs. Karper's stove and knew what was up. Since Sharrod was the only roomer in the house who was presumably going to be absent from the seance, the killer knew Sharrod would play the spook—knew that Mrs. Karper suspected Sharrod of having killed Miss Crowley. Fact is, Fred Duncan witnessed the killing. But in the dark, he mistook the killer for Sharrod. And Mrs. Karper and Duncan were—shall we say in cahoots?"

"The hell they were!" little McFee gasped. "Why, here I thought all along Duncan was paying hush money to Mrs. Karper just like the rest of us."

Wren silenced McFee with a look. His eyes moved around the circle of suspects. From Nahun Hitch to Jake Wister, Mrs. Karper's roomers were just a wee bit uneasy. Wren's eyes stopped at Martha Wister.

"Why did you burn your husband's pipe?" he asked mildly.

"Why did I—" Martha broke off, her blue eyes round as saucers. "I didn't burn Jake's pipe. It's right upstairs—"

"Martha!" Jake's eyes were stone cold, cutting into Martha's face. He was bailing desperately, but practically the whole bottom was out of his boat. "You sure as hell burned my pipe. You know you did. That's what Wren smelled in the bonfire—the vulcanite bit."

"The vulcanite barrel of the trick pen," Wren substituted. "Why lie about it? Hogan will find the metal part that fires the cap in the ashes. Hogan always sifts ashes."

Martha stood up from the sofa. She smelled of Jake and found him horrid. "So you killed Miss Crowley, did you? You thought you'd get at her money through Dad. You probably had it all figured out that the shock of Miss Crowley's death would kill Dad, then you'd get your hamburg hooks on the money. Well—"

Which came close to being Martha's last word. Jake sprang at her, caught her by the throat, and it was no necking party. Hogan and two uniformed police got at him from behind, dragged him off the gagging Martha, finally had to bang him on the head with a gun barrel to make him give up the struggle.

After that, it seemed that everybody was talking at once. Wren tried to slip out of the room, but got cornered by Sergeant Hogan.

The detective grinned around his mosquito bites, stuck out his hand.

"I'm going to be big about this, Mr. Wren. Thanks a lot. You've helped. You think Jake killed Duncan?"

"Quite likely," Wren agreed. "Duncan was an eyewitness to the shooting of Miss Crowley. Trouble is, it was dark. Duncan mistook Jake for Herbert Sharrod. The same bean-pole build, the same short-age of hair. But suppose Duncan discovered tonight that Sharrod was left-handed. He'd realize that Sharrod wouldn't have used the murder gun in his right hand. He'd know he'd made a mistake. Eliminate Sharrod and who's left who could be mistaken for Sharrod in the dark? Jake. Obviously Jake. So the Duncan-Karper combine turned the blackmail pressure on Jake. Jake killed to cover and to escape." He shuddered.

Hogan said: "Well, when we find Mrs. Karper, we'll get the dope from her. I suppose when you and Mrs. Osbourn found Jake and Sharrod fighting over that wax hand, Sharrod wanted to destroy the thing while Jake wanted it public so as to frame Sharrod."

"Precisely. Everything's open and above board with Jake. Wanted to hire me to find Miss Crowley originally. He knew Miss Crowley was a body, of course, but didn't know where it was. Couldn't cash in on the will if the body never turned up."

"Well, thanks again," Hogan said. "It'll all wash out when we get Mrs. Karper."

Wren frowned slightly, annoyed. "Don't think I'd tackle it that way. Wouldn't depend too much on Mrs. Karper. Better break a full confession out of Jake. Mrs. Karper mightn't turn up."

Hogan laughed. "A bad penny always turns up—"

Wren got through the door, out into the hall. Miranda Lestrard was there, with eyes all for Jeffery Wren. She said he was wonderful.

"But—say, wait a minute!" She tugged at the tails of Wren's jacket. "Where's that creepy Mrs. Karper all this time?" she asked.

He chuckled, deep and easy. "She vanished. Hadn't you heard? Went *pffft*. Forget about her. A bad penny, Mrs. Karper. But she won't turn up. Or call her a lead quarter." He went out into the cool dark of the early morning.

He was entirely right about Mrs. Karper. She never did turn up. Zoe Osbourn, who was more astute than most, did some further research on the subject of Mrs. Karper and came with her results to Wren's magic shop a week later. She leaned across the counter and glared at Wren's whimsically smiling face.

"All right, master-wit!" she began harshly. "None of Mrs. Karper's roomers remembers actually seeing Fred Duncan and Mrs. Karper together. How's that?"

"Remarkable!" he conceded, chuckling. "Explains why Duncan always whispered, since a whisper is the easiest method of disguising the voice. Explains why Mrs. Karper always wore felt bedroom slippers, since they were the only kind of feminine footgear Duncan could squeeze his big feet into. Explains why Mrs. Karper wore old-fashioned dresses, to hide masculine angles."

"And I can even explain Mrs. Karper," Zoe boasted. "The Karper end of the identity did the dirty work, the blackmail. When things got hot, Mrs. Karper would disappear and Fred Duncan came on the scene, probably posing as one of Mrs. Karper's victims. Right at the last, Duncan got rid of Mrs. Karper entirely, burned all the cast-off clothes and feathered hats he had got from Miss Crowley."

"Burned Mrs. Karper," Wren said, smiling. "Like any other old witch."

"And Duncan turns out to be a cashiered cop, believe it or not," Zoe continued, "so he knew the criminal records of Mrs. Karper's victims. Pretty darned neat, if you ask me!"

"Quite," Wren agreed. "Take out Fred Duncan's false teeth, put on the wig, the putty nose, the wax warts, the old dresses, and you've got Mrs. Karper. However"—he shrugged eloquently, "who wants Mrs. Karper?"

DIG A GRAVE FOR ME

"YOU'D *BETTER* LOOK IN THAT ENVELOPE," PURRED MYRNA, MY FOSTER-FATHER'S BIG MISTAKE, "BECAUSE WHAT'S IN IT WILL MAKE AN ORPHAN OF YOU AGAIN." JUST BETWEEN YOU AND ME, DAD HOGINS WOULD HAVE BEEN A LOT BETTER OFF IF HE HAD OPENED HIS PIX SHOP OVER THE FIRE STATION AND FALLEN IN LOVE WITH A HOOK-AND-LADDER WAGON, INSTEAD OF MOVING IN OVER CALVERIC'S DRUGSTORE AND MARRYING MYRNA CALVERIC—EVEN IF SHE WAS PLENTY COSMO.

CHAPTER ONE

THE PICTURE OF DEATH

IF YOU read anything besides *Li'l Abner* in the papers of June fifteenth and sixteenth, you noticed the item about the murder of Jonathan Quade of Hattersfield, Indiana. It was all over the front page with the war news.

But the papers didn't so much as mention my name. There wasn't anything like:

> Oswald Finch, age seventeen, who operates a molding machine in the foundry of the Quade Piston Ring Company plant here in Hattersfield, is of the opinion that Walter A. Hogins could not have shot and killed Jonathan Quade, because he has seen Mr. Hogins catch a fly that was bothering him and let it go outdoors to avoid swatting it.

Oswald Finch. That's my name, and nothing can be done about it. If you ran into me on Main Street and wanted to find out how to reach some address in Hattersfield, you'd begin with: "Hey, Fats." I know. Everybody does until they find out my name is Oswald, which strikes them a lot funnier, then it's "Hey, Oswald," from there on out.

Before I tell you any more about the murder, I ought to explain how it was with Walter A. Hogins and me, because that's the only way I can account for the crazy things I did that night. To most of the people in Hattersfield, Walter A. Hogins was just a stew-bum. I've heard Myrna, his second wife, call him an old stew-bum to his face about a million times. But he called himself a photographer, and I called him Dad because that's what he had been to me ever since my own father and mother were killed in an auto accident seven years ago.

I was a kid of ten when that happened, and Mr. Hogins, a widower with no children, took me under his wing. He was drinking then, but he kept it under cover. I'd come into the kitchen when he thought I

was out playing baseball and catch him with a glass in his hand. He'd squirm around in an old rocking-chair that sat near the stove, and give me a lopsided grin.

"Have to drink a lot of milk for my stummick ulcers, Ozzie, my boy," he'd say. "You never drink anything stronger than milk and you won't have stummick ulcers when you get my age."

But the fact was, he had gin in the milk and you could smell it a block away. He wasn't a photographer then, by the way, but worked, like nearly everybody else in Hattersfield, for the Quade Piston Ring Company. He had a job in Mr. Quade's office.

Which brings me to something else people said about Walter Hogins which burned me up plenty. They said he knew something he wasn't telling about four thousand dollars that disappeared from Mr. Quade's safe. There was enough talk about the missing money so that Dad Hogins gave up his job and opened this photographic studio

"I want you to dig the grave
for me, Oswald," he told me,
cocking the gun for emphasis.
"Dig it quite deep. Of course,
I'll fill it in afterwards."

above Calveric's Drugstore. That's how he began seeing a lot of Myrna, Old Man Calveric's daughter.

Just between you and me, Dad Hogins would have been a lot better off if he had opened his pix shop over the fire station and fallen in love with a hook-and-ladder wagon. Because Myrna had gone thirty-two years toward being an old maid, and it was too late to turn back then.

Not that Myrna didn't have the looks. She was plenty sharp and still is. A tall, brunet clothes-horse like they say Earl Carroll is looking for, and it's too bad he didn't find her before Dad Hogins did. Dad Hogins started acting about half his age and double his income, and before I knew it, Myrna had him.

About the first thing Myrna did after she and Dad Hogins were married was to try and get rid of me. Not with a bread knife or rat-paste or anything like that, understand. What she did was go to a mealy-mouthed stuffed-shirt named Peter Newsome and convince him Walter A. Hogins was an old stew-bum and not fit to bring up a child. Peter Newsome was chairman of the Civic Betterment League, and he threatened to have the juvenile court take me away from Dad.

All that came of it was that Dad Hogins started doctoring his "stummick ulcers" at his photography shop. And he'd frequently come home at night with what he called "an awful bad spell," so I'd have to help him to bed with an icebag, which, I noticed, he never applied to his stomach.

So he was an old stew-bum, Dad Hogins was, but the kindest man who ever lived, which made it hard for me to believe he could have shot and killed Jonathan Quade even when I saw the evidence.

You remember that on the night of the fourteenth, Jonathan Quade was the principal speaker at a Civic Betterment League banquet at the Shefford Hotel. You know how they found Quade—stretched out on the floor of a private dining room on the second floor, a bullet in his head and nobody standing around waiting to be arrested for murder.

IT PROBABLY would have been a shock to old Quade if he had known that the plant didn't stop running as soon as he was dead, because he really had his fingers in the business right down to the green sand in the foundry. But we had a war to win, and on June fifteenth every unit was going full blast as if nothing had happened.

Everybody was wondering who killed Jonathan Quade and why. Mostly why. The old man didn't have any family. I'd heard him say in a dozen speeches that Hattersfield, Indiana, was his family, and there was Quade Park, the Jonathan Quade Hospital and the Quade Public Golf Links to prove it. He didn't have any enemies, either, except a few he'd made when he'd backed Edward P. Lawler for mayor.

About five-thirty that evening, I turned up the approach walk of Dad Hogins' house on Pearson Street and found Peter Newsome just about six steps ahead of me beyond the lilac bushes. He jerked around, blinked against the sun and shook his head gravely.

"Horrible, isn't it, Oswald?"

I said yes, it was. I didn't have to ask what was horrible because in Hattersfield we were talking about just one thing.

"The worst eventuality which could befall our charming community," said Peter Newsome. "Mr. Quade was such an active man in civic affairs."

Civic affairs meant everything to Peter Newsome, and the term included anything that was not strictly his own business. I never could see how such a small nose could pry into so many places at once. He was a prissy, gray little man of about fifty, neat as a kitten, and he always wore a black bow tie. He was Hattersfield's leading undertaker, and you could never forget it. His standard greeting when he met me was: "You're looking healthy enough, Oswald." It was supposed to be a gag, see, because of my fat, but somehow he made it sound as though he was sorry I didn't have one foot in the grave and the other on a greased pig.

He walked with me onto the front porch. The door and the Venetian blinds were closed to keep Myrna cool, which made me think, honest to Christmas, I could have liked that woman a lot more if just once she would break out in a sweat. I must have taken my gripe out on the door, because it swung all the way to the rubber-nosed stop and bounced. Somewhere in the shadows of the living room there was a startled swish of skirts.

"Go on in, Mr. Newsome," I invited.

Peter Newsome stepped over the threshold ahead of me, but I think I saw Myrna before he did. She was sitting straight up in a lounge chair in the corner by the bookcase, elbows tight against her sides, one hand cramming something down into the crack between the cushion and the chair-arm. Sitting straight, I said, but stiff would be more like it. She looked scared stiff, her face pale except where the daubs of rouge stood out on her cheekbones like hives.

I don't want to give the wrong impression about Myrna's looks just because I don't like her. I'd say she had chiseled features—if Myrna had anything to do with them, I know they were chiseled. She had black hair which she wore pushed up as though any day now she expected to inherit a crown. Her eyes were big and gray, the kind you stare at a while before you start wondering whether they're looking at you or through you.

"My!" said Peter Newsome, taking off his straw hat. "How delightfully cool—" He broke off as Myrna stood up. His smile was the sort you'd expect if he'd called for the remains of your long-suffering grandmother. "Well, well, Mrs. Hogins! Good afternoon, dear lady. Is Mr. Hogins at home?"

Myrna put her hand out to Newsome as she always does, palm down, fingers limp. I guess she thinks that's cosmo, like the way she points at anything, with her palm up.

"How nice to see you again, Mr. Newsome," she said. And while Newsome was holding her fingertips as long as he dared, I got behind Myrna and plopped down in her chair just as though I didn't have any manners.

If Newsome hadn't been there, Myrna would have turned on me and said: "Oswald, get out of the only decent chair in the house! Do you want to break the springs in that one, too?" But she didn't turn, didn't say anything, though I could tell by the cock of her head that she knew what I was doing.

All I wanted was to find out what it was she had tucked down into the crack of that chair in such a hurry. My fingers closed on the ragged edge of an envelope that had been opened. I pulled it out, took a quick gander at the address side. It carried a Hattersfield postmark of 9:30 A.M., June fifteenth, which meant it had been delivered this afternoon. The handwriting directed the letter to Mr. Walter A. Hogins, and nobody could have possibly made *Mrs.* Walter A. Hogins out of it.

I stood up. Myrna was saying to Newsome: "Shocked? I was positively stunned.… Won't you sit down, Mr. Newsome? Mr. Hogins should be along any moment."

"Thank you," Newsome said and sat on the sofa. I mumbled something about having to wash up and started out of the room.

"Oswald!" Myrna said, as though now I had sat down in the best chair. Only there was something else in the way she said, "Oswald!"— as if I'd sat down in the best chair with a lively garter snake in my pocket.

I STUFFED the letter or whatever it was under the front tail of my T-shirt and turned. Newsome was sitting on the edge of the sofa, twiddling his straw hat. Myrna was a little in front of him, facing me. She had on a short, summery yellow dress. Even if she was all of thirty-five, some guys my age would have whistled at her from across the street, but not me, because she was Myrna, and with my short chubby build I'm not exactly the whistling type anyway.

I said, "Huh?" and watched her red lips thin and her nose spread. She had one hand tucked in a dinky pocket in the front of her dress, and if she'd pulled a gun and slaughtered me, I wouldn't have been surprised.

"Oswald, wouldn't you like to pull up a chair and join us?" Her voice was sweet enough. She knew I had the letter and she didn't want me to get out of her sight.

I shook my head. "I'm pretty sweaty." I used the word "sweaty" on purpose, because Myrna insisted that only horses sweat, while men perspire and women glow. She wasn't glowing. She was all poise and ice, and if you run that together to make "poisoned ice" that's all right with me.

"But Oswald, dear, we have company." She bit her lower lip.

I looked at Peter Newsome who waved his hat upwards at me. "That's all right, my boy, you go right ahead. I know what it must be like, working in a factory all day in this heat and humidity."

So I was excused. I went through the dining room into the kitchen. There wasn't much use looking around to see what we were going to have for dinner, because we didn't eat before eight o'clock. Myrna thinks an eight o'clock dinner is cosmo, but in Hattersfield, Indiana, it's just slow starvation.

My room was back of the kitchen, a place where Dad Hogins used to store some of his photographic equipment. And what I mean, it was my room, because ever since I got out of high school and went to work for the Quade Piston Ring Company, I'd been paying Myrna twelve dollars a week rent and board.

I took the letter out from under my shirt, put it down on top of the oak bureau which stood near the door. I weighted it down with a half of a piston that I'd picked up in the scrap heap at the plant and polished so that it made a real classy-looking paperweight. I intended that the letter should stay right there until I could hand it over to Dad Hogins. How I was going to explain why it was open bothered me a little, because you don't go up to even your foster-father and say: "Your wife has been reading your mail."

I skinned out of my shirt, which wasn't as easy as it sounds. I had just gone to the closet to dump the shirt into the laundry bag when I heard Myrna's high heels *tack-tacking* across the kitchen floor. She'd got rid of Peter Newsome and was on the hunt for me. I got back to the bureau and was standing there when she opened the door.

She didn't look at me, but noticed, instead, that I was guarding the bureau. Her gray eyes sharpened on the letter and she reached out a red-nailed hand for it. I was a couple of inches ahead of her, yanked the envelope from beneath the paperweight, and took two steps back to sit down on the edge of the bed. I grinned at her.

"Oswald, give me that," she said, biting off her words like pretzels.

I shook my head. "Nuh-uh. I'll give it to Dad when he comes in. And if you don't stop looking like that, Myrna, you'll get what no woman wants—namely, wrinkles."

She came around the edge of the door, and I remembered a cat I'd once had that came around door frames that way. She was in front of me, her back toward the bureau. She wasn't frowning now. Her gray eyes were narrow and bright. Her smile was so small I wouldn't have known it was there if I hadn't known Myrna. She leaned back easily, resting bare elbows on the bureau top.

I put the letter into my pants pocket.

"Well," she said, being chatty, "what do you think of it?"

"If you mean the letter," I said, "I don't read other people's mail."

"You're such a nice boy!" She was almost purring. "Why, you fat little slob, you'd *better* look at it so you'll understand you have to hunt for a new place to live. What's in that envelope will make an orphan of you again."

I didn't get it. All I knew was that she was up to something, and whatever it was, it wasn't good for Dad Hogins. I took the envelope out of my pocket. Inside was a photograph, a picture of a room, and the camera had been slanted to catch a portion of the floor. Against the dark carpet was old, white-haired Jonathan Quade wearing a dress suit. There was a dark, wet-looking stain on the upper portion of his face, and it drew black, crooked lines down his cheeks to his square jaw. In the foreground of the picture was a tall, skinny man, his right side toward the camera. What hair he had was black, salted with gray. His mouth hung open loosely, and even if it was only a profile view you could see the dumbstruck expression on his face.

The tall man was Dad Hogins, and he had a revolver in his right hand.

I looked up from the picture, stared at Myrna. I shook my head, which said everything I had to say. I didn't believe the picture. It was some sort of a trick. Dad Hogins wouldn't have killed the meanest man on earth.

Myrna was standing straight now, both hands behind her. She had that same ghost of a smile on her painted mouth.

"I think, Oswald," she said lazily, "that Mr. Quade found out who took that four thousand dollars out of his safe five years ago. And your precious Dad Hogins didn't want to go to prison."

I stood up. She was all wrong. The picture was all wrong. I clenched the photo and the envelope in my fist and shook them at her. "What were you going to do with this?"

Her slim black brows went up. "Why, send it to the police, of course."

I don't remember what I said then, and it's probably just as well. As I started through the door I noticed out of the corner of my eye that the half piston wasn't on the bureau. That must have been what she hit me with, because I don't believe that Myrna could have laid me out with only her bare fist.

CHAPTER TWO

DAD HOGINS' LAST "SPELL"

IT WAS the first time I had ever been knocked out. I opened my eyes for just a second and closed them again. I wished I was dead. I was flat on my belly—as flat as anybody with a belly like mine can get. My left hand clutched the rag rug that was just over the sill in my room, while my right tried to dig into the pattern of the kitchen linoleum. I had to hang on because the house was spinning and I was apt to shoot out the window any moment.

After a while, things slowed down a little. I could hear somebody moving around in the front part of the house. Myrna, I thought, and that brought me back with a jolt to the photograph and what Myrna had said she was going to do with it. I rolled over, sat up, but couldn't make it to my feet because the spinning started all over again. I leaned back against the door frame and sat still.

Somebody had opened the swinging door between the dining room and kitchen. A man's voice, one that I knew well enough, called: "Walt! Walt Hogins! Say, isn't anybody home?"

The man was Edward P. Lawler, who was not only the mayor of Hattersfield but held down an important job in the personnel office of Quade Piston Ring. Lawler handled the Quade employees' life insurance, which was one of Quade's pet ideas. You see, if you worked at Quade Piston Ring, you could get up to ten thousand dollars life insurance at low rates. It was a non-profit arrangement, backed by the Quade company. With what he got out of the mayor's job and the salary Jonathan Quade paid him, Lawler did all right for himself. He had a nice little house in town and a farm on the outskirts where he raised horses.

I'd often thought that it would be nice to look like Mr. Lawler when I got to be middle-aged. He was about medium height, lean through the waist, with a deep chest and square shoulders. He had the sort of skin that gets bronze in the summer instead of freckled like mine—bronze and sort of oily, as though maybe he was the skipper of a tramp steamer that made all the tropical ports. The only thing about him I wouldn't have wanted were those widely-spaced front teeth of his, and if I'd had a space like that I sure wouldn't have said "juvenile delinquency" as often as he did.

His dark eyes moved over toward me. His smile was quick and bright. I guess there's something funny about a fat guy sitting on the floor holding his head, but I couldn't see it from my angle. Then Mr. Lawler got serious all of a sudden.

"Sa—ay, Oswald!" That space between his front teeth didn't do my name any good, either. "Say, are you hurt?"

He came into the kitchen and let the door swing to. He had on a white suit, white shirt, and a dark red tie. He looked plenty sharp.

I couldn't think up an answer right away. I wasn't going to tell him that Myrna had hit me. Aside from letting family skeletons out of the closet, that wouldn't have sounded too good for me—a guy who is seventeen, weighs a hundred and seventy pounds, and goes into the Army next year.

I got onto my feet before Lawler could reach me. The floor started to move in the opposite direction from the one in which I was going. I plunged for the sink, hung onto it, got the cold water tap open. And then I darned near drowned, because about the time the sink was full of water I blacked out again. I came out of it with Lawler shaking me.

"Where's Walt?" he was asking. "Where's Myrna? What's the matter with you, Oswald?" His dark eyes were like hooks that got into me and kept me on my feet.

"Food poisoning," I said, and didn't have any trouble gagging. "Myrna opened a can of something. She's sick, too." I decided that was a pretty good idea. Maybe I could get Mr. Lawler to let me alone and go chase Myrna. Somehow, I had to get to Dad Hogins. I wanted him to say with his own lips that he hadn't killed Jonathan Quade.

Of course, if Myrna had gone to the police or mailed that picture, it wouldn't make much difference what Dad Hogins said to me or the jury. He'd be crucified in court, because the whole town was keyed up to a lynch-law pitch.

"You'd better go help Myrna," I said weakly and waved toward the door. "She was going for the doctor. Either Dr. Prescott or Dr. Morrison, and I don't know whether she'll make it or not. She was awful sick."

Lawler reached out a hand to the back of my head, and I ducked. He looked at me queerly, head on one side, half frowning and half smiling. "That's a funny place for food poisoning to show up," he said.

"I'm sick, see?" I tried to get it across. "Dizzy, Mr. Lawler. I must have fallen down and busted my head on something. You'd better go see if you can catch up with Myrna before she collapses in the street and gets hit by a truck."

Mr. Lawler put both big brown hands on my shoulders. He looked grave, as though he might sound off on juvenile delinquency any moment. "Look here, Oswald, you weren't brawling with a sneak-thief in the front part of the house? Nobody socked you?"

I tried to laugh, asked him where he got a notion like that. Lawler shrugged. He had a kind of foreign shrug that included his hands, his eyebrows and his mouth as well as his shoulders. Nobody, I thought, had ever called me a liar in fewer words.

"And you want me to go hunt for Myrna?" he asked.

I nodded. "She's seven shades greener than envy."

"O.K., Oswald." He smiled slightly. "I'm a public servant and you're the public." He turned, went out the side door which opens off the kitchen. I heard his footsteps on the walk that leads along the house and to the street. I was alone with my problems, the least of which was how to stay on my feet.

I SOPPED a tea-towel in the cold water, held that to the back of my head where Myrna had socked me. Across the kitchen, I opened the swinging door and right away I saw where Mr. Lawler had got the notion I had been fighting with a prowler. Somebody had gone hurriedly through the drawers of the buffet and china-closet and left them all standing open. I worked my way into the living room, hanging onto things. Myrna's writing desk, the one she would never let anybody touch, had been given the same thorough going over, and the wastebasket beside it had been turned over to spill the contents all over the floor.

I went over to the desk, stared down at the big brown blotting pad with its red leather corners. Maybe it was because I had been hit on the head, but I didn't need a mirror to make out the address Myrna had written in ink and then blotted on the pad. *Hattersfield Police* stood out just as clearly as *Sizzling Steaks* does in the front window of the Puritan Restaurant on Main Street. Myrna had done just what she had said she was going to do.

The little clock on the desk pointed to three minutes after seven. Myrna had probably put the photograph in the mail box by now, and there wasn't anything I could do to prevent the police from getting it in the morning. That left Dad Hogins a little more than twelve hours. I've known the time when twelve hours seemed like a lifetime, but not now.

I staggered back through the dining room and kitchen again, got into my room. My head was thumping so hard it was a wonder I could think at all. I got a shirt out of the bureau drawer and put it on. Then I lifted the mattress of my bed and got out the roll of bills I had hid there to keep Myrna's lunch-hooks off it, and then I went out the side door of the house and back to the garage. I got out the old jalopy I'd been driving to work every other day in a share-the-ride plan I had with another guy who worked for Quade Piston Ring. I let the ruts of the alley steer me out onto the street, then squinted my eyes against the lowering sun and headed for Main Street and Dad Hogins' shop.

Right next to Calveric's Drugstore was a parking lot which the auto accessory store used for tire service. I swung in there, killed my engine and got out. My head was still thumping but still figuring a way out for Dad. We could slip out of his place by the fire-escape at the back, cut across the parking lot, and get into my jalopy. I had a tank full of gas and enough "B" tickets to take us seven hundred miles in any direction. And we had twelve hours. I couldn't see any farther than that, and I wasn't sure I wanted to.

As I passed Calveric's Drugstore, I took a quick look through the screen, thinking maybe Myrna was in there spilling everything to her old man, but there wasn't anybody in the store except Marty Beecher who jerks sodas. I stepped to the door that said *Hogins Photo Studio* on the glass, pushed it open, started up the stairs.

All the way up, the walls of the stairwell were hung with framed portraits which Dad Hogins had taken recently—babies, sweet girl graduates, brides, some of the fellows I knew who were in the armed forces. Tomorrow, I thought, just about all of those people, except the babies, would be talking about me and about Dad. They were all smiling at me now, but tomorrow—I don't know, but it gave me a funny feeling as though right now they had started to whisper things that weren't true.

I reached the short hall at the top of the steps, went down it to the door of the reception room which Dad Hogins had fixed up as though he was at least half as rich as old Jonathan Quade. I pushed the door open, stepped across the sill and stopped cold in my tracks.

Dad Hogins was seated in a chair in front of his big walnut desk. He'd fallen forward onto the desk itself, his arms flung out. On the floor beside him was a quart bottle of milk. A glass on the desk contained milk, and I could smell gin all over the place even if I couldn't see it.

This was something I hadn't taken into account—the possibility that Dad Hogins would be having one of his "spells."

I said: "Hey, Dad, you can't—" and didn't get any further. Sore at him for getting himself tight at a time like this, I had taken a couple of quick steps into the room, and from this new position I got a view of Dad and the desk from another angle. His thin right fist was closed around the grip of a revolver and there was blood all over the right side of his face and down on the desk top.

I stumbled over to his side, dropped a hand on his shoulder and shook him. That didn't do any good. The sickening notion that nothing was going to do any good crept up on me. I must have stood there for quite a while, staring and swallowing.

On the desk, right in front of Dad Hogins' bald head was a sheet of paper weighted down with an open bottle of fountain-pen ink. His fountain pen, the cap off, lay right beside the bottle.

On the paper were five lines of Dad's neat-as-print handwriting, heavy at the beginning and scratching out at the end where the pen had gone dry.

> Red Keys:
> This isn't a poison-pen letter though I guess there is more poison than ink in my pen. But you know who stole Mr. Quade's four thousand dollars now, don't you?

That was all, and it didn't make much sense to me.

CHAPTER THREE

RED KEYS

THE TROUBLE with me is that I don't think along logical lines. I can remember how in physics class whenever I turned up with the right answer, I'd always got it by a different method than anybody else. So when I saw Dad Hogins lying there with a wound in the right side of his head and a gun in his right hand, I immediately began thinking along the lines of murder instead of suicide. Maybe that was because I didn't believe that Dad Hogins had killed old Jonathan Quade. Naturally, I didn't look upon the note on Dad's desk as a suicide letter. I thought, instead, that it was supposed to be some sort of a clue to the identity of Dad's murderer and maybe Jonathan Quade's murderer, too.

I picked the letter up, not without upsetting the bottle of ink all over the place, and took another look at it. I could see where some people might find it convenient to believe it was a suicide note and that Dad Hogins was actually referring to himself when he wrote: *But you know who stole Mr. Quade's four thousand dollars now, don't you?* Myrna would believe it was a suicide note, and possibly the police, but not if I fixed things up so that the scene didn't look like suicide. So I fixed things up.

At first, I thought I would mail the letter to the police station to arrive about the same time as the incriminating photograph. I got out an envelope, put the note in it, picked up Dad Hogins' fountain pen, started to write the address. But the pen was dry, which was maybe a good thing because it wasn't such a hot idea anyway.

The "Red Keys" at the top of the letter was both the name of a person and a place—a roadside tavern called "The Red Keys" which was owned by a man named Keys who had red hair. The tavern was located out on the banks of Cripple Creek near a spot where Dad and I had gone fishing some years back. I remembered Mr. Red Keys would sometimes come out of his roadhouse, stand on the bank of the stream, and ask Dad if he thought it would rain. That was about all I had ever heard him say, and the only thing about him that had impressed me was that he could stand on top of the bank and spit clear to the edge of the water.

Usually, after Mr. Keys paid us a visit, Dad Hogins would get restless. He'd say his stomach was bothering him again and that he guessed he would go see if Mr. Keys couldn't spare him a glass of milk. He'd come back in about an hour with some peppermints for me, though I suspect he had helped himself to the candy on the way to kill the smell of gin on his breath.

All this came rushing back into my thumping head while I was standing there, swallowing at the ache in my throat. What it had to do with my decision, I wouldn't know, but I stuck the note in my pocket and decided that I would deliver it in person to Mr. Red Keys and see what happened.

I worked the revolver out of Dad Hogins' dead hand and put it in my pants pocket. There was a laugh there if I could have seen it at the time, because I'd often read about a man putting a gun in his pocket and how surprised everybody is when he pulls it to shoot up a bank. It could be the way I am built, but in my pocket that revolver was about as inconspicuous as a turret gun on one of the Navy's big ships. I finally had to stick it, barrel first, down inside my belt and pull my shirt tail out to cover the grips of it.

I left Dad Hogins' studio by the back way, went down the fire-escape, into the parking lot. I drove off in my jalopy with the gun barrel jabbing me every time I worked the clutch pedal.

The sun had gone down red behind a bank of thick, black clouds by the time I rolled across Cripple Creek bridge and sighted the Red Keys Tavern just beyond. The building itself was big and rambling, and it would have been hard to discover which was the front door if a string of red-painted electric light bulbs hadn't led right up to it. Great plumy willow trees arched across the gabled roof. The place looked cool and inviting, which was good for my throbbing head. At the same time, it was shadowy and mysterious, which wasn't so good for my nerves. I was beginning to have nerves. Everything I had done up to now had been a part of a nightmare, but now the shock of finding Dad Hogins was beginning to wear off and I knew I was awake. All this was real: I was feeling less like a hero and more like somebody's victim. On top of that, I was sick.

I parked the car in the cinder lot with about a score of others, got out, followed the string of red light globes to the front door. The place was noisy with a big fan blowing a gale and Harry James taking the paper off the ceiling from a red, translucent jukebox. I opened the screen, went inside. The room was all knotty pine, red leather and chrome plate, so small that I started to wonder right away what Red Keys did with the rest of the big building. But then that's always been my trouble—I wonder too much.

There were five men at the bar and a few men and women paired off in the dimly lighted booths on the other side. Of the two men behind the bar, I picked out Red Keys right away, just as though it had been only yesterday that I had watched him spitting into the creek. He didn't seem quite as tall and broad as he had back then, but that was because I'd grown quite a bit in both directions since the last time I had seen him. Anyway, he was a big man with an expressionless, round, pushed-in face, hollow blue eyes, and shaggy, sandy brows. His red hair had faded to gray in streaks, but it was still coarse and brush-cut.

I got onto one of the leather-covered stools at the bar, as far away from everybody as possible, and let my left leg dangle so the muzzle of the revolver wouldn't jab me. Mr. Red Keys came mopping down the bar with a clean cloth after a while as though the mopping was far more important than waiting on any of his customers. He looked squarely at me, and said: "What'll it be, mister?"

I brought Dad Hogins' note out of my pocket, pushed it toward him, flattened it on the place he had just mopped. I said: "A coke, I guess."

HE TURNED a little way, stooped to reach under the bar and into the cooler. His hollow eyes were on the note all the time, and I would have studied the expression on his face if there had been one. He picked up a glass with a finger and thumb at the same time he was getting the cap off the bottle. He poured the coke fast so that it foamed all over the counter and he had to mop again. Somebody down the bar called for another beer, and while Mr. Red Keys was drawing it he was looking at the note. He slid the glass of beer along the counter and followed it without looking at me or saying a word.

I began to get that ache in my throat again. I didn't want to go home and I didn't want to stay here. As a detective, I couldn't put fish-oil on my shoes and catch a cat. I tried to drink my coke, but I didn't swallow so good. The red light from the jukebox was making my eyeballs feel hot. I don't know just what I would have done if Mr. Keys hadn't come back along the bar to take another look at that note. Then his eyes crawled over my face for an uncomfortable moment, dropped finally to about the middle of my shirt front.

"Where'd you get that, Fats?" he asked, and turned his thumb over toward the note.

"Mr. Hogins wanted me to see that you got it," I told him.

He jerked his head up and said: "Humph! What's it all about?"

I tried to shrug like Edward P. Lawler, managed all right with my hands and shoulders, but when I tried to raise my eyebrows my head pained me all the way from the bridge of my nose to the goose-egg Myrna had raised. Mr. Red Keys said, "Humph!" again and went off down the bar to wait on a new customer who had just come in and was sitting two stools away from me. He hadn't so much as touched the note, and I wondered if that meant anything. I decided it didn't, peeled Dad Hogins' letter off the damp spot on the bar, and put it back in my pocket.

The new customer was a man in a blue shirt and faded tan wash pants. He wore a straw hat and I didn't notice much about his looks except that his backside must have been even broader than mine. He hunched across the bar and spoke to Mr. Keys.

"Say, Red, have you heard? They just found Walt Hogins."

My heart took a couple of extra licks and the barroom started turning slowly and off-center.

"Found him?" Mr. Keys asked. He came over in front of me to reach down for a cold bottle of beer. "Didn't know he was lost. Under what table?"

My face got hot.

The man in the tan pants said: "Hell, he was in his own shop, shot through the side of his head. They say it looked like the same damn caliber of a bullet that killed Jonathan Quade."

I looked hard at Red Keys, but it didn't do me any good. His face hadn't altered in the least. He was wiping off the bottle of beer with his rag, taking his time.

He said: "I'll be damned! Walt Hogins was always a pretty white guy, I thought. They got any idea who did it?"

The man in the tan pants shook his head. "Naw. Them damn cops give me a pain in the—" He looked over his shoulder to see if there were ladies present and didn't say where his pain was. He took a folded newspaper, the Hattersfield *Chronicle* from his hip pocket, put it down on the bar to his right and about two feet from me. Red Keys put the beer and a glass down in front of the man, walked down the bar to disappear through a door at the back.

It's a funny thing that sometimes when your mind is full of a lot of little things you're trying to connect, your eye will light on something that drives everything else out of your brain. It was like that with me and the item on the right side of the editorial page of the Hattersfield *Chronicle*. It was headed: *LIGHTNING STRIKES*, in big black type, and my eyes read down the column of smaller type beneath:

> Everybody talks about the weather but how many do anything about it? Excuse us if we mention that severe electrical storm the night of June 12, but it was a humdinger. Lightning struck the garage on the estate of one of Hatters County's leading citizens, and the building burned to the foundation. Well, they used to say lightning was the sword of God, but that's considered old-fashioned.

Right underneath, set off as though it didn't have anything to do with the above, was another little item headed: *OUR SOCIETY EDITOR MISSED THIS ONE*. It read:

> Mr. Godfrey Peele left the evening of June 12 on an extended fishing trip in Canada. Mr. Peele motored.

Anybody in Hattersfield could have figured a connection between the two items. Godfrey Peele was auditor of Quade Piston Ring, but you'd have thought he was at least the governor of Indiana the way he talked and acted. He lived by himself in a six-room brick house on a secluded acre of land west of town, and he always referred to it as "my estate." It was a standard joke in Hattersfield. If you had a victory garden on a vacant lot you'd call it your estate, and practically everybody got the point.

But what the *Chronicle* editor was trying to imply was that Godfrey Peele must have used hoarded or black-market gasoline to take this motor trip to Canada while everybody else panted through the summer, and that maybe that was why the lightning had struck his garage.

I was staring at the paper when a white apron loomed in front of me. I looked up into the face of the fat, bald bartender who was standing there polishing a glass on a towel. He jerked his head toward the back of the room.

"Red wants to see you, Fats."

I got off the stool. Godfrey Peele and his garage fire were knocked completely out of my head. My heart was doing double-time, and every beat seemed centered directly behind my eyeballs. I was aware of a white apron following me, but on the other side of the bar, and at the back of the room the barkeep came around to push open a door for me. I walked down a hall toward the open door of a lighted room.

THAT room—it was plenty cosmo, what I mean! White fur rugs on the floor, red leather chairs, a big blonde maple desk. I half expected to see Humphrey Bogart standing there in a dress suit, cleaning a forty-five automatic with a silk handkerchief. But instead, there was Mr. Red Keys, his white shirt open at the neck, his sleeves rolled up to show a big red rose tattooed on his right arm, and beer spots on his creamy flannel pants. He was sitting in one of the low, red-leather chairs beside the desk. His hollow eyes started crawling over my face. I swayed, stumbled to the desk and clung to the edge.

"What's your name, Fats?" he wanted to know.

"Oswald," I got out. "Oswald Finch."

Red's mouth quirked at the corners. He had the thinnest lips I've ever seen. "O.K., Oswald. I remember you, now. You used to come out to the creek fishing with Walt Hogins. I thought you were his kid."

I explains that Dad Hogins was my foster-father and Red Keys nodded. He asked: "Did you know Walt had been murdered when you came here tonight?"

I nodded. "I came right from his shop out here. Because of the note. That was lying right on his desk."

"You didn't call the police?"

"Nuh-uh."

He stared at me until everything blacked out but his eyes. I could hear him saying: "That's cooking up a mess of trouble for yourself, Oswald. Suppose somebody saw you leaving the shop?"

It had never struck me before that anybody might think *I* had killed Dad Hogins. It struck me now, hard. I knew it was sit down or fall down. I let go of the desk, turned, started for a chair. The floor tipped up in front of me at about a forty-five degree angle, and I would have fallen on my face if Mr. Keys hadn't bounced out of his chair and caught me.

"Ozzie," he said. "Ozzie, what the hell's the matter with you? You didn't kill him, did you?"

I jerked away from him and collapsed in the chair. I looked squarely at him and shook my thumping head. "Nothing's the matter with me except that I cracked my head on something," I said.

He grunted, came over, fingered the nob on the back of my head. His thin lips grinned. "You got something there, son! How about a couple of aspirin tablets?"

I said: "That would be fine."

He went to the desk for the tablets. I studied his face and it was just like solid geometry to me. He said: "Walt Hogins and I were pals. Went to school together, Ozzie. You know that?"

I hadn't known that. I watched Red Keys pour water out of a fancy thermos bottle on his desk. He brought me the two tablets and some water.

"I've got a room here you can stay in overnight," he suggested, as I took the tablets and washed them down. "Maybe you'd better do that. Just until I can see how the land lies in town. Those Hattersfield cops get a lot of screwy notions, and they're all hopped up over the killing of Jonathan Quade."

"That's fine," I said. I certainly didn't want to go back home. Then I remembered the note in my pocket. "Mr. Keys, that letter I showed you— Do you really know who took Mr. Quade's four thousand dollars five year ago? Was it Dad Hogins?"

He shook his head, but his lips thinned out tightly as though that was all I was going to get out of him. He took hold of my left arm, helped me get to my feet. Then we went out into the narrow hall together and on back to a stairway that doubled back on itself going up. I thought that somewhere in the rear of the building there was a bigger crowd than out in the bar. There was that steady bumble of voices that goes with a crowd, and there was a mechanical sound, too—a clicking, as though a ratchet was being turned slower and slower until it finally stopped. Then the bumble of voices grew louder. I didn't think it was just the thing to do to ask Mr. Red Keys what went on in the rear of his big house, so I kept my mouth shut.

Upstairs, he showed me down the hall to a small room under a gable at the back. There was a good-sized window, curtained on the outside with willow branches. It contained an iron bedstead, a rocking chair and a bureau.

"It's pretty hot," Red Keys said.

I said that was all right and sat down on the edge of the bed.

He pointed to the chair. "You can hang your clothes on that, if you want to. Maybe you'd better do that, Ozzie. Stretch out and get some sleep. Maybe you'll get rid of that headache."

I thanked him for everything. Just before he snapped off the light switch and left the room, he gave me an over-the-shoulder glance which I didn't exactly like. But then I told myself that if he was solid with Dad Hogins, he was solid with me.

As soon as I was alone, I stretched out on the bed. The revolver that was stuck in the top of my pants bothered me, so I pulled it out and put it under the pillow. I was dead tired and the aspirin was making me sleepy. A cool breeze had sprung up so that the branches of the willow whispered lazily on the roof and on the screen of the window. I rolled over on my belly. I don't know why I sleep that way, but I do.

Just as I was dozing off, I noticed that I had a sharp pain in my chest, as though maybe I had a broken rib or something. I was startled awake, and I rolled over, sat up. My hand went up to my shirt front, pawed around where the pain was. I discovered a fountain pen clipped into the pocket of my shirt—Dad Hogins' fountain pen, I realized. I must have stuck it absent-mindedly in my pocket after deciding not to address that letter on his desk to the police. I pulled the pen out, reached to put it on the window sill. Just to show how tired I was, I missed the sill by several inches, the pen dropped to the floor, and I must have been asleep almost before I flattened out on the bed again.

I dreamed that Myrna insisted I was dead, just to get me out of the house, and that Peter Newsome had taken me to his undertaking parlors. I was trying to get up off his canvas-topped table and he was saying: "Lie still, Oswald, or you can't expect me to make you look very natural." His hands were moving over my back, prodding me gently here and there.

And then suddenly I wasn't dreaming any more. Hands *were* moving carefully up and down my back, prodding me gently. Somebody's breath struck chill against the sweating back of my neck.

CHAPTER FOUR

MORE POISON THAN INK

I LAY perfectly still like I had read you are supposed to do if you find a cobra coiled up in bed with you. My heart must have been shaking the bed, but there wasn't anything I could do about that. My right hand was under the pillow, my fingers just touching the metal of the gun, but I couldn't get a good hold on the revolver without giving out that I was awake.

The searching fingers fished into the hip pockets of my pants, came out, moved on up my spine. If they touched my neck, I was going to move—but fast. The hand crossed to my left side, went down to the mattress, wedged beneath me as though trying to turn me over. I decided I'd be accommodating and get it over with. I had to do something before I lost my nerve and let out a yell they'd hear clear over in the next county. I got my hooks on the gun under my pillow, yanked it as I flopped over on my back.

A knee gouged down into my chest. The breath *wooshed* out of me and didn't come back because a big hand closed tight on my throat. I hacked aimlessly at the hulking shadow above me, struck something, drew a smothered oath. The hand that wasn't busy choking me to death ripped a piece out of the front of my shirt. I kept hacking with the gun, and about the third try I must have hit the bull's-eye, because the man came all the way down on top of me and rolled over beside me on the bed.

I lay there gasping, thinking how lucky I was to be able to breathe again. Pretty soon I sat up and looked down at the still figure beside me. The dim glow through the window wasn't enough so that I could see the man's features, but then I didn't have to. One arm was flung out directly in the path of the bright moonlight that flickered through the willow branches, and I could see the tattooed rose on the arm of Mr. Red Keys.

Mr. Keys—my pal, Dad Hogins' pal, everybody's pal. I stood up, still breathing hard, patted myself all over to make sure I was all there. My wallet was safe in my back hip pocket. I had my key-case. Nothing was missing but the patch of my shirt pocket and that had been completely torn off. And then I remembered how those hollow eyes of Red Keys had crawled over my face and down to my shirt, and in a second I knew why he had so thoughtfully invited me to take off my clothes and hang them on the chair. He was after Dad Hogins' fountain pen that had been clipped to my shirt pocket. It was one of those thick jade-green pens and Dad Hogins had used it ever since I could remember.

I got around to the other side of the bed, went down on my knees, started patting the floor with my hands, trying to find the pen. On the bed, Mr. Red Keys was stirring slightly. I hunted feverishly, finally remembered that I was no cat. I stumbled back across the room, found the light switch, turned it on. The pen stood out, bright and shiny, against the dark oiled floor in front of the radiator under the window. I pounced on it, and this time I clipped it to the waistband inside my pants so that my shirttail hid it.

I took a final look at my pal, Mr. Red Keys. He was sprawled out on his back, his mouth open. A blow I'd landed with the gun had made a little red gash over one sandy eyebrow, but he was breathing heavily and groaning.

I gripped the revolver in my right hand, left the light on, and went out of the room, down to the hall to the stairway. At the foot of the steps, I noticed there were several doors in the hall. Mr. Keys' office door was open, but the others were closed and a mystery to me. I grabbed the knob of the one which I thought led out into the barroom. I thought it was stuck, tried twisting the knob in the other direction, gave it a yank and then kicked the bottom of the panel. The door gave suddenly because somebody had opened it from the other side. The somebody was short and thick, with a heavy, dark face and thick-lidded eyes. He started to say something, saw the gun in my hand.

"Geez!" he said, and stepped back fast. I just got a glimpse of the room beyond him. It had a low ceiling of cigarette smoke and there were a lot of people gathered around some sort of a table with a long fluorescent light tube suspended overhead. That clicking sound that I had heard when Red Keys and I had gone up the steps came from that table. Right away I knew what Red Keys did with all his extra space. The Red Keys Tavern was a gambling joint with roulette and everything except Humphrey Bogart. And until Humphrey came along, this short, dark person in the door looked hard enough for me.

I turned all the way around, hit the door on the opposite side of the hall. This one gave into the front room, and I'll give three guesses as to what fat guy with a headache left what taproom in nothing flat.

On the way back to town, I was trying to make big pieces out of little ones, and not having too much luck. I couldn't fit old Jonathan Quade in with the gambling at the Red Keys Tavern. No doubt the high-salaried young executives from Quade Piston Ring played there a lot, but they wouldn't have cared to have old Jonathan know about it. Dad Hogins didn't fit in with the gambling joint, either. I could picture Edward P. Lawler standing at the roulette table with one hand in his pocket, a smile on his bronze face as he carelessly tossed chips onto the board, but, for Pete's sake, he was the mayor who had got himself in office with backing from straight-laced Jonathan Quade! Then there was Myrna. I could see her slinking around in a long dress with no back, looking cosmo in Red Keys' casino, but where would she get the dough it took to play?

I decided I was thinking too much. I'd better stick to facts, which were: Dad Hogins' fountain pen had something to do with his murder. That Dad Hogins had been trying to get information to Red Keys whom he had apparently trusted. That Red Keys wanted that information but didn't intend to let anybody know what it was.

Mr. Keys had seen through that note of Dad Hogins' as soon as he had looked at it, but he had been playing cagy. And the whole business revolved around that four thousand dollars which had been missing from Jonathan Quade's safe for the last five years.

IT MUST have been close to midnight when I drove by Dad Hogins' house. The place was lighted up like Christmas and there were two cars out in front—Peter Newsome's solemn black sedan and Edward P. Lawler's gray convertible. I cruised to the end of the block, turned onto the side street, and drove up the alley to the garage. I wasn't too steady as I walked to the side door of the house, and consequently the screen door slipped from my fingers and banged loudly as I went in. The murmur of voices in the house stopped suddenly, as though maybe they were all talking about me. I crossed the kitchen hopefully on tiptoe, heading for my room, but Myrna came through the swinging door of the dining room.

She had on a pale pink housecoat that fitted tightly from the waist up and fell in frosty folds to the floor. She looked cool as strawberry ice cream, except that her big gray eyes were wide and a little wild. She had a black steel cash box under one arm. I'd seen the box before. Dad Hogins had pointed it out to me where it had rested on the top shelf of his bedroom closet. He'd pointed to it and said: "If anything ever happens to the old man, Ozzie—nothing's going to, of course— but if anything ever does, what's in this box will take care of things."

I looked from the box to Myrna's cold, lovely face. I said: "You never let any grass grow under your feet, do you?"

"Oswald, where have you been?" Her voice was an angry whisper.

"Out," I told her. "I want to talk to you. I want to know if you mailed that picture to the police. I know you addressed an envelope, but did you mail the picture?"

"Of course. It's in the mail right now. But the whole town knows about it. I've told the police, and Father, and Mr. Lawler—"

"I can bet on that," I cut in. "What happened to the envelope the picture came in?"

Her gray eyes wandered, searching over my face. "Why, it's in the wastebasket, I suppose."

I shook my head. "How did you happen to open it in the first place?" Funny, I thought, that I hadn't asked that question before.

She colored to match her rouge. "A perfectly natural mistake. I thought it was addressed to *Mrs.* Walter Hogins."

"Phooey! If it was a perfectly natural mistake, it wasn't because you thought the *Mr.* was a *Mrs.* It was because you recognized the hand-writing and had been getting letters written in that same handwriting."

Myrna paled so suddenly I honestly thought she was going to faint. *I thought, Go ahead and fall on your face, I won't stop you.* But she got hold of herself, stood straight and queenly.

"How *dare* you!" Her words slapped my face. "Why, you—you fat little—little—"

"Slob," I concluded for her. I was almost as cool as she was. I nodded at the steel box under her arm. "How's it feel to be a rich widow?"

Her scarlet lips opened and she laughed, the kind of a laugh that can be written, "Ha-ha!" She raised the box in both hands and flung it at me. She was short about a yard. The box struck the corner of the kitchen table, bounced, broke open at my feet.

"Go on, look at it," she urged. "Feast your eyes on the accumulated wealth of a lifetime!"

I got down on my knees on the linoleum, and as I did so I asked of Myrna: "Is this the box that you searched the house for after you knocked me out?"

Her eyes narrowed. "Searched the house? You're crazy! Search my own house? So you're trying to blame that on me, are you, when you know perfectly well you went through every drawer in the place! You've got a lot of explaining to do, Oswald Finch, and you can start right in explaining to Mr. Lawler."

Maybe she had a point there. Why would she go through all the drawers in the house? But if she hadn't, who had? Hattersfield has had its share of sneak-thieves, but they didn't usually operate in broad daylight.

I looked down at the stuff that had spilled from the metal box. Papers, mostly—old bills with little pieces of white scratch paper clipped to each one. I picked up last year's coal bill, thumbed over the sheets of scratch pad attached to it. Each sheet from the pad had a notation in Dad Hogins' careful writing, such as:

> George Perkins owes me twelve dollars for taking pictures of his two children 2/9/43

So that was how Dad Hogins had taken care of things in case something happened to him. For every bill he owed there were bills that were owed to him to cancel it. Maybe it seems pretty funny to you, but I could see how Dad Hogins would figure things just that way. Old Take-It-Easy Hogins who didn't ask for anything but to live and let live—he'd do things just that way.

I TURNED over some more bills, taking my time, because I knew I was irritating Myrna. In the entire mess was one life insurance policy for two thousand dollars. It named me as beneficiary, and clipped to it was another white sheet from Dad Hogins' scratch pad. On it was written:

> Ozzie, maybe this will help you get a start toward the desk you ought to have to go with that classy paperweight you made from half of a piston.

My eyes got hot all of a sudden, because this reminded me of a lot of other thoughtful things Dad Hogins had done for me. It reminded me, too, of a lot of thoughtful things I might have done for him and didn't. I looked at Myrna and she was just a pink blur. I stood up. My hands clenched. About all I could do for Dad Hogins now was find out who had killed him. I turned toward my room, but Myrna swooped across the kitchen and caught me by the wrist.

"You're going right into the living room and talk to Mr. Lawler," she said. "You've got a lot of explaining to do, Oswald Finch."

I batted her hand down, turned toward the dining room door. I said: "O.K., Myrna," and walked ahead of her through the dining room and into the living room.

When I entered, Peter Newsome was saying: "I do hope it *does* turn out to be suicide, Mr. Mayor, because that will settle everything right away."

Newsome was sitting on the sofa, twisting the brim of his straw hat. Mr. Lawler was pacing the floor like the skipper of a tramp steamer caught in a heavy squawl. He even had a short black briar pipe clenched in his white teeth.

"Hi, fella," Mr. Lawler said to me. "Where've you been?" There were grin-crinkles in the corners of his dark eyes.

Mr. Newsome got up, came toward me with his hand outstretched. His eyes blinked rapidly, and I guess mine were blinking some, too.

"Oswald, I know that nothing I can say will lighten the burden of your grief, but I do feel the loss of your foster-father as everyone in the community must feel it."

I don't know what got into me, but I snapped right back at Mr. Newsome with: "Well, you can't say Dad Hogins was active in civic affairs anyway!"

Mr. Newsome stepped back as though I'd punched his button nose for him, and I followed right through with: "That's so much canal water, and you know it! Nobody'll feel the loss of Dad Hogins except me As for you, if nobody died around Hattersfield, you'd starve to death!"

"Oswald!" That was Myrna's voice, coming from behind me. "Apologize to Mr. Newsome at once!"

I looked over my shoulder, and she was still just a blur of pink. "Nuts to you, Myrna. If you'll give with the name of the party who mailed that incriminating photograph of Dad Hogins and Jonathan Quade's corpse, it'll clear up a lot of mystery. You must have recognized the handwriting on the envelope. Some guy who has been writing to you secretly, I guess. It's either that or you'll have to admit you made a habit of opening other people's mail. And besides—"

That was as far as I got. Mr. Lawler was on me in a couple of strides. He caught me by the shoulder, shook me a little—about as much as he could shake a guy of my build.

"Now listen, fella—" he began, and what that pipe and the wide space between his front teeth did to the *s* in "listen" was something you could call a dog with. "Now, listen, I don't want to get hard-nosed about this, but I've a couple of questions to ask you. Did you go to Walt Hogins' studio this evening before the body was officially discovered?"

"No," I lied to him. His black eyes hooked into my face and he shook me again.

"Because," he said, "that photograph will prove Walt Hogins murdered Jonathan Quade. And the police have already concluded that the same bullet that killed Quade also entered your foster-father's head. And there were powder burns on Hogins' temple around the wound, which means the shot was at close range, possibly with the gun in Hogins' own right hand. You *did* enter the studio, didn't you, Oswald? And you did find Walt Hogins a suicide. And you framed it to look like murder because of that life insurance policy—"

I broke in with: "What are you talking about? What insurance policy?"

His shrug called me a liar. "The one that named you beneficiary. It was in the steel box. Didn't Myrna show it to you? Walt Hogins just took that policy out four months ago, and if it could be proved he killed himself, you wouldn't collect on it because the suicide clause remains in effect for six months to two years, depending on how liberal the issuing company is."

I shrugged right back at him. "I didn't know there was an insurance policy until about five minutes ago."

He said: "O.K., Oswald. I'm just the mayor—not the police force. You'd have made it easier for yourself, talking to me, though." He picked up his Panama hat from an end table, smiled at Myrna. Peter Newsome sidled over toward the door. Myrna showed the two men out, and there were sympathetic murmurings at the threshold. I thought I could do without all that, and I stepped into the dining room, went back through the kitchen and into my bedroom. I locked the door, removed Dad Hogins' fountain pen from where it was clipped to the waistband of my trousers.

I DIDN'T have to reread that letter which Dad Hogins had written to Red Keys and which somebody had thought would pass for a suicide note. I remembered that it had mentioned that the note wasn't a poison-pen letter though the pen contained more poison than ink. And it hadn't contained any ink. Which meant, of course, that the pen contained something else—something that was poison to somebody.

I took the cap off the pen. There was a pair of pliers in one of the drawers of the bureau, and I used them to get a tight grip on the black rubber part that held the penpoint into the jade-green plastic barrel. I twisted and the black rubber finger-hold came out of the barrel. There was a piece of silk thread tied to the ink feed inside, and when you pulled on this that pulled a tightly rolled piece of photographic film from the portion of the pen barrel that usually contains the rubber sack.

The film, a fully developed negative, didn't mean a thing to me at first. For a long time I held it so that the light penetrated it and tried to make something out of it. It was a picture of the front of somebody's garage—a double garage with a cupola in the center of the peaked roof. There was a lot of shrubbery, a straggling old pine tree in the background. The garage was of frame that showed light gray in the negative. In front of the garage door stood a man, his back toward the camera. His head was turned just a bit to the left, and maybe in a print you could see something of his features, but not in the negative. He was apparently in the act of opening the garage door. On the ground beside him was one of those five-gallon gasoline cans with a pouring spout. The man wore a long coat—a rain slicker, I thought, which made me look twice at the pine tree and the shrubbery. Tree and shrubs were bent far over as though by a high wind. I started to think about the last big storm we'd had. That was the night of June twelfth—

My mind streaked back to that item I had seen in the paper spread out on the bar in the Red Keys Tavern. On the night of June twelfth, lightning had struck and fired the garage of Mr. Godfrey Peele, auditor of Quade Piston Ring! Lightning—or was it this guy in the picture that Dad Hogins had snapped?

I rolled up the negative, jammed it back into the pen. I was putting little pieces together again, and this time I was coming out with the whole thing. Dad Hogins and Red Keys both knew who had stolen that four thousand dollars from Jonathan Quade's safe five years ago. Maybe they hadn't had any proof. Dad Hogins had simply been trying to find something which he could pin on the crook and make him confess to the theft of the money. This photograph was the evidence which Dad Hogins had supposed could force the crook to do just that, and in case of Dad's death, Dad had wanted Red Keys to take the same evidence and act on it. But maybe Red had figured he could do a little blackmail business if he could get the evidence away from me.

I could go quite a bit farther than that. I could see how Dad Hogins had approached the crook with this evidence and tried to get the man to confess. Then what had the crook done? He had invited Dad to the Shefford Hotel, the night of the fourteenth, maybe to talk things over. He'd got Dad drunk. Then he had got Jonathan Quade into that private dining room on the second floor and murdered Jonathan. He had taken Dad Hogins to the room with the corpse, pressed the murder weapon into his hand, and snapped a flash picture. He then had evidence of his own—framed evidence—to check any that Dad Hogins had dug up against him.

The killer had mailed a print of that picture to Dad Hogins the following day, just to show Dad that he had the whip-hand. Myrna had opened the envelope and had sent the print to the cops. And that wasn't the way the killer had intended things should pan out. Maybe he had come to our house, had seen the police station address on the blotter, and had put two and two together just as I had. He didn't want the police to arrest Dad Hogins, because that meant the evidence which Dad had against the killer would be brought into the open. So he had gone to Dad Hogins' studio, killed Dad. Failing to find the negative which Dad had concealed in his fountain pen, the killer had come to the house. He had come while Myrna was out and while I was lying unconscious on the floor, and he had given the place a thorough tossing, still without finding what he wanted.

But just exactly what was there about the picture which Dad had taken that had scared the killer into taking a chance on still another murder? Maybe it proved the killer had fired Mr. Godfrey Peele's garage on the night of June twelfth. So what? So Dad Hogins could say the killer was a fire-bug? I didn't know, unless—

I was thinking so fast I couldn't keep up with myself. But suppose the picture Dad Hogins had taken of the man standing in front of Peele's garage meant a lot more than appeared on the surface. Suppose it meant that the killer had also murdered Godfrey Peele, concealed the remains in the garage, and set the whole thing on fire? That, I decided, was the way it had to be, the only way things would stack up to make sense.

I clipped Dad's pen back to my trousers' waistband and left the room. I don't know where Myrna was at the time, but I didn't have any reason to stick around and bid her a fond good-by. I went out the side door, back to the alley, and got into my jalopy. The only missing link in the murder chain was the charred body of Godfrey Peele whom everybody supposed was having himself a time in Canada.

CHAPTER FIVE

DIG DOWN DEEP

THIS GODFREY PEELE really thought he owned an estate, and one of the things that convinced him of it was the elaborate gate across the crushed-stone drive. I parked my car in the dusty weeds at the roadside, got out, walked back to the gate, which was unlocked. The house came at you all of a sudden just beyond a group of Scotch pine planted at a curve in the drive. It looked big, black and sort of menacing, scowling down at me from the top of a little knoll.

I moved around the house and saw plainly, against the dim sky-glow, the straggling pine that showed up in Dad Hogins' negative. But the garage was nothing but a heap of blackened rubble. It struck me then that I'd have a fine time trying to locate a charred corpse in a mess of charred timbers without a flashlight, but, as it turned out, I didn't have any worry on that score because somebody was there ahead of me—somebody who had had the foresight to bring a light.

I saw the beam finger through a skeleton of burned timbers, drop down and disappear. I stood there, waiting for it to show again, but it didn't. I pulled out the revolver I'd been lugging ever since I had taken it from Dad Hogins' dead hand, started toward where I had last seen the light. I tried to work my way around the remains of the burned building so as not to make any sound that would give me away. I saw the light again, or rather rays of it shooting up from behind a section of roof that slanted at a crazy angle. I headed for it.

I got behind that section of roof without making a sound that I was aware of. It was a piece maybe six feet square that the storm had blown from the blazing building before it had burned through. On the other side of it, where the light was, I heard a sound that might easily have been a quiet footfall. I took a couple of quick steps to the right and around the end of the piece, the gun gripped in my right hand.

"Put 'em up—" I began before I realized that I'd been taken in by the oldest trick in the book. There wasn't anything behind that section of roof except the flashlight, and I stood full in the beam of it while somebody in the shadows on my right slammed me across the right wrist with a length of timber. I lost the gun and for a second I thought I'd lost my right hand along with it. The man on the other end of the timber rammed me in the tummy. I sat down hard on the earth, stared like a prize dope while Edward P. Lawler picked up the chips.

The chips he picked up were the flashlight and the gun. He turned both on me, his dark eyes grave, as though he was going to deliver a lecture on juvenile delinquency.

"Oswald!" he chided. "What are you doing here?"

"I thought—" I gulped. That was just my trouble—I'd thought too much. I'd thought myself right into an early grave. Because Mr. Lawler was the man who showed up in that picture Dad Hogins had taken. True, it was mostly a backside view, but the raincoat hadn't hidden his big square shoulders entirely, and I didn't know but what, when that negative was blown up and printed, the left side of his face would show enough for positive identification.

So I'd thought too much. But since there wasn't any way to back out now, I kept right on talking.

"Why," I said, "I thought maybe you'd come out here and move Godfrey Peele's remains. Because of that item in the *Chronicle* tonight. You don't know but what the gas rationing authorities might come snooping around to see if the fire was caused by hoarded gasoline. As long as that picture Dad Hogins took of you just as you were about to fire the garage is still in existence, you wouldn't want the charred remains of Godfrey Peele to turn up."

Mr. Lawler cocked his handsome head on one side, frowning a little, giving everything I had said a lot of consideration.

He said: "Damn it, Oswald, have you seen that picture?"

Seen it? I had it on me! More than that, it was the only thing that could keep me alive. I nodded my head.

"That," he said quietly, "is unfortunate, Oswald."

I said: "If you ask me, it's lucky for you. Because if Red Keys had got hold of it, he'd have blackmailed you out of your eye-teeth."

"Stand up, Oswald," he ordered.

What could I do? I said, as I stood: "You don't think I'm dope enough to travel around with that negative on me, do you?"

He didn't say anything, but dropped the lighted torch to the ground, stuck the gun in my middle, and started patting my pockets. His fingers passed right over the fountain pen, and I could have chuckled except for the gun pressing into me. Then his searching fingers went up to my shirt pocket which had been torn clear off by Mr. Red Keys. His hands stayed there, just a fraction of a second, and right away I discovered I didn't have any monopoly on thinking. Because his next move was to snatch Dad Hogins' pen from the waistband of my pants.

He said: "Well!" and sounded pleased with himself. "I ought to have thought of that before."

"Don't be a dope, Mr. Mayor," I said, bluffing. "I took the negative out of the pen about an hour ago."

He recovered the flashlight and turned it on me. He uttered a short laugh. "I don't think so. You're shaking in your boots." He motioned with the light a little way toward the left, spotted a long, shapeless sack of burlap. And I remembered the time I had admired Edward P. Lawler's flashing smile!

"Oswald, you can be pall-bearer. Godfrey Peele probably counted on having at least six vice-presidents at his funeral, but he'll have to be content with a foundry laborer."

I STUMBLED over to the sack, with Edward P. Lawler and his gun right behind me. I said: "You don't think you can get away with this, do you?"

"Why not?" he asked, mockingly. "Pick up the sack, Oswald. Over under that pine tree will make a nice place because it's mossy. You can transplant moss over a new grave and it heels over in a hurry."

I hoisted the sack to my back. It wasn't as heavy as some of the molds I had to lift at Quade Piston Ring, but I grunted some.

"Because of Mr. Red Keys," I said. "That's why not. He's not dead yet, and what I've seen of him, he won't be a pushover like Jonathan Quade, Godfrey Peele, and Dad Hogins. He knows about the four thousand dollars you swiped from Mr. Quade's safe five years ago." I was thinking again, and I was going to keep right on thinking until Mr. Lawler put a bullet in my brain.

"He does?" Lawler sounded bored.

I started walking toward the tree with what was left of Godfrey Peele a dead weight on my back.

"He does," I said. "I figure it was like this. You lost more money than you could afford at that game room in the back of the Red Keys Tavern. You were scared that Red and some of his men would make you pay through the nose. So you swiped the money from Quade's safe to pay to Red Keys. When Dad Hogins and Red got to comparing notes, they found out that you made the payment right after the money was missed from the safe. There wasn't any proof, of course, and Dad Hogins was suspected of stealing the money. But Dad was laying for you, waiting to get something—"

Mr. Lawler wasn't paying any attention to me. He said: "Right here, Oswald. I've got the spot picked out. See that shovel sticking in the moss?"

I saw the shovel standing there about six feet from the trunk of this old pine tree.

"I want you to dig the grave for me," Mr. Lawler said pleasantly. "Dig it quite deep, you understand? And, of course, I'll fill it in."

I let the sack down carefully to the ground, looked over at Mr. Lawler. He was standing with his feet widely spaced, the gun in his hand. He was grinning something like Basil Rathbone might grin in the movies if he ever won a duel with the hero.

He said: "Get the shovel. And don't—please, don't, Oswald—don't make me shoot you until the grave is dug."

I walked over toward the shovel. My legs felt like stumps of wood. I had an ache in my throat. This was it—you know, *it*. I put my hand on the shovel handle, pulled the blade loose from the ground.

"Look," I said, and I wouldn't be surprised if my voice broke. "I'm damned if I'll do it!"

I gripped the shovel as though I was going to vault with it and ran straight at him. If I had tried swinging with the shovel, he'd have got me sure, but there was something about the cold steel coming right at his head that unnerved him. He shot at my head, and if anybody asks what chewed that piece out of my left ear, it was Edward P. Lawler's bullet. He tried to duck the shovel, but didn't try soon enough. It took him somewhere in the face. We went down together with Lawler screaming. He'd dropped his flashlight, of course, and we went over and over in the dark. His gun let go a couple of times, but he might have been aiming at the branches in the top of the pine.

It was about that time that I realized this was no private squabble. Three men came running in from the road and around the Peele house. They turned out to be one Hattersfield cop, a reporter from the *Chronicle,* and an OPA investigator. What they were after was some evidence that Peele had hoarded gasoline in his garage, but what they got was a three-time killer.

I still wouldn't mind looking like Edward P. Lawler when I get to be middle-aged. That is, like Edward P. Lawler looked before I tried to feed him the large end of a shovel.

Why had Mr. Lawler killed Godfrey Peele and Jonathan Quade? Well, if your guess is as good as mine, you hit it right on the nail. He'd been gambling a lot. This time it was horses, which had turned out more expensive than roulette at Red Keys Tavern. He had found he could make up his losings by withholding the premiums which the Quade employees paid him on their life insurance. He'd got in deeper and deeper, had tried to cover up on his books. But the auditor, Godfrey Peele, had found him out, had gone to him the day before he (Peele) had intended starting on his vacation. Lawler thought maybe he could make good if he had more time. So that night he'd killed Peele at Peele's house, using the well-known blunt instrument. That was the night of the big storm, so what could be sweeter than just to hide the body in the garage and fire it?

It was the next day that Jonathan Quade thought he'd play auditor for a while. Like I said, he really had his fingers in the business at Quade Piston Ring, and he could pull a pattern in the foundry, direct a meeting of vice-presidents, or even balance books. So Lawler had to have still more time, which meant killing Quade.

All that came out at the trial. The gun which I had taken from Dad Hogins' hand and which, later, Lawler had used on me, was the gun that had killed both Quade and Dad Hogins. Just about all of my private deductions seemed to hold water, and I was pretty well pleased with everything except the fact that Myrna's name scarcely entered the thing at all. You can't tell me there wasn't something fishy between her and Edward P. Lawler. They were birds of a feather, what I mean. You know—smooth. Cosmo.

THE TURN FROM THE TRITE

G.T. FLEMING-ROBERTS

DURING THE PAST ten years, I have had my workshop on the second floor of my home, on the first floor, and, at this writing, I am relegated to the basement. So far as I know, there is nothing lower in this life. I think I could play this into something emotional—me, cast into the basement like an old anything after ten years of faithful service—but to be perfectly honest, this is a very nice basement with a supposedly sound-proof ceiling, knotty pine walls, an asphalt tile floor, fluorescent lighting, comfortable furniture. It has an all but invariable temperature the year round, and I like it.

In this my latest workshop I meet a nice class of people—men who read meters, change over oil burners, and the plumbers who unclog the drains. Each and all, at one time or another, have discovered that I have no keeper, have learned that I am down here for the bloody business of writing murder yarns. Some have been kind enough to say they have read my stuff. And after that comes the inevitable question:

"Where do you get your ideas?"

I get the same question from beginning writers. But asked wistfully. The plumber is never wistful, because he knows when he's well off. But the beginning writer is always wistful and will frequently add to the inevitable question, "Editors tell me my situations are trite. What's the rule for avoiding the trite?"

I asked Merle Constiner whose characters people the pages of *Black Mask* and *Dime Detective* regularly. "After the ten-year stretch you've served at writing," Merle replied, "you just naturally avoid the trite like poison ivy."

The same question addressed to C. William Harrison, who generously spreads his talents over the entire western and detective fields, brought the following: "You don't avoid the trite. You use it and give it a new coat of paint."

Both are right, of course, but neither is particularly helpful to the beginner.

Let's consider the subject of a doorknob—that now famous glass doorknob Arthur J. Burks told us all about in the *Writer's Digest* many moons ago. Mr. Burks was demonstrating how he could take any object in his hotel room and produce a plot idea from it. Glancing at his glass doorknob, he conceived the idea that a valuable diamond could be concealed in it, and therein was the nucleus of a detective story plot.

I distinctly remember that after Mr. Burks discovered the possibilities of his doorknob, the entire detective field became cluttered with stories concerning stolen diamonds concealed in anything of cut glass from Lady Windfall's punch bowl to Milady's perfume bottle stoppers. In imitation of Burks' doorknob, I thought up a honey of a stunt. It came in a flash at the dinner table just as I was about to wolf a dish of lime gelatin. Why not conceal emeralds in a dish of lime gelatin?

That little bit of dinner table inspiration netted me one of the few absolutely unsaleable duds on the pantry shelf. But I learned something. I learned that while Arthur Burks could write from inspiration, I couldn't. And I further decided that the average detective story reader on reading a yarn that concerned a stolen diamond and a cut glass doorknob—or lime gelatin and my own gem—comes to the identical conclusion that the inspired writer did when the idea first hatched: that the diamond is in the doorknob.

Whenever I am struck with something like that diamond-doorknob gag, right there is where I make an abrupt turn. I set the idea aside, put a gift card on it labeled, *Ixnay Icksiepay*. Then I start off across uncharted wastes, seeking an entirely different significance for the doorknob. Call the method "reverse reasoning" if it has to have a name. I have no patent on it, and I'm convinced that all professional detective story writers use it.

Merle Constiner has never said anything to me about using reverse reasoning, but watch that author's mental gymnastics carry him far away from the trite in the McGavock yarn "Why Meddle With Murder?" in January *Black Mask*. It's a doorstop we are concerned with this time—not a doorknob. Merle's doorstop is a red, carpet covered brick which immediately attains importance in the story by being mentioned in somebody's will. Stolen jewelry also figures in the yarn.

I'm willing to bet that when Author Constiner first hit upon a carpet covered brick doorstop as his plot nucleus, it occurred to him that such a doorstop would make a swell place to hide something of value. Exactly the same idea would have struck the beginning writer provided he happened to stumble over the doorstop in the first place, so it might be said that beginner and professional start out with the same equipment.

Some ten thousand or so words after the doorstop has been introduced and dangled intriguingly in front of the reader's eye, Merle's detective, Luther McGavock, gets his hands on the doorstop, rips the carpet covering off, and reveals what's inside. The stolen jewels? Oh, no. Beneath the covering is the last thing the reader—or the beginning writer—would think of—an honest to heaven, common alley variety of brick. And on that brick the author builds his highly original and logical conclusion.

How many packs of thoroughly smoked cigarettes went into the ash barrel before you got that solution figured out, Merle.

Anyway, Merle Constiner's brick demonstrates the reverse reasoning process. It is essentially a simple stunt, consisting of discarding the first easy-come inspiration and getting right down to using the old think tank. You can use the trite idea if you reverse it—thus the reader comfortably expecting that he has outguessed you, is utterly fooled.

THE AMATEUR WRITER doesn't lack novel situations at all. He simply refuses to work out solutions to those situations, even discarding valuable material because there is no easy solution filed away for ready reference. In fiction, no situation is without a possible and logical solution. Any tantalizing situation that you hit on can be explained, and in leisurely working out this explanation, you may unfold your story. To find that solution frequently means much backtracking and revising to replant a *means* for the solution. But the result is frequently gratifying and not apt to be trite.

Back to Burks' doorknob for a moment, because the darned thing haunted me for years. I finally decided that the only way to lay the ghost was to write a doorknob murder yarn of my own. I started with a brass doorknob, just to be different. Since doorknobs are generally found on doors, reverse reasoning prompted me to put mine somewhere else. The tapered cylinder of a paper drinking cup would, I decided, hold a doorknob very nicely. The most logical reason for the doorknob being in the Lily cup seems to be that this particular doorknob is plastered with latent finger prints and whoever put the knob in the cup did so to keep the finger prints from being smudged, believing he could get the cup out before it dropped to passerby.

Immediately the whole course of the story practically falls into my lap. There will be murder and its motive will be blackmail. My victim will be the man who put the knob in the cup and the finger prints on the knob will be blackmail evidence. Naturally, the man whose finger prints are on the knob is the person who is being blackmailed and he will also be the murderer.

Fine! A nice broad highway, straight to the conclusion. But right here is where I turn off. Let the reader take the broad highway while I jog off along a bumpy sideroad. I devise another motive for murdering the man who put the knob in the cup, do plenty of mental backtracking to supply the necessary clues and plants. When the pay-off comes, my detective can carry the reader right through to the solution of the blackmail angle, clear up the business about the doorknob, get right up to the thoroughly obvious villain—and then pounce on the actual murderer to disclose a greed-jealousy motive instead of the fear motive suggested by the blackmail angle.

No, it wasn't particularly easy, competitor-to-be, but Popular Publication's Alden Norton made my efforts worth while.

Recently, in working out one of the Green Ghost mystery stories which I do for Leo Margulies, I found myself with a deadline to meet and nothing in my head but a title—a crazy bit of alliteration, "The Case of the Bachelor's Bones." The title obviously suggested that some unfortunate bachelor would be murdered, possibly burned so that there would be very little left of him but his bones. Applying the reverse reasoning method, I immediately pulled away from that first inspiration. In the end of the yarn I would reveal that a pair of dice the bachelor owned would be much more important than his skeleton

This started me on some research into the subject of loaded dice, and this, in turn, suggested that my unlucky bachelor would be a gambler. A dishonest gambler, since he was using loaded dice? Not at all, not at all. Make him an honest gambler and then figure out why he would be using loaded dice. From that point on I was off along a bumpy sideroad that led to one of Mr. Margulies' phenomenally fast checks.

Let's see if the reverse reasoning method will furnish that new coat of paint for a thoroughly trite situation as C. William Harrison has suggested. Now, as probably everybody knows, there's no device which has been used any more frequently in detective stories than the murder committed inside the locked, practically hermetically sealed room. It is still a good gag, and there must be a number of as yet unexplored ways in and out of that sealed room. But in a yarn I was working on not so long ago, I found myself with a locked room, a dead man inside it, and no new way up my sleeve for getting in and out. In fact, I had used the very old gag of working the lock from the outside by means of a piece of thread manipulated to turn the key on the inside. Unfortunately, the gag had to come quite near the beginning of the story. I felt certain that if that old hackneyed situation could be saved, the rest of the yarn was sure money. There was my detective and a number of other people standing outside this room in an office building, and everybody, including the reader, was perfectly aware there was a corpse in that room. There had to be a corpse in there, or my story was a dead duck.

Detectives, as you've probably noticed, have a couple of tried and true—and trite—methods of getting into locked rooms. They smash the panel with burly shoulders—or maybe it's the more logical fire ax—or they pick the lock. My shady detective was more the lock-picking, skeleton-key type. But instead of doing the expected, my detective simply looked at the door and said, "To hell with it. If I open that room now, every time some rat nest of an office in this building is burglared, I'll get the blame." And he walked away.

Disappointing to the reader? I don't think so. I think that turn from the trite saved a situation that might otherwise have ruined an acceptable story.

There is some truth in the beginner's frequent complaint that he cannot recognize the trite unless he has done a great deal of reading and writing, but if he accepts this premise as gospel he immediately erects an insurmountable barrier for himself. So far as basic situations are concerned—and by basic situation I mean the tested formulae of the "boy meets girl" variety—there is certainly nothing new. But the beginner has in William Wallace Cook's *Plotto* a complete list of all these basic formulae, and all of them, as stated in *Plotto* are trite, since they were taken from published stories. Erle Stanley Gardner uses this storehouse of plots one way; but to me, *Plotto* is an excellent text on what is trite—a book which beginners should carefully study before they decide to sell it to pay the grocery bill. Let's pick a typical *Plotto* formula, examine, and see what can be done with it as a springboard for a complete skeleton plot. For example, try paragraph 819, page 111:

> A, a burglar, seeks to aid B, who was his friend before he went to the bad. A, friend of B, breaks into a building for the purpose of committing robbery, and finds a trusted employe, A-5, B's husband, dead at his desk, a defaulter and a suicide. A-5 has left a note explaining his guilt. A, in order to save his friend B from disgrace, destroys the letter that would have proved B's husband, A-5, a defaulter and suicide, 'blows' a safe and pretends to have committed a robbery.

I think everyone must know that a detective story based upon straight suicide is highly disappointing to the reader, so let's make that our first important change. The death of A-5 is *framed* to look like suicide by X, a murderer. A, completely taken in by the framed evidence of suicide, reframes the scene to look like murder without being aware that it actually is murder.

Thus, a different basic situation—and a more intriguing one—begins to show up. Let's tinker with it some more.

Instead of making A a burglar, why not make him an ex-burglar? Why not make B a girl who befriended A *after* A "went to the bad," that is, after he got out of prison? We shall not meddle with the self-sacrifice behind A's death, because that is good for an emotional pull, but as the motive for that deed now stands it can be strengthened considerably. Instead of making B the wife of A-5, let's make her a sister of A-5. Suppose that B is being wooed by A-2, scion of a wealthy and aristocratic family. A is also secretly in love with B, to give us a triangle with B at the apex and A and A-2 at the other two points. We can explain A's secret passion for B on the grounds that A's devotion to the lady coupled with A's "past" leads him to the conclusion that he isn't good enough for B. On discovering that A-5 is apparently a defaulter and a suicide, A decides to frame the job as robbery and murder in order to save B from disagreeable publicity which might make her unwelcome in A-2's family.

But what about the love triangle in a detective story? Its easiest solution—and the first to pop into the designing author's head—is that one point of the triangle may be disposed of by making that person the murderer. Since we are presumably beginners and can't know that such treatment of the triangle is trite—trite to the point of being a taboo in some editorial offices—we must trust reverse reasoning and decide at once that A-2 cannot possible be X, the murderer. We can play up to the reader's natural thought process by making A-2 look like the murderer. We might do this by revealing in the course of the story that A-5 is blackmailing A-2, thus providing substantial motive for A-2 to have done the job, but under no circumstances must A-2 turn out to be X.

Let's revise the old *Plotto* formula to include the changes we have made:

A, an ex-con, seeks to aid B whom he loves and who has befriended him since A got out of prison. A discovers A-5, B's brother, dead in an office, *apparently* a defaulter and suicide. A, in order to save B from disagreeable publicity which would wreck her romance with A-2, member of an aristocratic family, frames the scene to appear as robbery motivated murder, little suspecting that it is actually a case of murder, and that A will be chief suspect in the eyes of the police.

There is a new basic situation from which any number of new plots may be built. Consider its possibilities. When it is revealed that the job is actually murder, A must, in self defense, find the real murderer. How is A to get rid of the supposed suicide weapon? Shall robbery be the real motive for the killing? How is the love triangle to be broken down in order to achieve a happy ending? Shall this be accomplished by making A-2 a second murder victim about the time the reader has decided that A-2 is the murderer, or shall we let A-2 be suspected to the very end of the story? Ask the questions and settle upon the *least* obvious answers. Bring in material bits of "business" such as doorknobs or what-have-you. Chances are, you'll have too much fresh material for a single story. It won't be easy, but then, friend competitor-to-be, plotting a detective story never is.

www.ingramcontent.com/pod-product-compliance
Lightning Source LLC
Chambersburg PA
CBHW061522020726
47502CB00006B/2193